HOTLINE HEALERS

GERALD VIZENOR

HOTLINE HEALERS

An Almost Browne Novel

Wesleyan University Press

Published by University Press of New England

Hanover and London

Wesleyan University Press

University Press of New England, Hanover, NH 03755

© 1997 by Gerald Vizenor

Printed in the United States of America

5 4 3 2 1

CIP data appear at the end of the book

ACKNOWLEDGMENTS

A shorter version of "Headwaters Curiosa" was first published as "Monte Cassino Curiosa: Heart Dancers at the Headwaters" in *Caliban*, number 14, 1995, edited by Lawrence Smith. A shorter version of "Hotline Healers" was first published as "Hotline Healers: Virtual Animals on Panda Radio" in *Caliban*, number 15, 1996. "Naanabozho Express" was first published in a different form as "Oshkiwiinag: Heartlines on the Trickster Express" in the journal *Religion and Literature*, spring 1994, and in *Blue Dawn, Red Earth*, edited by Clifford Trafzer, Anchor Books, Doubleday, 1996.

IN MEMORY OF

JOHN CLEMENT BEAULIEU

CONTENTS

AN ALMOST BROWNE NOVEL

The Browne Barony

Almost Browne is a rather ordinary person in many ways. Ordinary in the native sense of natural reason. His stories are an eternal rush of creation, the trusty tease of chance, and a tricky solace.

Almost wears four ordinary wrist watches, and the hands are set at arcane hours. His clothes are borrowed, bright, loose, and wrinkled, from neck to ankle. He never wears hats, socks, or undershorts, and his outsized shoes are tied with copper wire.

"We live forever in stories, not manners," he teased a newspaper reporter last year. "So, tease the chance of conception, tease your mother, tease the privy councils of the great spirit, and always tease your own history." Yes, my cousin is outrageous, notorious, wanton, a natural bother, and he is a mighty hotline healer in his stories.

Almost has a sure hand, heart, and eye of survivance. He has never been a separatist or a coach of victimry. The traces of his native ancestors are always tricky, but never tragic. Almost is my closest cousin, and he was almost born on the White Earth Reservation in Minnesota.

That chance of birth is the source of his ordinary nickname. He was raised by our grandmother on the barony, a natural meadow of native ceremonies and tricky stories. Some readers may find our barony hard to believe at first, but once there, one shout over a panic hole, and the outside world is never the same story.

Almost reasons that we are almost never the same even in our own stories. What we hear, what my cousin almost always talks about, is chance, the unnameable creation of natives. "We are healers on a native hotline, almost unnameable," he told students at a commencement ceremony. We have always been unnameable. Our native presence is unnameable in the histories of the nation. Almost is unnameable, and some of his best stories were told on the first reservation railroad, the Naanabozho Express.

The Baron of Patronia, Luster Browne, and Novena Mae Ironmoccasin, raised ten children at the barony on the White Earth Reservation in Minnesota. The nicknames of their children are Shadow Box, Mikwan, Blue Heron, Rain, Bones, Aristotle, Galileo, and Swarm. Mae and Rose, twin daughters, died in an influenza epidemic.

Shadow Box Browne married Wink Martin, his second cousin. The nicknames of their nine children are China, Tune, Tulip, Garlic, Ginseng, Mime, Slyboots, Eternal Flame, and Father Mother. Ginseng married Li Yan, from the People's Republic of China, and the nickname of their daughter is Liberty. Eternal Flame renounced the convent, and the nickname of her son is Almost. Father Mother was an ordained priest. He renounced the order and married the novelist Sharon Mary Greene. Their son is the unnamed narrator of the stories in this novel.

Ashigan Browne and Luster are brothers. Luster remained on the reservation and became the Baron of Patronia. Ashigan was removed from the reservation by federal agents and lives on an island near the international border. Gesture, the nickname of his son, is an acudenturist and the owner of the Naanabozho Express.

Griever de Hocus is a distant relative. China Browne is the public information director at his Wanisin Elephant Casino in Macao. Gracioso Browne is another distant relative. Cozie Browne was an abandoned child, raised as a cousin at the barony.

Pure Gumption, Admire, Chicken Lips, Casino Rose, Agate Eyes, Ritzy, Cranberry, Hawk, Curly, High Rise, and Poster Girl, are the nicknames of the active mongrels in the stories. Ritzy, for instance, was the first mongrel to drive an automobile. Later he was an instructor at the Animosh Driving School.

1

Teaser of Chance

Almost Gegaa Browne is rather ordinary, as you know, and a homely person in many ways. Ordinary in the sense of natural reason and native sovereignty. His tricky stories, even as a child, were heard as dares, the trusty tease of chance, the ruse of extremes, and the constant motion of creation, but you might think otherwise in his actual presence.

Almost teases everyone, a natural sense of mercy that others sometimes misconstrue as censure outside of the barony. He wears four ordinary wrist watches, and the hands are set at arcane hours. His clothes are borrowed, bright, loose, and wrinkled from neck to ankle. He never wears hats, socks, or undershorts, and his outsized shoes are nicely tied with copper wire.

"We live forever in stories, not manners," he teased a writer for the *New York Times*. "So, tease the chance of conception, tease your mother, tease the privy councils of the great spirit, be a natural pirate, and always tease your own history." Yes, my cousin is outrageous, notorious, wanton, a natural bother, as you know, and he is a mighty hotline healer in his stories.

Almost creates his intimate celebrations of contradictions, the traces of natural chance, the turn of seasons, a thunderstorm, and yet he amounts to much more than humor, a tease, and a generous memory at the end of his own stories. He is a hotline healer with a sure hand, heart, and eye of survivance. Almost has never been a separatist or a treasonous coach of victimry.

Almost is my closest cousin, and he was almost born on the reservation. That chance is the source of his nickname. Almost is *gegaa* in the language of the *anishinaabe*, but only a few elders ever use that native name in their oral stories. He was raised by our grandmother on the barony, a real landscape of native ceremonies and tricky stories. Some readers may find our barony hard to believe at first, but once there, one wild shout over a panic hole on the meadow, and the outside world is never the same story. The uncommon soon becomes natural, the ordinary on the barony. My cousin reasons that we are almost never the same even in our own stories, and that is the natural tease of chance.

Patronia, the name of our barony, is a native land allotment located north of Bad Medicine Lake on the White Earth Reservation in Minnesota. Patronia is near the source of the mighty Mississippi River. The Indian Agent, more than a century ago, at the time of federal land allotments, gave my great grandfather an official document that created the barony. "Now know ye, that the United States of America, in consideration of the promises, has given and granted, and by these presents does give and grant unto said Luster Browne, *primus inter pares*, and to his heirs, the lands above described, and the title, Baron of Patronia; to have and to hold the same, together with all the rights, privileges, immunities, and appurtenances, of whatsoever nature thereunto belonging, unto the said Baron Luster Browne, and to his heirs and assigns forever."

Almost teases me about the stories in this book, and he warned me never to portray his body, the color of his eyes, the estimate of his weight, or other such obvious descriptions. He has a mighty heart, and the rest of his manner, motion, and appearances, you can imagine in his stories.

Actually, there is nothing really unusual about the way he looks. Maybe the copper shoelaces are marvelous, and his nose is enormous, but these are hardly singular descriptions. The caution about his portrayal is another tease, and that much, the natural tease, is a rather common practice on the barony. Motivation, descriptive body features, and brand names are seldom used in native stories.

The descriptions of characters and causal reasons of their actions are not very important in trickster stories. What counts the most is the tease of chance and the motion of native sovereignty. Not much is ever tragic in native stories, as there are no aesthetic treasons, no last lines to prove the cause of discoveries and cultures. My cousin, in this sense, was never more than a tease of chance, a comic trace at the natural leave of his own tricky stories. Tragic closures, essential last lines, and the cultural romance of a denouement, inevitably begets the invention of traditions and ceremonious representations, as you know, and almost the subversion of chance, creation, and native survivance.

The most romantic representations of natives are the advertisements of cultural dominance, not the natural sources of motion and sovereignty. The tragic creases of one culture can be the ironic chance of other creation stories. So, countenance, the tease of manners, and motion, are closer to creation than the hue of cheeks, the tragic crack of ancient bones, the body size, shape, weight, or the ethnic portrayal of the flesh and blood of characters. Anyway, tricky stories are creations, a native presence not an aesthetic discovery. Tricky stories are the sovereignty of motion and creation, never the dead letters of cultural inventions, or the classy causes, tragic closures, and motivations of discoverers.

Almost, born at the side of the road to the reservation, is evermore the natural roamer. You could always hear the healer dealer on the free reservation railroad established by our great uncle, Gesture Browne. That luxurious seven car train circled the reservation once a day and stopped at several stations, including one near the barony, and the Ozaawaa Casino. My cousin created and told his tricky stories on that native train. He said his best stories were always told in motion on the Naanabozho Express.

Almost has never been a member of any societies, associations, or privy councils, none secret or otherwise. "Secrets attract the curse of envy," he told me. "The evil of envy haunts the liver and heart, not the mundane or tricky, no matter the nature of secrets, and our lives are shortened by the curse of envy." Those who practice evil and bear envy are overcome by the emotion and humor of the native *debwe*, the heart dance ceremonies held at the *gichiziibi*, the great river. The earliest *debwe* was an erotic dance with animals, a native passion play that was described in a rare monastic manuscript, the *Manabosho Curiosa*.

The Monte Cassino Passion was enacted at the headwaters of the great river by monks in the fifteenth century. The liturgical, artistic, and literary sources of that play were combined and transformed by the native *debwe* heart dances.

The original "play is the earliest surviving Passion drama in the West," wrote Robert Edwards in *The Montecassino Passion*. "The work was composed at the Benedictine abbey during the middle of the twelfth century by an anonymous playwright who was probably a member of the order." Three centuries later the *debwe* heart dance became an erotic conversion of monks and animals, a pleasurable passion at the first monastery near the headwaters.

These new heart dance ceremonies are the stories of the *oshkianishi-naabe*, the new *anishinaabe* natives, and my cousin created these new ceremonies of truth, nature, and harmony on the barony. The *debwe* starts in the autumn at the sound of water drums and lasts for seven wild nights of chance and creation.

Actually, my cousin created the *oshkidebwe*, the "new truth," the new *debwe* on the barony, a ceremony of natural reason, that buries secrecy, greed, evil, and envy, in panic holes. The native word *debwe* means "to tell the truth" in *anishinaabe* stories. The ceremony is a dance that overturns the burdens of traditions, unties the inventions of cultures, and creates tricky stories that tease the manners of dominance. The heart dance is our natural reason, the reciprocity of natives and nature.

"Long life is not a secret, not a tradition, my life is the sovereignty of motion," my cousin told an anthropologist. "The shouts, the dance, the stories, rush over the secrets of tradition and raise the memories of those who have returned to live with the animals, if you know what that means?" Hardly anyone ever asked my cousin what his stories might mean. Almost every native who hears stories knows that the meaning of one story is truly another story, and so the sovereignty of natural reason and literary motion.

Almost was summoned once to be a member of the *midewiwin*, the Grand Medicine Society of the *anishinaabe*, to learn the secrets of herbs, songs, and manners that would heal and lengthen our lives. The *midewiwin* leaders, shamans who were moderate but secretive, were sure to mention the seven temptations of natural reason and native wisdom. They teach that right living, a gentle manner, good behavior, native songs, and the knowledge of herbs, are the secrets that prolong life. These old men of the *midewiwin* teach that evil is sure to backfire on the posers.

My cousin teased the old men and their secret traditions, and learned how to outsmart the seven temptations on his own. He created a new version of the *debwe* ceremonies and practiced the reversion of violence with tricky stories. The outcome of his renunciation and conversion is not peace but the reciprocity of humor, and humor of the heart is natural reason. My cousin has reversed theft with bounty, dishonor with praise, greed with meditation, competition with masks, dominance with panic holes, and envy with stories of native sovereignty.

Almost teases me with the obvious, that "lust is the foretaste of creation, that our tricky stories of remembrance are the chance healers, and envy is a bad memory." He pauses in stories and conversations to say *maanoo*, a signature *anishinaabe* word that means "never mind." Naturally, his response to the translation of his tease words is yet another metaphor, and always tricky.

The obvious has more energy to heal than secrets, manners, and tradition. So, the tricky stories that outwit evil with humor, and overturn envy with empty poses, are the same stories that tease loneliness, heal the wounded, and, at the same time, scare the soul wanderers who torment others with their secrets. "Tricky stories are not enough either, you must learn how to fly out of traditions in a virtual reality," said Almost.

"What do you mean, to fly?" asked an anthropologist.

"How else, but *maanoo*," said Almost.

"What does that mean?"

"Never mind," said Almost.

"Sacred traditions?" asked the anthropologist.

"What else, *maanoo niizhing*," said Almost.

Almost bears no more secrets than chance and the tease of words, as he said in response to the cultural anthropologist, *maanoo niizhing*, which means "never mind, twice." Obviously the anthropologist never once heard the natural and merciful tease. Almost said the man was lost in the creation of stories, "burdened with the secrets of a *maanoo* culture."

My cousin never wrote his stories. He was pleased that his signatures, the names of native authors that he signed in our series of blank books, were almost the only words he ever wrote. The signatures were the tease of secrets, and he forever teased me about my need to write and publish stories. Almost said, "the best stories are in our blank books."

You know, we must write tricky stories too, because the names have been so abused in translation and the course of dominance. The tragic rights of discovery continue to be heard in common names and native stories. The reader has entered into the wages of dominance in most stories about natives. Most, but not in our stories. How is a reader to hear our tricky stories over the crush of advertisements, the curse of envy, the abuse of cultural representations, the history of revolutions, and over the misconstrued missions of a constitutional democracy?

"Remember *maanoo*," said Almost.

Tricky stories amuse, never abuse. That much is a natural tease in the sovereignty of motion. At the same time, secrets, envy, and the most common representations of dominance are overturned in the tease of native names. There must be a natural reason of motion, a native genre that is not a romance, not a pious revision of victimry. Natural reason is a tacit chance, the reciprocity of readers who bond in native stories. A genre that traces the native tease that heals in literature. A genre that teases the reader to hear the author in an unnameable presence.

Tricky native stories tease the reader to loosen the dominance of manners, and the closure of names, a tease that would overturn the cultural inventions of natives, and liberate the reader from racial causes and the declaration of grand motivations. What we hear, what my cousin almost always talks about, is chance and the unnameable creation of natives. We are the unnameable. We have always been unnameable. Our native presence in stories is unnameable.

"Remember *maanoo niizhing*," said Almost.

2

Heirs of Patronia

Almost Browne was born on his way to the barony. He was born on the road in natural motion, the actual start of his sovereignty and native creation stories. My cousin is almost a crow, almost a bear, almost a flea, almost the leaves, and almost the heat of the primeval stones. He teases the seasons, the memories of ice creatures, and he has been on his way ever since the first bruise of winter.

The missionaries were versed to hear blasphemies in his creation stories, and so his adverbial nickname was cursed by the abbess as the wicked cause of almost every backwoods nuisance and mischance. Sudden storms and black ice were blamed on this natural child, and whatever might happen to anyone on the shoulders of the reservation roads was inevitably his fault. Nothing since his birth has ever been obvious on the way to the barony.

Almost Browne was born in the backwoods north of Bad Medicine Lake on the White Earth Reservation in Minnesota. The true story is that cousin *gegaa* was *almost* born there in the late autumn. That much is the natural start of other stories and the true source of his natal nickname. Almost, you see, is my closest cousin, a native crossblood, and he was born on the road, almost intact, and almost indivisible on the reservation and the barony.

Almost, in fact, was born in the back seat of an unheated station wagon. Eternal Flame, his mother, was driving alone, on her merry way home to the barony, when she was overcome by the unmistakable rush and heave of birth. She stopped on the shoulder of the road and delivered her natural child almost on the White Earth Reservation.

Eternal Flame told me once that many crows circled the car at the instant her son sent out his first cry. My aunt said she knew at the time that the crows were there as natural allies, and now she wonders who they really were, and if they knew the secret name of the father, a name no one has ever heard. "Crows marched on the narrow road, bounced on the hood, and then, as sure as the crow of my son's voice when he was born, the crows flew me back to the barony."

The exact location of his birth, as it was recorded on the official certificate, became a serious controversy. The agency nurse wrote the literal truth, "*gegaa*, almost on the reservation," as his actual place of birth, but the family, three mission nuns, and even the mulish federal agent, protested the slight of location and the certificate was changed to be *almost* accurate.

Almost, naturally, has turned that station wagon into a celebration of native motion and sovereignty, his observation car on the universe, and a natal monument that has moved his mother to wonder about his material associations. He has been in the back seat with his mongrels doubtless more than he has ever been anywhere else on the earth. The crows, of course, have made that rusted car their benchmark on the barony, and caw in a very peculiar manner whenever they fly over the meadow.

Eternal Flame has forever teased her son that his fascination with "an abandoned birth station" has caused her to be "insecure, even jealous of the back seat." She assured him that he was "probably not the only kid to have a junk car as a mother, and you're probably not the first kid to have a crow as a father, but you are the first bird on the reservation who pretends to be born again every day in the back of a station wagon." Almost made it clear to everyone that he would *never* abandon his station wagon, "not for any reason, not for anyone, almost."

One summer, a few years ago, we were hounded by a strange pack of international anthropologists on a tour funded by the government. The federal agent was always sending tourists, film makers, and curious academics to the barony. My cousin almost never hesitated to show them the exact location of his birth in the back seat of the station wagon. He would point to a lonesome brown stain on the seat, and then, like the big hands on a clock, the naive academics would turn to me for a wise native explanation. Naturally, these moments were precious, ever primitive, to be sure, and so easy to convince the anthropologists that the heart of native traditions was not in the wild curses of shamans, not at casino slot machines, but in a rusted station wagon with no wheels or engine, a new culture to discover outback in the thistle and sumac. Sometimes, if the visitors showed a generous spirit, even the slightest sense of humor about that stain of tricky deliverance, we would show them the *ininishib*, or the mallard ducks in *madoodoo*, the natural sweat bath pond, and later, a tour around the statue of the Trickster of Liberty.

Almost is almost brown, a crossblood savant of tricksterese, that wild banter of native chance, and the wise reversion of uninvited envy. He would give anything and everything away to avoid envy, but not the natural world, not the *ininishib* or *madoodoo*, or his birth place, the station wagon. He wanders in and out of my memories, a natural at native reason and tricky stories that almost never end. Our grandmother said if he could fly the way he talks he would be a hummingbird, and so *nenookaasi* was his nickname for a time. Such a name was not that uncommon on the reservation, but when we called him *nenookaasi*, the birds answered and flew around him everywhere, as if the hummingbirds heard the word and almost became the name.

My cousin taught me many tricky things, but to outwit envy was truly a stroke of genius and the cross hairs of native wisdom. He even teases his own bones, ducks his own shadows, and misnames the traces and seams of his native ancestors to avoid the envies of others.

Almost traces our native surname and honorable descent to the inimitable backwoods hunter Luster Browne. The entries of these names have never been certain in the most obvious reservation documents. Naturally, all names are stories, and the native stories we heard as children show that more than a century ago there was a very angry young man named Panic Hole. His native nickname, it turned out, was an insecure translation of three *anishinaabe* words, *wanaki* or *danakii*, to live in peace, *waanikaan*, a hole, and *babaamendan*, to worry, and, to obscure the stories evermore, he was given two other nicknames by rival missionaries on the reservation.

Father Constantine, the Roman Catholic priest at the mission, and doubtless the most verbose man who ever lived on the reservation, named our great grandfather Lackluster, because of the "instancy and insipidity of his stories." He told that same story every time he saw me or my cousins because we lacked the same luster in his eyes.

The Episcopals at Saint Columba's Church, on the other hand, were more propitious and named our great grandfather Brownie, for the night sprite, and native trickster. Panic Hole, in his own time, resisted both missions, but the two clerical nicknames were connected by chance on government allotment records at the General Land Office.

I have heard, over the years, many versions of these stories about the man who, when he was worried, shouted into a hole in the earth, a panic hole. These were common reservation stories with many original and unusual turns. To this day some natives continue to shout at holes in the world, on natural meadows in his name, and even into the concrete. They shout, and shout, and shout, to land their memories, to be healed, and to tune the temper of the earth.

Almost, when we were children, started a story that lasted for seventeen days. He told me that "once, not so long ago, our mongrels were healers," and insisted that "they were silent shamans, almost." This was not his choice tease of church or state, you understand, but the shaman mongrels were in his heart and continuous winter stories. He convinced me, at the end of the second week, that the very first bark of the night was by a mongrel who was worried about priests and other missionaries in black gowns. Since then that original bark has been carried forever by other mongrels around the world. You could say, and we did many, many times, that missionaries were the panic holes to the tricky mongrels, and in our stories the mongrels did more than bark in those mission holes.

Pure Gumption, one of our mighty mongrels at the barony, was a true healer, and we wondered if our shouts into panic holes were trickier than the eternal barks of mongrels, and who was the first shouter, man or mongrel? We were never short on shouts or stories at the barony.

I read the federal documents many years later, in the course of my own search for records of family allotments, and learned that Panic Hole, because of his fierce resistance, was named Luster Browne, the Baron of Patronia. He shouted at the priests, renounced the missions, sneered at the malevolent federal agents, and, despite their censure of his "intractable nature," he became a nobleman, the first baron in reservation histories, and by order of the President of the United States.

Panic Hole was handed a land patent that the government agents thought would banish him forever to the outback on the reservation. That ironic warrant has become another tricky document in the histories of native survivance. The "fee simple patent" was printed on bond paper with the watermark of the Crane Paper Company of Dalton, Massachusetts. The document bore the red embossed seal of the United States General Land Office. The Indian Agent had not seen the remote land, but he was certain that the certificate of the untamed allotment, between the metes and bounds ascribed, was mere muskeg, as worthless as the peerage that the officials pronounced that summer afternoon, and with a flourish for the first time, in the name of Luster Browne.

"Whereas, there has been deposited in the General Land Office of the United States an Order of the Secretary of the Interior directing that a fee simple patent issue to Luster Browne, a White Earth Mississippi Chippewa Indian, for a quarter west of the Fifth Principal Meridian containing one-hundred sixty acres in a Township named Patronia:

"Now know ye, that the United States of America, in consideration of the promises, has given and granted, and by these presents does give and grant, unto said Luster Browne, *primus inter pares*, and to his heirs, the lands above described, and the title, Baron of Patronia; to have and to hold the same, together with all the rights, privileges, immunities, and appurtenances, of whatsoever nature thereunto belonging, unto the said Baron Luster Browne, and to his heirs and assigns forever.

"In testimony, whereof, I, Theodore Roosevelt, President of the United States of America, have caused these letters to be made Patent, and the seal of the General Land Office to be hereunto affixed."

The government agents were mistaken about the value of the allotment on the reservation, and untrue about the virtues of a dubious backwoods barony. Patronia is almost a paradise, not a barren muskeg, and the many heirs who trace their descent to that native noblesse have created an honorable and distinctive history.

Patronia is a natural wide crescent north of *maazhi mashkiki*, Bad Medicine Lake. The *madoodoo ziibi*, or sweat bath river, rushes at the bend of the crescent south to the lake, and carries the ancient scent of cedar, birch, white pine, and willow. The riverbank bears the eternal rumors of glaciers and the great granite boulders that once tumbled out of creation stories. There, at a turn in the river, the greens are tender, and the beaver nose the curves and traces of the seasons. The rare moccasin orchids bloom in the moist shadows of an eternal summer near the river.

The sunrise rushes over the crescent in waves of blues, and then brighter on the boulders, widens and treats the natural meadows. Flies arise in teams of light, circle in the moist weeds, and then in several columns lean to the sun. Closer, on the wide reach of the crescent, warm water pours out of the earth into a natural pond, and then two tributaries carry the constant overflow to the *madoodoo ziibi* and Bad

Medicine Lake. That steamy lake is the only naturally heated water on the entire reservation. We swam there with the mallards and geese in winter, sauntered with blue herons in the great reeds close to shore, and we tried to skate with the water striders out of season.

Truly, the barony is marvelous, more generous and humorous than our memories, almost a natural paradise on the earth. That romance, as you know, is a contradiction and the source of our many tricky stories. We named the pond *madoodoo*, an obvious and natural sweat bath for ducks, herons, and other creatures, but the missionaries warned that the warm water was the unnatural influence of the devil in winter. Luster considered their curse his deliverance, the *madoodoo* a native mercy seat, as the missionaries would never, in their pious consideration, come near the natural heat of water, much less tread with ducks and mongrels on the barony. However that may be, our grandmother told stories about the priest who secretly cured many, many nuns of winter hives in the warm water. Grandmother Wink said his nickname was *gichibangan*, or "big peace, and when the sisters pray for peace, they mean more than what they say." Some of the natives were worried too, because no *madoodoo*, or sweat bath, had ever become a land patent, not to mention a back-woods barony.

The old men of the *midewiwin*, the native healers of the *anishinaabe*, told stories that the water must be heated by four great stones, each one hidden by *naanabozho*, the original *anishinaabe* trickster. Hidden in tricky stories, in the pond, under the mountains, and in the blue mire of creation. The old men of the *midewiwin* were assured that their eternal ceremonies would renew the breath of creation. They were healed by the fires that heated the stones and by the mist in the *madoodiswan*, the sweat lodge, and by their tricky stories. The healers were never care-worn, as were the missionaries, by stories of stones, native creation, and the crescent waters warmed out of season. Naturally, they turned that mysterious heat into their own ceremonies as healers. Summer in the winter is a marvelous tease of creation, a chance in the stories of the native healers. The *madoodoo* was a natural heat, not demonic, not even a sacred romance in *anishinaabe* stories and ceremonies at the barony.

Tricky stories, of course, were almost our natural paradise. My cousins never resisted a chance to return to the barony in the winter. We returned to our families, the stones, and the warm water, and always we came back for the taste of grouse and venison. Shadow Box, our grandfather, was a racy outdoor cook. Many times he baked grouse with chokecherries, and venison with rose hips, a delicious combination of colors and flavors. Whenever we were at the barony we heard over and over again the stories of the land patent, the new ceremonies over the panic holes, and how our great grandfather Luster Browne, the most among equals as a baron, first met our great grandmother, the intensely independent Novena Mae Ironmoccasin.

Novena was so named because she was born premature in a wild snow storm on Advent Sunday. The child's young unmarried mother died from exposure, as many natives died in those early days of cruel winters on the reservation. "She died alone, in silence behind the mission, but never in shame," said my aunt Eternal Flame.

The Benedictine sisters at the boarding school cared for the tiny child, and when she opened her eyes for the first time on the ninth day of their prayers in eighteen ninety-two, the nuns named her for their novena. She was a dark and distant child, a serious student who chanted the missal in a clear voice and with a bearable, haunting passion. She was devoted to the sisters at the mission, but she turned down their clerical summons to become a nun and teacher in a consecrated community. Instead, when she was only fourteen, she wounded as many trees behind the mission to create a wild Stations of the Cross. She heard voices at each tree, and then retreated to the *madoodoo ziibi*, the sweat bath river, as her mother had once done, north of Bad Medicine Lake.

The Baron of Patronia came over the meadow almost every day and buried his lonesome voice in panic holes. There, in many, many panic holes, he was sure that his words would nurture the flowers and trees, in the wild sound of his noble names. He planted his voice in this manner, and praised every touch and turn of the seasons. In summer he shouted into panic holes near the moccasin orchids, his solace blooms. He shouted on the blue meadow in spring and autumn, and in winter he turned to panic holes under the cedar near the river.

The barony was more than ten miles from the nearest houses, and he was certain that only the mongrels and other animals ever heard his shouts on the meadow. Not that he was troubled to be heard, but he reasoned that his shouts were closer to creation when he was farther from other humans. The crows shouted right back at him from their high perches in the birch and white pine.

Novena Mae heard his shouts and watched his shadow moves over three seasons. Luster was loud and sudden, his voice was wild, his breath blanched, and blued on the rise of light over the meadow. She was hushed and courteous, hidden at the treeline, at a natural escape distance, but that autumn she moved closer to the *madoodoo* and his cedar house on the crescent. She listened to this man of natural panic and counted the seasons since she had last seen the sisters at the mission.

Eternal Flame said her grandmother, more than anyone, was a natural healer, and "she knew the stories that heated bones and the stones." Novena Mae remembered the scent and sounds of the months she had been alone, the distant crack and thunder of ice on the coldest nights, the mice in the dried oak leaves, blue bears at sunset on the ancient river boulders, the dance of water striders in the warm rain, the crash of lightning in the white pine, and her heart beat under moss, under water, under the memories of her mother and the sisters at the mission. Many years later she told her children that they would never be ruined by their memories of the seasons or their stories of chance. They would be mocked in the world, of course, but never ruined by the native tricksters.

Luster Browne and Novena Mae Ironmoccasin were never married in the mission sense of union, but they raised ten tricky children on the crescent of the barony. He was hoarse and bounteous as he shouted the nicknames of his children over many, many panic holes, and for each child he built a cedar cabin on the meadow.

Shadow Box, their eldest son, and two daughters, Mikwan and Blue Heron, lived their entire lives on the crescent, and never ventured outside the barony. Rain and her brother Bones were the first to leave. They studied art and became eminent painters in New York City. One was an expressionist, and the other a native naturalist. Swarm, their eldest daughter, vanished in a thunder storm. Mae and Rose, twin daughters, died at age two in an influenza epidemic.

Aristotle and Galileo, twin brothers, shared the same nickname because their feet were almost webbed, and because of their silence, mime, and obscure hand language. The Creature Brothers were soldiers in a native company mustered from the White Earth Reservation. They died in a shallow trench in the battle of Belleau Wood at the bitter end of that wretched Great War.

Shadow Box married Wink Martin, his second cousin, who lived with her brother, Mouse Proof Martin, on the shores of Bad Medicine Lake. Shadow Box and Wink were our grandparents. Mouse Proof was our weird great uncle who earned his nickname in a federal boarding school. The first two words he learned to read were on the metal pedals of a bellows organ. The word "mouse" was forged on one pedal and "proof" on the other, and these words became his nicknames. Many native families embrace brothers, sisters, uncles, aunts, and cousins who were related by chance, not blood, or who were conceived in name, but not descent. We never heard the same story twice about how and why our grandparents were cousins.

Gesture Browne, my great uncle, was born outside of the barony, at Wanaki Point in Lake Namakan. Ashigan, his father, was born on nearby Ghost Island. Gesture is an acudenturist, a modest man of precise memories, and he is the first native ever to own a private railroad on a reservation. This acute denturist told everyone who sat in the dental chair, as he fixed their teeth in the luxurious parlor car of his own train, that trickster stories come out of the heart, not the mouth. "My heart hears the silence in stones, but your teeth are rotten, so what does a wimpy smile mean that covers rotten teeth?"

Gesture poked, drilled, filled, and pulled thousands of teeth and never charged anything for the service. He wanted to be sure that natives on the reservation could show a good smile. He knew everything about teeth, but he had never studied at a dental college. The federal agents and politicians on the reservation were suspicious of my great uncle because he would not answer to their authority. They tried to tax his railroad and close his practice because he was not a licensed dentist, but we organized a boycott of the casino and that caused the greedy ones to think twice about the source of their smiles.

Gracioso Browne, a distant cousin, is an economist and historian who lives on the Leech Lake Reservation in Minnesota. He always wears a black business suit and two wristwatches. The mongrels pose in his presence, they cock their heads, and raise a leg, because he records animal behavior with a portable video camera. He also records panic holes, and marches on the meadow with his camera aimed at the hardy blooms. Pure Gumption, Admire, Chicken Lips, and the other mighty mongrels, bounce at his side, always ready to be cast in any scene.

Eternal Flame heard the confessions of many men in the Patronia Scapehouse. Gracioso, you can be sure, was there as a penitent more than once. Hail Marys were common remedies, but she ordered him to masturbate with an animal of his choice. Almost told me how he would listen to men night after night announce their erotic loneliness to his mother in the scapehouse. She told mercy stories about masturbation with bears, beaver, and mice, and then they would leave with a signed picture of Mary Magdalene and two or three very expensive copies of *Manabosho Curiosa*, the monastic manuscript of erotic pleasures with animals.

Gracioso told us that he recorded the best shouts of our great grandfather at the barony and then sold his shouts to the California Transportation Department. The shouts were broadcast on highway medians, and the oleander bloomed overnight. Others learned of the native shouter and played the recording in their gardens. The magnolia and wisteria matured in a few seasons. Many, many copies were made of that original tape recording. Soon the shouts were feeble and so were the blooms in gardens. Luster, for a time, earned residuals as a shouter and became the richest man on the reservation.

Almost lived with our grandparents as a child, at about the same time that my father returned from his parish and then traveled to England. I was always happy to be at the barony in any season, but to be there in the winter was a natural paradise. Almost was very close to our grandparents. He was not their favorite, but doubtless he was the tricky hint of creation, the tease of native survivance in the stories of our ancestors.

Wink, our solemn grandmother, was short and stout, and she had a very smelly breath. She covered her mouth with one hand when she spoke or laughed, to hide her rotten teeth, but the stink was so strong that even the river mosquitoes circled at a great distance. My aunt swore, in the best humor, that our grandmother could drop an insect in flight with a single puff of poison breath. Maybe so, but we would rather give our blood to the mosquitoes than take the chance of being hit by her breath.

My grandmother never mentioned the word dentist. She lived with pain and pried her own teeth loose with a hickory crow. As you know, she vowed never to leave the barony, but the train was the fastest way to the new casino. Wink would not show her teeth on the train, never mind that the dentures and the ride were free, and she would never trust her teeth to a relative, even if he was an acudenturist, because, she said, "real dentists are never on trains, and besides, railroads are the wicked work of missionaries."

Chicken Lips and the other mongrels at the barony were very tolerant of human odors, to say the least, but even they turned away when she breathed in their direction. Sometimes she shooed flies, mongrels, and children outside with her breath. Almost said he collected several bottles of our grandmother's tobacco spittle over the years and used it to chase away mosquitoes and black flies. A mere trace on the station wagon was the best protection on humid summer nights. Naturally, he was often asked by strangers to share some of this native essence. He was generous with anthropologists, of course, but never revealed the source.

Shadow Box and Wink raised nine children at the barony. China Browne, their first born, became a writer and has traveled almost everywhere in the world. She earned her nickname because, as a child, she bound her tiny feet with ribbons and silk scarves. She meditates with visions of lily feet.

Tune Browne, their eldest son, lived alone for a few years in an anthropology museum and, at the same time, established the New School of Socioacupuncture. Later, he became a celebrated photographer and was named the Oshkiwiinag Distinguished Professor of Simulations at the University of California, Santa Cruz.

Tulip Browne is moved to tears by natural power, but *never* men, and the *never* is literal and absolute. She builds miniature windmills, and she owns her own detective agency in San Francisco. Garlic, her closest brother, studied at an agricultural college and, with a generous government grant, developed a distinctive hybrid bulb, the mammoth Patronia Garlic.

Ginseng Browne was born with a nose and instinct much better than most of the mongrels. He snuffled and unearthed wild ginseng on the barony, but not much more. His dubious ginseng trade agreements with the People's Republic of China resulted in a pledge, on their part, to build a bronze trickster on the barony, but only half the figure was ever constructed. The Chinese have a bronze foothold on the reservation, but nothing more.

The Trickster of Liberty, an enormous statue on the meadow, was, we learned later, a negotiated bribe for an exclusive contract to control the world market of Madoodoo Amber Ginseng.

Mime Browne was born without a palate. The sounds she made as a child were seldom understood by anyone outside the family, so she learned how to mouth words in silence, and to imitate hand and facial gestures. She told great stories about native hand talkers with her hands. Sadly, the night after she attended the ground breaking for the trickster statue, she was raped and murdered behind the mission water tower. The crime has never been solved. Tulip investigated the murder for more than a year, but she has never revealed what she found, or who she might think is a suspect. The most hated priests were accused at first, and even a few nuns, but the only evidence my cousin made known was a casino coin.

Slyboots Browne, the most clever and devious trickster at the barony, graduated from college and then founded a factory to build microlight airplanes on the barony. He trained native pilots for an airborne revolution. The microlights were great, a fantastic liberation flight, but the unusual native revolution never got off the ground on any reservation.

Eternal Flame Browne renounced the convent and established a fashionable scapehouse on the barony. Almost, my closest cousin, is her only child. She has never told anyone the name of the father, but most people think he was a priest. Cruelly, at one time or another, our cousins named the oldest and most despicable priest, and then every other man on the reservation as his father. We even wondered for a time if we were brothers by blood and cousins by name. Sister Flame, once the most sensitive nun in the order, earned her nickname at the cloister. The abbess censored the wild passion in her letters to her cousins and noticed the natural blush on her neck and cheeks. The Patronia Scapehouse is a haven to wounded women, and a station for men to confess their sins on the reservation.

Father Mother Browne renounced the priesthood and ordained the Last Lecture, a tavern and sermon center on the meadow at the barony. Father Mother, in fact, is my real father, and there has never been any secret about my mother. Sharon Mary Greene is a church historian and novelist who once lived with her family on the Isle of Man. My father first met her at the Canterbury Cathedral in England. My birth was a secret, not mentioned for three years, and then my father left the church, married my mother, and returned to the barony.

Father Mother was an ordained priest in the Order of Saint Benedict of the Roman Catholic Church. He might have been a shaman in an earlier generation, or an ecstatic, but evensongs, the glorious instrumental music of the church, and the heat of confessions, moved him more than the native flute or the mere heart beat of the water drums. The ascetic and lonesome nuns were ever tender at his side as a mission student, and later more earnest than ever to hear the natural treat of his litanies as a priest. The mongrels leaned to the warm shimmer of his body. He had the hands of a healer, and his numinous touch was no secret at the mission. The bishops were worried, as they must be about a native healer, and banished him to a remote parish. Many stories at the mission traced his scent to the spring willow, to bears at the river, and to the heat of musk and blue mire. My father was a man of creation, and his native fate was most feared at night.

Father Mother is a natural healer, but the stories of his native heat were never told as true testaments at his first parish in Fortuna, North Dakota. The church was built at the turn of the century, and the stories of the past priests were lost in the storms and maneuvers of the parish-ioners. My father, one bitter winter night, was invested in the narrow chapel as a potent member of the Flat Earth Society.

Father Mother and my aunt Eternal Flame were both tricky healers. My father was one of the healers on the prairie, not with promises of ec-clesiasticism or casinos, but with a shout and the everlasting praise of mongrels. The sick and lonesome came over the prairie to hear his new creation stories, to shout into panic holes, and to be healed at last in the Cathedral of the Flat Earth.

Pure Gumption, the mighty shaman mongrel, healed with her smooth tongue and rough paws. She licked the twisted hands and blue arthritic thighs of the bent and tormented, and nosed the tortured dis-tance out of the prairie children at the chancel. They shouted their in-terior distance into many panic holes. In the natural heat of these com-munions, my father and the mongrel healers chased the enormous shadows of prairie silence out of the cathedral, and shouted those wicked shadows right over the edge of the earth.

Then, one humid afternoon, the beams creaked in the clerestory, the air cracked in the nave, and the birds shivered at the rose windows. Lightning sheared the meadow at a distance, and thunderclouds towed the prairie into night. The wind and rain beat on the doors, and the sud-den storm turned the outhouse over at the back of the cathedral. Trees were down, the water tower listed to the east, and the wind sheers moved several houses on their flat earth foundations.

My father was blamed for that storm, and for the trouble over the panic hole shouters who came to town to be healed. He was accused be-cause the worst storms seemed to come with the new priests. The last three priests were seen as the cause of wicked storms that blew the school down twice and carried the wooden courthouse into the next county. Birth, marriage, property, and death records, court documents, and pages from geography textbooks were found in shreds on the prairie more than a hundred miles east of town. The documents were unfurled on fences and decorated the windbreaks. The collection was tedious, but each recovered note has become a source of community gossip to this day. Since then storms have been associated with the priestly pres-ence of the Roman Catholic Church in Fortuna.

That storm, the fourth one blamed on the priests, you might say, brought my father and mother together. My father was driven by threats and curses from his first parish, the Cathedral of the Flat Earth. He returned in silence, the mighty mongrel healers forever at his side, to the barony. He waited at night, many nights, on the blue meadow to wear the morning star, his spiritual conversion at the barony. Later that summer he met my mother for the first time on a tour of Canterbury Cathedral in England. She was there doing research for a historical novel about the murder of Thomas à Becket.

Father Mother returned to meditate at the barony. His mission, of course, would never be the same. The winter was bitter, the seasons lonesome. His memories were never hurried in the *madoodoo*, as he waded in silence with the herons. He was a celebrant, a communicant, and a mourner at many wakes in the spring. Then, on the summer solstice he had a vision to ordain a new mission, a tavern and sermon center on the barony.

The Last Lecture was constructed in three months on the meadow near the scapehouse. Outback of the log tavern my father carved a precipice and named it the Edge of the Earth. There, seven public telephone booths were anchored to the crest. Each booth had doors on two sides. One door faced the back of the tavern and the other opened out over the escarpment. Visitors were invited to present their last sermons, their very last lectures to an audience of natives in the tavern. Many people came to end their native poses in one last lecture and then walked out the back and over the edge with new names and identities.

Cozie Browne, our cousin, had been abandoned in the last telephone booth at the back of the tavern. She was a few weeks old, at most, wrapped in a bright blanket at the bottom of a brown sack. The word *minwaajimo*, printed on a tavern coaster, was tucked in the folds of the blanket. The word means "tell a good story." Overnight, lost or found, she became our cousin. We teased her at every turn, with our best stories, but she heard the literal causes, not the tease. Once we told her about a winter paradise, an ice house that can hold every native ancestor at one time. "That's why natives drive out on the ice in winter, to dance with their dead relatives."

Cozie said our stories were not true. We persisted with our tease and told her that "the ancestors return from the dead to the ice houses, they rise out of ghost holes in the ice." Finally, she counted the natives who drove out on the ice one day, and decided our stories might be true. So, she walked out to a house alone one winter and watched a hole in the ice for three days. Sadly, she waited, and waited for her lost mother to rise in the ice.

The Last Lecture was a tavern for those tired of their poses and native identities. Cherokee charlatans walked over the edge as Irish, Blackfeet impostors turned Greek, Hopi peace fakers studied to be Italian, and Chippewa posers turned back their identities to be French.

Father Mother learned of my birth and renounced the priesthood. At the same time, he returned the telephone booths and closed his contentious mission at the Last Lecture. My parents were married that autumn at Canterbury Cathedral.

So, as the natives of the canon, my cousin and me were conceived by chance, and that became our sacred bond at the barony. Almost was the son of an anchorite and an unnamed father. My mother is a novelist and my father a priest. Nothing, you see, ever seemed uncommon in our experiences and stories at the barony.

Almost convinced a blond anthropologist one summer that he was born by chance in the bottom of an aluminum wild rice boat. He told her that he learned how to read in a limousine. She was amused, and with extreme manners attentively recorded every word he said in narrow blue notebooks. She wrote that he was raised by mongrel healers as they sat in the back seat of his birth car. The only story she ever doubted was the creation of the *madoodoo* on the barony. She noted that the heated pond "could be an overstated sense of mythic presence, as he never revealed the sacred location."

Almost told her more than anyone could ever remember, more than could have happened in a century on the barony. Really, and we were doubly amused when he stole her notebooks and then insisted that they start over again. He could not retreat from her patience and serious surveillance of natives. Naturally, he told her different stories, and declared the most obvious contradictions to see if she remembered anything from the first round. His stories were bettered on the second performance. She was dedicated, a cultural anthropologist, and without a trace of irony, she recorded his stories as true representations of native traditions.

Almost learned how to read on his own, from books that had been burned in a fire at the Nibwaakaa Library on the White Earth Reservation. The building, once the residence of federal school teachers, was struck twice by lightning and burned in minutes, right down to the stone corner blocks. The few books rescued from the ashes were burned on the sides, the corners rounded by the fire. Almost learned to read the centers of the books and then he imagined the stories from the absence of words, from the words that were burned.

Grandmother Wink had never crossed the border of our reservation, but she told convincing stories about how the government was run on manners and nonsense, otherwise, "politicians would never wear a headdress to win votes." She taught us to understand that the real world runs on four natural deals, as in the common sense of barter and chance. In this way we learned that tradition was an undecided deal between memories and native stories. "Memories are real, stories are the seasons, so remember the deals," she insisted.

Wink told us that the first deal was chance, "remember chance," as things happen without manners or causes, "just like the big deal of creation." The best deals are not the causes. "The shamans see to that," she said, "so leave the causes to the lonesome priests." We meant to ask her about the cause of her foul breath, and then she turned and laughed in our direction. We ducked, held our breath, and the poison passed right over our heads. The second deal was the natural deal of pictures. "Words are pictures, the way we see with animals in stories, and the pictures we see with the sound of the words." She said the third deal was to eat *real* food out of the natural world, not a picture or tasty description of an entrée or dessert on menus. The last deal was the very best in our memories. She said we must tease manners and liberate our minds with trickster stories. "Tricky stories are the best games of liberation." Almost took the fourth deal more to heart than anyone else. Believe me, he is the most liberated native that ever lived on a reservation, almost.

Almost is a natural deal of his own. My cousin is a mighty teaser of worried hearts, the poser of survivance, and a healer with warm hands and native reason. He could easily turn stories of chance adventures into motion and action, as he has done so many times at the barony. Once, however, his persuasive stories about blank books landed us in jail, and it was our very first business experience in the city. We had established a mobile bookstore with borrowed money and a station wagon with a weak battery and bald tires. We promoted books by native authors, of course, but my tricky cousin insisted that we stock more blank books than otherwise, as we could earn more money. We folded and bound our own books and sold them at regular book prices. Every other book on our portable shelves was a blank book, and some of them, our special "trade books," had bright calico cloth covers.

We drove to the city, parked here and there in loading zones, opened the back of the station wagon, and sold a few copies of *The Way to Rainy Mountain* by N. Scott Momaday, and a few more of *Faces in the Moon* by Betty Louise Bell, and one customer bought seven signed copies of *Bone Game* by Louis Owens. Almost never hesitated to sign the books as the author, and now and then he would sign another author's name for the association value. Once he signed several copies of *The Sharpest Sight* as John Steinbeck. He boldly signed *The Map of Who We Are* by Lawrence Smith in the name of Maxine Hong Kingston. On the title page of *The Light People* by Gordon Henry he signed as the novelist Ishmael Reed.

Naturally, we sold most of our books at the University of Minnesota, but not the books you might think students would buy. We parked the station wagon on the circle in front of the literature and humanities center and sold hundreds of blank books in a single day. Almost was right about our real business, but we never could decide why students were so eager to buy empty pages bound in cloth covers. True, the students were curious about reservation natives in a mobile book business, but we never played native to the audience, and we certainly never conveyed the blank side of our calico books. My cousin told students that the best stories were heard in the absence of printed words. "The orality of a blank page is worth a thousand printed words," he said and almost convinced me.

Wiigwaas Trade Books, the brand name of our empty books, was a great success and we never had enough of them on the shelves. The *anishinaabe* word *wiigwaas* means birch, as in birch bark, and we wondered if the students thought our books were made of native birch bark. The books were hand made, no doubt about that, but not of birch bark. We bought large sheets of paper from the same company that supplied the university and folded the signatures by hand, so the pages in each book were uneven. The students seemed to like the feature of a featheredge.

Thomas King, the novelist and photographer, arrived at the barony one day with his "culture trunk" tied to the back of his car. The trunk was packed with fake native costumes and fantastic turkey feather headdresses that were used in various posed pictures of anthropologists. He also collects books by native authors and surprised us with an offer to buy first edition signed copies of our Wiigwaas Trade Books.

Several versions of that story, however, did not keep us out of jail. We had just sold the last of our trade books one day when the university police arrested us, then and there, for consumer fraud, false advertising, and conducting a commercial business on state property without a license. We would have moved the bookstore sooner but the battery was dead, so we waited for a student to return with jumper cables. The deal was chance, and if our battery had not gone dead we would not have been arrested, and we would not have gone into the catalogue empty book business. We were taken to jail and the borrowed station wagon, our bookmobile, was impounded by the police.

Professor Monte Franzgomery told the judge at our court appearance the next morning that he was there to support our book business at the university. His hair was white, and he wore a black silk shirt that filled the entire courtroom with the smell of too much laundry perfume. Almost remembered that the professor was the one who danced around the bookmobile to the sound of shaman drums. He was the one who leaned to the side and danced in circles. The tape we played held the attention of students on campus, but we had no idea that an elderly professor would dance to our tune. He never bought a book or said anything at the time. What a deal, you never know who might stand by the chance of our memories and stories. Naturally, we were grateful that he was there at our bookstore, and we were beholden that he was in court the next day.

"These boys are natives and they must have the natural treaty right to conduct their business on the campus of a land grant university," the professor shouted in court. He stood at the wooden bar and never moved his hands. Almost, however, thumped his fingers on the wooden table. The professor leaned to the side and moved his feet to the beat of the shaman drums. "We are the real trespassers, your honor, because, as you know, the land of our university, of this state, of this nation, was stolen, and the receipt of stolen land, as a land grant or mission, is no less a serious crime."

The judge listened to the professor and then ordered the bailiff to verify his credentials and identity. No doubt the judge had heard so many crackpots in court that he could no longer trust his own sense of truth in character. "Professor Franzgomery, does your presence mean that you are here to pay the fine, or to instruct me on the legal theories of sovereignty?"

"Indeed it does, your honor," said the professor.

"Indeed what?" asked the judge.

"I am here to support these boys and their books," said the professor.

"Five hundred dollars," said the judge.

"Wait, wait a minute, that's more than we made on the entire sale of our books," shouted Almost. The judge was stolid and waited as the professor wrote a personal check for the amount of the fine. The deal was more cause and less chance than we wanted and we were in debt over our first serious commercial enterprise.

"You boys have much to learn about the ways of business in the city," said the judge. "You might try your hand at the casino back on the reservation." He smiled, and we knew what he meant about native casinos.

"*Maanoo*," said Almost.

"What was that?"

"The chance of justice is a native casino," said Almost. We smiled back at the judge and then rushed out of the courtroom before he said anything more about reservations. Almost burst into laughter and his voice echoed in the rotunda of the courthouse. He hardly ever worried about anything.

Professor Monte assured me that our blank books made more sense to him than anything he has read in the past decade at the university, and he would require his students to buy our calico trade books for his course in romantic literature. "In that way you can stay in business and pay me back at the same time." He said our books were a source of inspiration, and the blank pages were a "spontaneous overflow of powerful feelings." Actually, we were never sure if he was a tricky professor or just cracked with age, but such distinctions never mattered very much because the deal was chance, and there were hundreds of others much stranger than him on the reservation. Not only that, but he loaned us money to establish a mail order catalogue business in blank books. Our second business was located on the barony. Coincidentally, he loaned us money on the very same winter day that he waded in *madoodoo* with the herons.

"What a deal," said our grandmother.

Almost told him stories in the warm water about how he learned to read burned words, "the ashes of native literature." The professor was so impressed that the two of them became instant brothers in a name. Almost never mentioned that most of the books in the reservation library were those condensed novels published by Reader's Digest Books.

The catalogue sales of our blank books has grown every year, as more university courses require our empty titles. While our business booms we never know how students use our books. Last month, for instance, the best and most expensive calico cloth edition of our blank books, marbled and with a fore-edge painting of our mighty mongrels, was assigned in a cinema course on "race and courtesy cultures" at the University of California in Santa Cruz.

A few years ago we introduced blank books with literary autographs. My cousin, you remember, signed the names of various authors, but most of the native authors whose books we once sold gave us permission to duplicate their signatures, and for the dead writers we either found a facsimile or we created a distinctive signature. Almost, for instance, signed for Jesus Christ, Crazy Horse, Geoffrey Chaucer, and William Shakespeare.

Monte loaned us money, but it took us several months of other deals to double that amount so we could rescue our impounded bookstore. We paid the fine, but the battery was dead, of course, so we waited for a chance. At last two police officers, amused by the bumper stickers on the back of the station wagon, came by and told us that they hunt bear and deer every autumn on the reservation. "What This Country Needs is a Good Injun Tune-Up," the most obvious message on the tailgate, the one that always embarrassed me, was exactly the one that amused the police and resulted in a jump start. "Words are never more than chance, and you never know what deal might be funny," said Almost. He has always assumed that there is as much chance in the mundane and stupid as otherwise.

We hold four blank book conferences every year, one each season, in our main office, located in two abandoned station wagons. The first is the original birth wagon with the sunroof, and the other is our bookmobile, double parked forever on the barony. My cousin has never come to any of our conferences without a sense of chance, wild reason, and tricky stories. We have traveled together many times, and we see the same situations, but his stories are almost never the same as mine. Some of his stories might cause you to think that we were never in the same time or place, much less the same memories. Our book conferences were like that every year.

Almost would rather tease his own presence in stories than bear a customary rank or honorific title that might encourage envy. Priests and politicians duck his tease and elusive presence, but children love his transformations because he never worries them with manners and pretensions in stories. Clearly, children everywhere are liberated by his stories, the native savant of tricky stories.

He is heard by some elders as more earnest and believable than tricky, a native of mere chance and coincidence, and others hear him as elusive, wily, and dangerous. You might believe the worriers and wicked backbiters on the reservation, but his stories are closer to the truth of native reason, or at least his tricky stories are the absence of the cultural concoctions of sacred traditions. Otherwise, the tame and obvious would be our best creation, and chance a mundane casino romance.

Almost is a head turner, even in his own family, as no one has ever been able to predict the outcome of his experiences, adventures, or stories. He is not elusive to me or our cousins, but he is his own instance of reason, a natural wild reason. Shadow Box and Eternal Flame are convinced that he inherited the tricky spirit of our great grandfather Luster Browne.

Almost is almost the vision of motion in every word, that sense of sovereignty in every sentence. His stories are the continuous creations of his visions and memories, and his stories never end, a natural absence of causes, closures, authenticity, and authority. What a deal, and he told me the "world is seen in tricky stories, so we are the tricky reason that nature is created in stories and not discovered with envy."

Politicians on the reservation say he is far too negative, an "unreliable native," because his stories never end in the familiar tragic tune of dominance. What they never say, especially the casino politicians, is that there are no native immunities to the diseases of corruption. Almost is almost the tricky cure, never the disease or envy. The one thing his family knows for sure is that nothing, not even the *madoodoo*, matters more to him than humor, the humor of chance, and the natural deals of tricky stories. He might even vanish one day in his stories, not end, but come to naught, and that might be one of his best stories.

Almost teases others to move and shimmer in their own stories. He was born in motion and has been on his way ever since. He created a rare curiosa manuscript, bound and sold blank books, chartered a hotline healer service of natives on cellular telephones, taught at a private college, and he has been invited to lecture at many native conferences and commencement ceremonies. My cousin teases his own stories, the hotline healer of survivance.

3

Healer Dealer

 The Mississippi River starts out north of the barony. There, at the headwaters of the *gichiziibi,* the great river, you can almost hear our creation in the traces of the stones and the bruises of the seasons. You can hear our stories in the seams and creases of the clouds, and tease the crows in the tender reach of the birch. Our presence wavers on the river, in the wake of beaver, in the slow and certain rise of cranes, and the secret march of the unnameable blue and silver creatures in the reeds.

Almost Browne was on his way to the absolute source of the great river that autumn. He leaned over the water to catch the crows in the birch, in the course and shimmer of the clouds, and noticed the obvious, the virtual reality of native histories. Many years later he leaned over a simulated poker machine at the casino and, in the rush, much the same as over the river, he created the native *mizay* laser, a signature hologram of virtual memories. Now his creations beam and shimmer the tricky traces of our histories, and the traces over the river stones are almost the same as the laser characters over the barony.

Grandmother Wink named the laser natives the *mizay,* because the traces of the trickster over the crescent reminded her of the tactile whiskers of the freshwater burbot. Almost never hesitated to use that nickname for his signature creations.

His laser simulations of characters, once heard and seen in stories, were seen at last over the great river in native histories, over the crescent on the barony, and at the roulette tables in the casino. Almost has traveled many times in visions and dreams, and out of ordinary situations in meditation, but his *mizay* natives, the creation of virtual reality, that visual presence in the consciousness of others, are more precise and memorable to many natives than some of the characters in his tricky stories.

Well, as you know, he almost created a native presence in the virtual reality of laser characters. Almost told stories that created a simulated presence, and many natives have sworn that some of his characters were absolutely real and even won money at roulette and the slot machines in the casino. His stories, and the visions of other natives, were almost virtual realities, so we were not taken unaware when he created *mizay* laser characters. The mission nuns covered their heads with black hoods in the presence of the laser, so as not to be seen by the pagan holograms. On the other hand, natives came from many communities to see wild tricksters shimmer in the air. The luminescence of native stories were seen and heard on clear nights over the entire crescent on the barony.

Actually, he created virtual reality and the *mizay* laser holograms for at least four very practical reasons. The first was to influence judges and juries with virtual evidence, tricky stories, and native histories in courts.

Almost, for instance, once invited a federal judge to wear magic socks and laser moccasins so she could enter the shadow realities of native consciousness. Naturally, she resisted at first, but then she consented to be the first judge to travel in a native world of virtual realities in her own courtroom. The evidence of this visual native presence was not the mere competition and arguments over facts, but a creation of the moment in the visual sense of tricky stories. My cousin pointed out that legal strategies and procedures are no less tricky than the virtual realities of native stories.

The judge wore a helmet with a miniature television screen, magic socks and laser moccasins as she moved behind the bench. "Your honor, this could be the wave of the future for witnesses," said a native. The socks were woven with miniature beads and electrosensitive fibers that were more responsive to touch and muscle movements than flesh and nerves. The beaded sensors were even activated by heart beat, perspiration and changes in blood pressure to create a simulated visual reality.

Almost asked the judge if she could see animals. Yes, she said, "a panther, and there are three wolves." Then she sat in silence, and leaned back in the chair behind the bench. The judge perspired and moaned in a sensuous pose, and then she leaped out of the moccasins and slammed the helmet on the bench.

"What did you see?" asked Almost.

"Never mind," said the judge.

"Whatever you saw was virtual evidence."

"One is virtual and the other is the truth," said the judge.

"Did the panther scare you?"

"No, monks were masturbating with the wolves."

Almost persuaded her to try the moccasins once more, "this time the native scenes will be evidentiary." He stimulated the electronic beads and created the crescent near the headwater as the first scene. The judge saw birch, red pine, a black bear in the distance, and natural meadows with a man shouting into panic holes. Then she entered the shallow river at the source. The shiners nibbled on her toes. She reached down to touch a smooth red stone, reached through the clouds, and pushed under the clear water. She swam with the fish close to the bottom of the river, over the bright stones to the last seam at the source. The judge saw my cousin at the source, and he told her tricky stories about native sovereignty.

The second reason he created the *mizay* laser was to be a virtual presence at the casino and never, never lose. Almost was a virtual genius at roulette, a presence and laser perception that favored him to see the colors and read the numbers in advance. Casually, he was a virtual winner, and he taught me to be a virtual gambler, to enter the memory and concentration of croupiers, to tease and win at roulette, blackjack, and slot machines. The trick, of course, is to be close enough to the tables at the casino to rush over the moment the virtual presence wins to be the other, the winner, the real other to collect the money. We almost never lost at virtual reality, and never at the casino.

Naturally, natives are worried about the *mizay* laser simulations of history, but when they see the stories of their survivance in a sublime luminescence, and when the characters are cast wiser, wittier, and more humane than natives have ever been presented in other stories and histories, their worries vanish forever. Almost virtually created a literature of survivance and a better native history.

The third practical reason my cousin created virtual presence was to travel and be seen in many places at the same time. This, he said, was laser shamanism, and the mastery to be seen more and more was much better than once, because "wicked tongues are more active in our absence than in our presence."

The fourth reason was that natives could visit the very best doctors, dentists, bankers, barbers, professors, and presidents, with a virtual easement. You know how difficult it is to get an appointment with a doctor, and how much it costs to see anyone named a specialist or an expert, not to mention a late lunch with a rich banker, or even a conversation with a distinguished professor, or an audience with the President of the United States.

Almost created memorable names, scenes, and cultural calendars with his virtual reality visitations. President Richard Nixon, for instance, promised that my cousin would become the next vice president if he raised a revolution of "American Indians to overthrow Fidel Castro." The Great Pumpkin, or *gichi okosimaan* in *anishinaabe*, one of the many nicknames we gave Nixon, was obsessive about a native covert action to liberate Cuba. We gave him many other nicknames too, such as *ozhaawashkwaabi*, or "black eye," and *giiwanimo*, or "deceptive," which became the Great Deceiver. Almost has an audio transcription of that presidential warrant to prove the conspiracy.

President William Clinton invited my cousin and me to be a virtual presence at a cabinet meeting and later to a private conversation in the Oval Office. Almost introduced me as a virtual administrative assistant and then, in an unusual diplomatic gesture, posed mundane and bottommost questions to the president about a balanced budget, education, medical care, and a lasting peace in the world. We avoided any mention of veto measures or notice of showdown politics in the Democratic Party. "How would this be perceived overnight by our adversaries," my cousin said and then cocked his head, ready for an executive response. The use of the possessive pronoun worried me, but the cocked head was even more worrisome, virtual or not, because it was his tricky inquisition pose. He cocked his head to the side and said, "Mister President, who gave you that dumb, dumb, dumb watch?"

Nobody ever seemed to listen to anybody else, so our virtual presence was hardly noticed that afternoon in the White House. Really, we were convinced that the government, virtual or not, was a matter of chance because no one hears anything without a political standpoint, not even their own stories. The president pretends to listen to his trusted advisors, but they never really speak to him, they speak to the imminent documents of history. No one was really there with us that afternoon, not even the president, but who would care? We were the virtual visitors, the virtual presence of the reality of natives. So, our virtual presence was a reality, as natives have always been political simulations in the world. The president might have been there in the same sense, elected in virtual reality, and then his presence turned real, a myth in the mirror of his own history.

Strange, but my cousin might have been heard when he cocked his head and posed a dumb question about the president's wristwatch. At first we thought about giving the president a nickname. Ghost Legs, or *jiibay nikaadan*, came to mind, but we decided to see if he had a sense of humor about time before we announced a native nickname. "Mister President, what time is it?" asked Almost. The president laughed and then looked at his watch for the longest time. "You know," he said, "no one has ever asked me that since my inauguration." We told him that native shamancy and the presidency were virtually the same, at least in the sense that both conditions were the end of ordinary time.

We tried to convince the president that his ordinary black digital watch was a conservative conspiracy. He seemed to listen, but had no idea what we meant. What virtual time would the president notice? The next day he wore ordinary numerals, and we heard that he might try a watch without numbers. Then, at the close of our virtual visitation, we presented the president with a pair of beaded virtual reality moccasins. He pressed the moccasins to his nose and seemed pleased to learn that the leather was cured with the brains of a deer.

Almost assured the president that if he wore the moccasins late at night on the birthdays of past presidents he would be able to walk and talk with them in virtual reality. The president wore the moccasins then and there, and asked his secretary to provide a list of presidential birth dates.

"Andrew Jackson's not worth the trouble, and wouldn't you know, he's the one who does the most talking about states rights on his birthdays," said Almost. "Harry Truman, on the other hand, has to be coaxed to say anything about the presidency, but tell him you really like his daughter's voice, and the tune of her novels, and he might say you're a fool, but a damn good one, and start talking straight away about how to outwit the demons of greed and political piety."

"Now, there's a new idea," said Clinton.

"The Great Pumpkin has more than a few promises to keep, and when you walk on his birthday, remember to consider me as his vice president," said Almost. "Fidel Castro lost the revolution to native sugar cane."

President Clinton said he would be dancing in his moccasins come the very next presidential birthdays in the spring. Once again, the stories of our virtual visitation with the president are much more pleasurable than an elected presence in the Oval Office. The best of our native memories are never measured on a causal clock.

Almost is convinced, or so he says, that natives created presidential politics, and reservations, federal schools, missionaries, and even the most treacherous Indian Agents. "Otherwise," he said, "we might be struck stupid by too much praise as natural healers and feathered shamans."

"Almost is overly suspicious, and for reasons," said an agent.

"The great temptations of noble savagery," said Almost.

"Natives are never suspicious enough to be great at anything."

"*Maanoo*," said Almost.

More than once, on stage at a graduation ceremony, my cousin has said as much and more about suspicion and savagism in the context of the inventions and simulation of natives. No matter, the students who were moved to tears by victimry could not bear to hear irony, and they loudly hissed the mere mention of the word savagery.

Almost was his own teacher, or as he told my father, "the healer dealer of my own bright memories." His education was by chance, as he seldom sat for more than an hour in any school and never completed even one whole grade of instruction. He was never tested and never finished an academic examination on anything. Everyone at the barony thought he was endowed with native wisdom because he avoided schools and became a natural healer with his own stories. As you already know he learned how to read from the burned margins of library books. Astronomy came to him in a similar way, through the sunroof of an abandoned automobile. Naturally, he had his own nicknames for the planets and stars as they passed through the open sunroof, and the rest of the universe was imagined. Our many mongrels, the bears, herons, and shamans, turned the earth and traced the stars, planets, and seasons at the barony.

My cousin teases academic audiences with his own creation stories, obscure notions, and wild metaphors, such as "the ears of ancient animals beat nature and the river in my heart." Some students have swooned over his "native memories," and others hear him as a natural wizard. Consider his story that universities are the same as burned books, because "nothing can ever be known but the unnameable, and the best of books, libraries, and universities is in the imagination of what is not there, the burned bits are the real bits, the real is the unnameable." Absence and the burned bits are natural metaphors in his stories, but the ancient ear in the heart is not a common strain to me, not even an unnameable beat.

Almost made his name as a native scholar on the road. He soon became a master of short lectures to large classes in history and literature at many universities in the country. His nickname, for a time, was *akwanaamo*, or Short of Breath. This nickname was true because he lost his breath in front of academic audiences. That fear remains to this day, but hardly anyone notices his many disguises.

Almost started his peripatetic lectures in humanities courses at Bemidji State University in northern Minnesota. More natives were students there than at any other university we visited. In other words, he started out with a critical and sardonic audience, and the humor was much wiser in a native presence. Then, in a few months, he moved his wild notions and lectures to the same campus that gave us our dubious start in the blank book business, the University of Minnesota.

Professor Monte Franzgomery invited my cousin to lecture in his course on romantic literature. He introduced him as the "native master of the spontaneous overflow of the unwritten." That gave me the chance to try out other nicknames, such as the Spontaneous Unwritten, and the Blank Master. Almost lectured for a short time about moths, and the great dance of the moths at night. He created fantastic moths in his stories, and then landed in a flutter with the notion that the natural camouflage of moths was the same as the pleasures of romance in literature.

"The disguises of the moth are the double adventures of nature in our other nights," said Almost. Monte was astounded at the creation of a moth metaphor of romance, "a true return to the romance of nature," and insisted that we both sign blank books for his students. My cousin autographed several books as William Wordsworth and others in the name of Samuel Taylor Coleridge. Later we were treated to a lunch at the faculty club on campus. We ordered walleyed pike with wild rice and spread the fine bones on the monogrammed carpet.

Soon the peripatetic romancer was invited to lecture in the Ivy League. Karl Kroeber at Columbia University said my cousin was "one of the subtlest of trickster artists" in the native tradition of long nights and slow mornings. Elaine Jahner at Dartmouth College introduced him to an introductory literature class as the "natural deterrent to academic boredom, and our native traces of the last slow train out of town." Ishmael Reed, the novelist, said my cousin was a "talking book." Henry Louis Gates at Harvard University compared his spontaneous stories to the best tricksters of natural reason in the native reins of structural orality. "This 'inner dialogization' can have curious implications, the most interesting, perhaps, being what Bakhtin describes as 'the splitting of double-voiced discourse into two speech acts, into the two entirely separate and autonomous voices.'"

Almost was almost famous for his wild stories and creative lectures. He never pretended to know more than creation, more than the instance of his stories, but he never discouraged others who might have assumed that he knew everything. In this way he could pose a wise denial and start another story. Only children could break the tricky thread of his creation.

"Whatever you hear in my stories comes out of the natural air right here," said Almost. "You hear my stories on the run, in a vision, and that is the creation of sovereignty." Even when we wrote his lectures out in advance he never read what was there. He created other stories from the ones that were written, a creation from the absence, not the presence of words. His stories are never the same in sound or otherwise.

Amherst College in Massachusetts was the only academic institution my cousin was ever forced to leave. Certainly others worried about his tricky presence, but he was seldom in one place long enough to be removed. Amherst, however, measured manners by the minute. One student said there was a "manners clock" in the president's office that ran four times as fast when natives were on the campus. My cousin wears four wrist watches, as you know, but not to see time or manners. He told the students that he wears watches in the same way that curators exhibit ordinary native sticks, stones, beads, leathers, and feathers in museums.

Almost was almost more outrageous than he had ever been at other universities, and in such a short time. Extreme actions are sometimes roused by the weather, by a wicked breach of manners, by teases, tricky stories, and obvious lust, but in this situation the extremes were aroused by nothing more than common masturbation.

My cousin told his stories about bears, mice, and moths, and that the real measures of a hunter are his disguises, lures and traps, not the cold body counts. Then, a male feminist professor asked my cousin about his "position on animals." Almost assumed the professor meant a sexual position, and was eager to show several positions described in the *Manabosho Curiosa*. Naturally, my cousin mimicked bear onanism. How could he resist such an obvious invitation? The wild masturbation scene aroused the audience. That, however, was not the specific reason he was removed from campus. My cousin teased seventeen students, thirteen men, and four women, to masturbate with a wild animal in mind. The students masturbated at the rail in front of the stoical portrait of Calvin Coolidge in Johnson Chapel. That was the end of his time at Amherst College. Later we learned that the college president removed the portrait and painted the chapel a severe white.

Almost is erratic, to say the least, and his influence on others is nearly as memorable as his stories. Belinda Swithen at the University of Michigan, for instance, wore a simulated prickly pear cactus costume and danced in wide circles on stage as my cousin told stories about fleas and social scientists. "Anthropologists are the ectoparasites of our creation and literature, and the lowly fleas are better friends because they choose our company to raise their families. The fleas of chance are buried in our hair, but even a hundred flea bites are more memorable than the curiosity of a cultural anthropologist." People in the audience were scratching their heads by the time he finished his stories.

Kimberly Blaeser at the University of Wisconsin in Milwaukee introduced my cousin at a convocation on "Buried Loot, Indestructible Breeds, Trickster Landmarks" with a compendium and a poem she discovered for the occasion. "Trickster is not distinctly human, animal, or god, but has magical powers, including the ability to change shape at will. So, as a cultural figure, trickster makes the transition from mythic to modern times and remains not fully one kind of being," she said and then read a poem in a vibrant tone of voice.

> almost is twice our other eye
> the hotline healer
> teaser of nicknames
> never the true touch that ends
>
> mongrels dream our stories overnight
> forever out of breath
> rush the shadows on the meadow
>
> we might never last to hear the end
> trickster traces of creation
> our lonesome stories
> tease the same unnameable seasons

Alan Velie invited my cousin and me to say a few words about natives and literature at a faculty meeting of the English Department at the University of Oklahoma. Velie introduced Almost as the "Gimpel the Fool of the Chippewas," and then talked about lovable idiots, pathos, and natural humor, in native literature. "Great comic authors are often moving as well as funny, but only the greatest—Shakespeare and Faulkner, for instance—are both at once." His voice was loud, clear, and fast. Louise Erdrich's "account of the way Lipsha and his grandmother accidentally kill Nector Kashpaw is reminiscent of Shakespeare's account of the death of Falstaff in the way it combines humor and pathos."

Velie is magnanimous, a generous, direct, brisk, ready, and funny man, but we had no idea what he was talking about at the time, so we asked a hesitant faculty member near the door. "Rugbyese," she said, "and there are no timeouts in his literary game." Velie is a master player of Rugby, and his mother tongue of action is rugbyese, a field of crash words that takes no subjects or objects.

Almost talked about books, the barony, and told the faculty that our blank books were required reading in many university courses. Someone asked for the name of the author, and then another faculty member shouted out from the back of the room, "Golem, he's the only author of blank books worth reading in my book." Velie doubled over with laughter. The rest of the faculty, with a few exceptions, broke into a haunting silence of wild tics and nervous turns of the head. One professor, a stout native poser who wore a stained hat with a beaded eagle on the visor, ticced and moaned as he turned in his chair. He moaned to his right for every native who died of the pox, ticced to the left for the natives who died on the road, but he never said a memorable word to anyone at the university. Ruby Blue Welcome, the resident Bureau of Indian Affairs agent and professor of native medicines, carefully explained that he was "touched by prairie mold, a condition that causes foot and mouth tics, withers and moans, and the curse of native malaise and victimry."

Velie bought seven copies of our calico edition of blank books, and we signed each one with a distinctive flourish in the names of Isaac Bashevis Singer, N. Scott Momaday, Louis Owens, Eudora Welty, Maurice Kenny, Linda Hogan, and Geary Hobson.

Louis Owens, professor of literature at the University of New Mexico, walked into the auditorium backwards that afternoon and introduced my cousin at a conference on "The Literature That Matters Out of Place," sponsored by the Southwestern Symposium of Aesthetic Landscapes. "Almost is that eternal brother we must see in our dreams," he said with his back to the audience. "Never perfect, never electable, never holds back the sunrise, and that makes him almost more real than our own families." We gave him two copies of our calico editions inscribed by Jack London and John Steinbeck. "Louis Owens knows more about my novels than anyone alive in blue jeans," wrote Steinbeck. London's inscription was in the name of his hero Buck. "Now we read the same blank pages, and we share the same pleasures of the mongrel named Custer."

Almost was invited by N. Scott Momaday to talk about his animal stories at a seminar on creative writing at the University of Arizona. My cousin wore a short maroon skirt, bulky wool sweater, and a rubber mask that resembled Jay Silverheels. "That's not the actor, he looks more like Ward Churchill," said a student. Others who had seen the actor in movies and heard the writer at conferences were not convinced that the simulated countenance was the same. Momaday, in turn, wore the adventurous black mask of the Lone Ranger. He told the filmmaker Matteo Bellinelli that he was interested in appearances and loved masks, "I like people who wear masks, whose faces are masks that reinterpret realities behind them."

Almost told pleasurable stories that hot afternoon about the native shaman named *gaaskanazo*, a nickname that means "whisper." She was an old woman at the headwaters of the great river who taught the monks how to masturbate with animals. Momaday told the eager students that my cousin was "almost a man made of words." The stories he told were comic, erotic, and obscure trickeries, but many of the students, poised to hear the litanies of native creation and victimry, never heard much of the humor. Maybe it was because no one could bear the stench of animals that came from the sweater he wore. His sweat simulated the musk of creation, a much trickier story than the students could imagine at the moment, but no one laughed until my cousin removed the sweater and sat at the head of the seminar table in a black lace brassiere. A mongrel sneezed over the wet wool sweater. "Indeed, almost a woman made of words."

Canterbury was the start of my stories, the place where my parents met for the first time, and the actual place of my conception. Professor Robert Lee had never met my cousin, but he heard about his lecture and stories at the conference "The Literature That Matters Out of Place" in New Mexico. He immediately invited my cousin to meet with his students at the University of Kent in Canterbury. Bricky Lee, a nickname he earned in California, was a lively lecturer on ethnic literature and wanted my cousin to talk about native oral stories, "and be as tricky as you can be in a word."

Almost was amused that someone had heard his name in another country. He never forgot some of the tales he read by Geoffrey Chaucer, and was ready to tease the fowl and good women of his memory, but at the last minute he changed his mind about the lecture. The true reason is that he has never applied for a passport, and, as you know, he would never bear his own picture, embossed by the government, to prove that he was a real person. Remember, one of the natural deals we learned from our grandmother was not to eat the pictures on menus either. So, that was my chance to be my cousin and me at the same time and see Canterbury Cathedral.

Roberta Rose Eelpout, a friend of the university, met me at Heathrow Airport in London. She was an independent scholar, editorial writer, and former librarian, who told me as she drove that she had read many books about natives. She was most certain about common virtues, the recitation of manners, and the precise summaries of people, places, and family events. Certain to a fault, and yet, as she drove, she never paused once for anything between her constant and intense stories. Eelpout was a maniac on the road, as she must have been at the circulation desk in the library. She weaved, passed, and shouted at other drivers, and the entire time she told me one romantic native stereotype after another. She had an ear for the obvious, and she almost convinced me to believe in the primal kitsch and great native insights of Jamake Highwater, Lynn Andrews, and the notable Carlos Castaneda.

Eelpout asked me about my native identity as she caught her breath and entered a wild roundabout. I told her my father was a priest, my mother was a novelist, my grandmother had rotten teeth, and we lived on a barony. She was not interested in my family and circled for almost an hour trying to find out something about my exotic and sacred culture, but each round inspired more stories about the crescent, the *ininishib madoodoo*, and my uncommon cousins. She heard nothing repeatable of native romance or traditions.

"Almost is a name to conjure with," said Eelpout.

"Eelpout is a rival entrance."

"Surely your name is more than an adverb?"

"Almost, and nearly more, but not quite."

"Fowler, you know, entered your name as an incompatible."

"Almost incompatible."

"What about blood quanta?" she asked abruptly.

"Native blood, however minimal, is pure and simple, and much lighter than the blood of others." She watched me in the rearview mirror. I caught her critical eye for an instant and winked once, twice, but she was not one to smile easily, and quickly turned away.

"Lighter, do you mean color?" asked Eelpout.

"No, not the hue, the stories are much lighter."

"What then, native stories about blood?"

"Science has proven that native blood is lighter."

"Nonsense, surely you don't believe that?"

"Millions of natives have been bitten by mosquitoes over and over in the past hundred thousand years or so, and in all that time not one mosquito has ever been grounded with heavy blood." I waited for a response, but she clucked her tongue and said no more. "You see, even the stories are much lighter."

Two or three rounds stimulated other stories about the barony. She circled, listened, and clucked, circled and clucked to the center, closer, slower, and then, only when she heard the word shaman, the native practice over panic holes, and animal masturbation, did she cluck too much and leave the roundabout on the road to Canterbury. I told her about how to balance the earth in a shout over a panic hole, but she was probably distracted by the thought of monks masturbating with animals and wanted to leave me as soon as she could at the University of Kent.

Bricky Lee waited at the campus corner to welcome me. Eelpout raised her thin white eyebrows, a sign that she was not charmed by my humor. Bricky, however, was more than tickled by the masturbation stories, and asked me to do the same at the convocation that afternoon. I mentioned the monks and their lusty way with the animals, a new erotic totemism, and told other stories of bears and squirrels, and the mighty mongrels of the barony who were natural healers.

Pure Gumption, in fact, became a mongrel saint in the stories about my father and his first parish on the prairie. I told the students that my father heard the shouts over panic holes as confessions, and the mongrels pawed, healed, pawed, healed, but there was never an end to the soul sickness on that endless prairie.

Masturbation, as it turned out, did not seem to be a subject that interested the students that afternoon. My best stories were heard in silence, as the students were much too serious and romantic about natives to consider the ironies and contradictions of my royal family on the barony.

Bricky Lee invited me to the private wine cellar at his college. We drank rich and rare red wines, an academic treat, told more stories about masturbation, bricks, bats, and pigeon toes, and then the night crashed on our memories. I mentioned my cousin only once or twice by mistake in our lively conversations, but quickly turned the pronouns around, and he never suspected that my presence was almost as real as my cousin, a virtual visitation. Much later, of course, when he and his wife visited the barony, everyone was almost there in the same name. Bricky wore a few feathers to get even, and was so taken with the *ininishib madoodoo*, that we ate lunch, thin slices of venison cured in honey and blueberries, heavy bread, and rose hip custard, served on floating trays. We asked him about the real story behind his nickname, but he revealed no more than "the art of bricksmanship is an elevated experience." That night, over wild rice wine, he told my cousin that his father advised young men to carry a brick on every date. "Almost once is never enough," said Bricky Lee.

John Purdy persuaded my cousin and me to visit his seminar on native literature and that evening to celebrate his appointment as the head of the English Department at Western Washington University at Bellingham. Almost does not like parties of any kind, and even less attractive is an academic party, but we went along for the promise of good food. Purdy teased us with a native menu, salmon on cedar in his backyard on Mosquito Ranch Road.

Almost told the faculty and their wives around the fire that he was born and raised in a native salmon hatchery on the Strait of Juan De Fuca. The family mongrels were at his side, and pushed him ever closer to the fire with their wet noses. "We were at sea for a long time, a common salmon tradition," said my cousin. The mongrels licked his hands on both sides. He turned to the fire and his eyes caught the flash of the coals that night. "A few salmon would not return to the hatchery with the others, as was our promise and custom, instead we started a salmon resistance and swam right up the rivers and streams into the mountains, and that resistance was a trace of our lost tradition. We swam in the clear mountain streams between the great bear paws and the sudden shadows of eagles, but at the very end the other salmon shunned us because we had escaped from the hatchery. We were not admired for our resistance in their pristine mountain streams."

"So much for uppity river coups," said a postmodernist.

"The end of your resistance?" asked a modernist.

"Resistance, the end is in the name," said a language poet.

"Hatcheries are pristine, so clean, indeed hatcheries are salmon heaven," said a scholar of children's literature. "So, why would any young salmon from a hatchery take pleasure in your story?"

"Our resistance landed in the bears," said Almost.

"There's no resistance in this meal, because this is the bear's story now," said Purdy. He served the salmon as he roared with heart and humor, and in return the faculty toasted their new chairman. Everyone was amused by the stories, the responses, and the salutes to health. We ate with pleasure, and then leaned back in the shadows. The hungry mongrels, excited by the stories, and toasts, circled, barked, and crowded their master right into the center of the fire. He roared, lost his balance, and then landed on his back in the coals.

Purdy was in pain, and yet my cousin turned the severe burns to humor in the emergency room at the hospital. Almost told the story that the faculty, incited by one of the past heads of the department, "pushed the new chairman into the fire, and then, a pack of hungry modernists turned him over on the coals a few times to see if he could survive the heat of the deans and university administrators." The mongrels licked him clean and healed his burns, of course, and since then he never leaves for a faculty meeting without a good licking by the mongrels.

The University of California at Berkeley was founded on stolen native land and racial treacheries. Nothing new that land was stolen, but when the thieves were honored as the founders their names, not native nicknames or stories, became the haunted landmarks of terminal histories. Almost said that much the first time he was invited to lecture at a transethnic studies convocation. He assumed the land was stolen, and stolen native land was almost the true cornerstone of every public university. When his comments were published in the student newspaper a professor of physics responded, in a critical letter to the editor, that such "historical inaccuracies are slanderous to the good name of our university." My cousin never worried about responses to his lectures and stories, and so he never noticed that the letter by the physicist was corrected by another professor who cited the actual documents and history of land theft. So, the university was founded on land stolen more than once, and the professor warned that ignorance of that history is no less a crime.

Berkeley was our lecture station that winter. Our tricky stories and the mongrels on campus might have healed the lost students, but they were caught in examinations at the end of the semester, and could not hear the mongrels. The natural food and fruit juice on every corner, the scent of wet acacia, and the bloom of magnolias, turned the memories of our seasons around and nothing was ever the same.

Almost listened to hundreds of healers on the campus, and he tried almost every new age cure. One day he was cornered and healed with crystal energy, and later his past lives were tuned to perfection by the chants of transpersonal monks who wore turquoise and tight cowboy boots. At last he was almost prone to colonic irrigation. That first winter he told everyone about his experiences with healers, and never failed to mention the sensation of the stainless steel irrigation pipes. He intruded on many campus lectures with his colonic stories. Most of the students were amused, but not their professors, who reported the colonic intrusions to the police. In fact, the campus police once told my cousin to leave a lecture on philosophy.

Professor John Searle is a philosopher of mind, consciousness, and the intentions of language, so my cousin was certain he would not mind a perceptive metaphorical intrusion in his lectures. He started his intrusions at the back of the classroom, and then moved slowly down the aisle as he spoke.

"Sir, philosophy is colonic irrigation, a true metaphorical instrumentation and intentional state of mind and body, but the intrusion is neither a vision nor a simile of consciousness," said Almost.

"Who are you?"

"Almost."

"Indeed," said Searle.

"Sir, the intrusion is intentional," said Almost.

"Indeed, an ironic utterance."

"The *sir* is ironic," said Almost.

"Sentences and words have only the meaning that they have."

"Philosophy, then, is colonic," said Almost. The students were surprised at the play of language and must have reasoned that the intrusion was an intentional structure of the lecture. Their heads turned with the words, one intrusion to the next.

"The problem of explaining how metaphors work is a special case of the general problem of explaining how speaker meaning and sentence or word meaning come apart," said Searle. He was precise and very determined, as if his intentional utterance had been written in advance. "It is essential to emphasize at the very beginning that the problem of metaphor concerns the relations between word and sentence meaning, on the one hand, and speaker's meaning or utterance meaning, on the other."

"Almost the other," said Almost.

"Quite so," said the professor.

"Sir, would you answer a question about identity?"

"Doubtless an ironic utterance," said the professor.

"John Searle is Cherokee, is that an irony or a metaphor?"

"Neither literal nor figurative."

"The meaning must be in your resistance," said Almost.

"That utterance is not literally true."

"The *San Francisco Chronicle* reported in a story about affirmative action that you said, 'Look, as it happens I'm part Cherokee. What relevance has it to the quality of my work?'"

"What is your question?"

"John Searle, part irony or Cherokee?" asked Almost.

"What could be the relevance?"

"John Searle said that 'sentences and words have only the meaning that they have,' and if the meaning of 'as it happens I'm part Cherokee' is not literal then it must be an ironic or metaphorical utterance," said Almost. "Why would a distinguished philosopher choose a native identity only to announce in public that it has no relevance?"

"The metaphorical utterance does indeed mean something different from the meaning of the words and sentences, but that is not because there has been any change in the meanings of the lexical elements, but because the speaker means something different by them," said Searle.

"*Maanoo,*" said Almost.

"Speaker meaning does not coincide with sentence or word meaning," he continued, as if his comments had been twice revised. "It is essential to see this point, because the main problem of metaphor is to explain how speaker meaning and sentence meaning are different and how they are, nevertheless, related."

"How are you related to your sentences then?"

"Word by metaphor."

"Gemma Corradi Fiumara wrote in *The Metaphoric Process* that the 'paradox of a metaphor is that it seems to affirm an identity while also somehow denying it,'" said Almost.

Searle seemed to reach, in silence, for a wiser metaphor, but the reach was ironic because the course period ended. The students gathered around my cousin to continue the conversation about metaphors and identity. The students wondered where he had studied philosophy. That encounter, no doubt, was one of the reasons the students later invited him to present the commencement lecture.

Almost was bound to the creation of stories, and in stories he posed the ironies of manners, the contradictions of cultures and traditions, teased the tiny aesthetic turns of scholars, and untied the hypocrisies of education. He cocked his creation stories at philosophers, but had the most ironic pleasure with those teachers he nicknamed the "tiny master-workers," because their sense of stories was so narrow, so literal, and precious, that native literatures were never mentioned in their courses. His stories are memorable, and in this way he has touched the humor of many thousands of university students over the years.

Almost was paid thousands of dollars for his stories and lectures, but he never took any of this attention very seriously. Somehow he spent almost everything he earned in a few days. "The money from stories is never real, so take the money and make more stories," he told the students at an overnight conference on "Gaia Shawomen, Fairies, Golems, Winsome Witches" at the University of California, Santa Cruz. He bought clothes, and gave them away. He bought new books and gave our best blank ones away. He gave money away, especially to students and street people who wanted to eat or travel somewhere.

Almost insisted that we travel first class everywhere. We hired limousines and ate at great and expensive restaurants. Chez Panisse in Berkeley, for instance, created an "almost green sandwich" in honor of my cousin, or at least they served him that story. He never ate greens on a plate, but would turn the salad into a sandwich, and then wipe the plate clean, very clean. Soon, of course, the owner served my cousin his salad in two narrow sandwiches. He is never without a tricky nickname, as you know, and one of the four deals was not to eat pictures or names. He ate everything the waiters served and never worried about the names.

Chez Panisse turned us away the first time because we brought along four street mongrels, and they were mighty healers with great tongues, to share our dinner. The owner was more than curious, you might say, about my cousin but not the mighty healers at our heels. She told him to return soon again, but not with the mongrels. We walked around the block and the mongrels ran with two children into a nearby delicatessen.

So, we returned that night to the restaurant and waited our turn to eat. Almost was never any real trouble in restaurants, but the humor ended abruptly with his farts. He would sense the moment, turn to the side, raise his first finger, break wind, and then name the native sway and scent. Garlic, bean, onion, and oat winds were the most nauseous and memorable. He had another habit that brought pleasure to the mongrels at the barony, and later bothered most customers in restaurants. Actually, we both crunched on bones and then threw the remains on the floor. Children did the same thing, of course, but we never saw our behavior in the same way. When we told these stories at the barony our relatives wondered why we were ever served a second time.

Almost thought we were an absolute pleasure to serve, and that, because we were uncommon natives with a natural romance and great stories. Peculiar and extreme, maybe, because he gave money away on the streets, but my cousin would never leave a gratuity at a restaurant. "You buy the meal, not the favor to watch me eat," he told the maître d' at Lalime's in Berkeley.

Masa's Restaurant in San Francisco was not amused in the slightest by our native presence or stories. We ate there twice to the tune of several hundred dollars, but we were told by the headwaiter never to return without a bonded custodian. First, we were not pleased because we had to wear neckties, a dress code to eat, but the meal was the very best and the most expensive. The maître d' directed us to a small round table in the center of the restaurant. Every table was under a bright spotlight.

Almost turned everything into a sandwich, as usual, no matter how precise the preparation, and we threw bones around on the carpet in the darkness at the side of our table. They turned the spotlight out over our table when dessert was served. We sighed, smacked, slurped, and made other noises in the dark. Almost never could understand how the parvenus and blue bloods could eat under a spotlight in almost total silence.

Actually, we almost threw the bones on the carpet. You see, our presence in the restaurant was more than real, and our stories are tricky. Memories are that way, uncertain from one creation story to the next, uncertain enough that you better not mention our names in any restaurants.

4

Fifth Deal

 The Transethnic Situations Department at the University of California invited my cousin to create a native ceremony of truth, reconciliation, and harmony. The department, at the time, was an obscure cause, a transethnic marker in white water, and the faculty was so undecided they could not even agree on an academic mission statement.

Native American Indian Studies, one of the three academic centers in the department, was almost in ruins. The romance over shamans and warriors would be the last to wane, but the lavish shadows of native literature, and a native presence on the campus, were erased by the soul wanderers, those who hunted and haunted the lonesome and wounded faculty. One native professor was told to leave, with his worrisome dick in hand, and several other faculty members, disheartened by yet another generation of treasons and dominance, were on their way to positions at other universities.

Governor Pete Wilson, in his wicked reach for the presidency, turned his back on the integrity of ethnic diversity and affirmative action at the University of California. We were there on the marker at the time to hear the academic pietism, the many failures of learned words, the political extortion of race and rights, and we encountered the dirty white lies of the governor.

Almost named the governor *mangindibe nichiiwad,* the "big head catastrophe." My cousin is almost never overcome by easy vows in a hoarse voice, not for any reason, as you know, because he teases the pious with trivial names, and he forever mocks the manners of ideologues and opportunists. The most perverse posers, however, were those in the race for the least power, the puny ducks of a poached dominion.

President Andrew Jackson, for instance, practiced a perverse and vicious mode of victimry. He held to his promise that if elected he would act in the interests of the rights of the states over the federal government, and so he ordered the removal of the native Cherokee from Georgia.

Jackson, Wilson, and others, have ducked and slithered behind state sovereignty in their cruel and ironic pursuits of the constitutional power of the presidency. Jackson caused the Trail of Tears. Wilson has no cause to mention more than his old political sores and scores.

Natives are forever betrayed by wicked politicians, because their power is based on the laws and lies of stolen land, and the abuses of sovereignty. The mutant electorate, never the heirs of native land, are outsmarted at last in the stories of the shamans and healer dealers.

Almost heard many times the stories of *gaaskanazo*, the old *anishinaabe* woman who was a shaman in the fifteenth century. She is the one who created the heart dance or *debwe* ceremonies. My cousin heard many times how the monks had established a monastic library at the headwaters of the *gichiziibi*, the great river, and how *gaaskanazo*, a nickname that means "whisper," taught them how to masturbate with the animals as the pleasurable restoration of natural harmony.

The *Manabosho Curiosa*, the monastic manuscript that describes the *debwe* heart dance and other erotic ceremonies, was discovered by an antiquarian book dealer at an auction in London. Many scholars have studied the stories and are convinced that this rare manuscript is authentic. To say otherwise is to deny the truth of eroticism and tricky stories. My cousin was moved by these stories and started a similar heart dance festival at the barony. There was no need to teach natives how to masturbate, or so he said at the time, but the other curiosa ceremonies were converted and revised as a native festival to ease the tension of worried hearts, tease the pious, the most serious, trick the lonesome, and dance back our harmony. We learned how to shout over aesthetic panic holes, the most sacred of our histories, but we shouted louder at television, and danced later with a native beat, and overturned the obvious missions at the time of the *debwe*, as if there were obvious missions and manners to overturn at the barony. We danced to outlive the burdens of traditions and the power of victimry. We danced for seven nights and anything short of that was almost harmony.

Almost started the *oshkidebwe* festivals, the new *debwe* heart dances, and other ceremonies in native studies centers at many universities, but some radicals, casino nationalists, and the new crossblood nativists, constrain any tricky stories or natural moves in a dance. The *debwe*, to some natives, is a perversion of sacred traditions, but stories are not sacred and traditions must endure the sovereignty of native motion. Our tradition is the heart dance, not the silence of posers, or the stoic pout, and not that native grimace over the wide drums on the Fourth of July.

Academics pout too much over the aesthetic panic holes of history, but my cousin never likens academic ruins to panic holes. Obviously, not much comes of shouts at universities, and even more risky, academic natives are haunted by the soul wanderers. Not even postindian fry bread could save the day. The grievous nativists, bent to a spiritual silence, were cornered in the academic ruins of their own essential victimry.

The Transethnic Situations Department was an ironic creation of academic extremes, no less than the angry politics of peace. The diverse faculty was driven by chance, doubts, suspicion, envy, and aesthetic vengeance, for more than two decades of ethnic poses and politics. At last, the tenured faculty had nothing more to lose than the ornamentation of humor, and so they summoned an outsider, the native master of antienvies and tricky festivals, my cousin, Almost Browne.

Whisper created the *debwe*, as you know, and my cousin created the *oshkidebwe*, a new heart dance of truth to counter the temptations of envy and secrecy. As a matter of fact, my cousin practiced the new academic truth festivals first at the barony. He wanted to be sure the tricky motions worked with classical music and his favorite bullroarer.

The Last Lecture, in a sense, was the actual start of the academic *debwe*, the contested truth of native identities, and even the confessions at the scapehouse were similar to the truth ceremonies. Naturally, when my father closed the tavern many natives lost their connection to the obvious, the salute of their communities, and turned to the new casino cultures. They waited and were ready for any reason to shout the truth at a heart dance. So, the tricky toasters of the old tavern were eager to practice their shouts over the poses and common envies of learned professors.

Almost practiced the *debwe* festival with recounted academic situations and real faculty names. Grandmother Wink pretended to be the head of the department, and other relatives posed as the rest of the faculty. Shadow Box was the dean overnight, and when he danced the faculty and students were truly liberated. Our academic truth festivals were great pleasures, as you can imagine. We mocked the most envious scholars in the department, and turned academic gestures into various sexual positions with animals. The practice festival lasted for seven nights, and at the end we were convinced that universities must be some of the best, and most ironic, sources of tricky stories.

Grandmother Wink has always been the one who casts the right moment to start the festival at the barony. So, one night she starts the distinct beat of the water drums. Our hearts rise to the beat, and we dance. No one should ever be shamed or envied at the erotic heart dances. My cousin said, "stoic silence is the faux pose of shame and victimry."

We shout over panic holes, and dance, dance, dance to the erotic memories of the first *debwe* ceremonies at the headwaters. We dance out the lost and lonesome soul wanderers overnight. Wicked memories forever hover in the winter trees, and ice blues the windows with tiny envies. We shout and dance, otherwise the soul wanderers might crush our stories of survivance to hear their own miseries and victimry.

We hear the sound of the water drums in the early autumn and that is the natural start of the *oshkidebwe*, the new truth of the heart dance. Ready or not, the silence ends, and the festival lasts for seven nights. The beat carries to the headwaters of the *gichiziibi*, and in the other direction the beat can be heard as far away as the Ozaawaa Casino on the White Earth Reservation.

Almost always traces the sound of the drums with his willow bullroarer. He circles the meadow and whirls that aerophone overhead with tremendous force. The sound, as you know, is haunting, and at night the roar could have been the voices of our spirits at the heart dance.

Then, the tricky stories of creation start, and native shamans catch the eye of animals and lead them back to the barony. The shamans can be treacherous, unstable, and touchy, but only the envious mistrust their visions. Who knows, a tricky vision might even heal the university. The treasons of others are the cause of more misery than uncertain visions. Shamans are worried about poses and power, and yet they wear strange costumes to the heart dance. My cousins never tease the shamans, at least never in their presence.

Almost taunts creation, the obvious and mundane, but never the shamans. Sometimes he wears an enormous wooden *niinag*, or penis, trained to his waist, and teases those who are too serious about creation. Frequently he crossdresses as a nun and masturbates with animals. No one has ever denied the stories that some of my relatives were easy cross-overs with various animals at night. My cousins have arisen as beavers, brothers come out as sisters, our fathers dance as mothers, and the best nights are the heart dances of sensuous motion, erotic animals, and almost a natural harmony.

Family treasons are absolved overnight in the *madoodoo*, and we dance natural reason and the truth out of breath for seven nights. Sharon Greene, my mother, who was once very serious, brave, and rather cautious, became a new woman at the heart dance. She was a novelist, as you know, and somehow that seemed to be a good introduction to the festival. At one dance, for instance, she carried two snowshoe hares, one over each shoulder like a clerical tippet, and wore nothing more. My father wore his clerical vestments more than once to the dances, and teased our absolution with erotic gestures and unruly humor. Later, at the end of the ceremonies, my mother always worries that so many others have been denied the pleasures of such harmony.

The *debwe* festival is a dance of truth, a native agreement that anything can be said, any manner mocked, any secret revealed, any traditions overturned, and any erotic affection or emotion performed without fear of censure or retribution. Well, almost any manner, as you know we never tease the shamans. What a deal we made with our shouts and ceremonies. Naturally, my cousin named our heart dances the "fifth deal of the barony."

The Patronia Scapehouse never closes, not even on the usual holidays, but no one is ever there to hear confessions during the *debwe* festivals. There is no real need because everyone is in constant motion at the dances, an absolute avowal of shame and guilt. Heart dances are the true stories, the most reliable memories, and the best admission anyone ever heard on the barony.

Eternal Flame, my aunt, is always the wildest dancer. She wears many tiny bells tied to her waist, thighs, and ankles, and the sound of those bells never seems to end, night after night a constant jingle for the entire festival. Our family, no matter the cause of trouble or the distance, always returns to the annual *debwe* heart dance at the barony.

Gesture, our acudenturist, parks his marvelous train at the end of the line near the headwaters, and every year he mounts that ancient dental chair on the meadow, right over the panic holes. He wears a black opera cape, dances, doubles over with lusty stories, extracts, patches holes in molars, and creates false teeth with tricky smiles, the toothy signatures of the heart dance. Years later almost everyone remembers the dance by the color, curve, and peculiar angles of the dental plates. Some natives can even name the precise summer of the signature dentures, based on a certain earthy turn of the teeth. For instance, some false smiles were overbites, other new teeth were uneven, spaced too wide, or twisted to the side, and the colors were never the same. Not mere coffee or to-bacco stains, but some dentures were blued, marbled, veined as stones, and others blushed with the hue of roses. "Why, that's a smile created at the casino harmony," my cousin said to an old man in line for ice cream. "Seven heart dances back," said the old man with a wide smile. His teeth were speckled.

The Mormon Church started the run on dentures many years ago. They sent several young missionaries out to convert the natives on the reservation, but their gifts and generous attention were always returned, and that ended any sense of obligation. Dressed in business suits the missionaries chauffeured native elders here and there, but a ride was worth at least a fresh blueberry pie, or a beaded necklace. The Mor-mons were never able to bait the natives with transportation, but what did the trick was free dentures. The elders were pleased to be seen at services with new homogenous teeth. The dentures were cultured pearls, a signature of the church.

Gesture, at about this time, started his fantastic free railroad on the reservation, the Naanabozho Express. He knew the elders would pose their smiles at a few services to match the cost of the dentures, and then return to their own community churches. He was right, of course, the perfect milky teeth were worth about thirteen services.

Gesture, who resisted missionaries, anthropologists, shamans, and wolverines, in that order, was surrounded by identical, insipid toothy smiles, molded for the elders by the Mormon Church. The churchly smiles were unbearable, and soon became the source of constant mock-ery, so he created original signature dentures that were clearly native. The stories of the denture wars have endured as a measure of resistance on the barony.

The elders honored the acudenturist with many mighty mongrels over the years, an ironic gesture of gratitude for their signature teeth. The cost to feed the mongrels was more than the cost of the dentures, but the mongrels became a signature of the train. They leaned out of the coach windows and barked to the children at the side of the tracks.

Ogin, the old woman who sang, "I am as beautiful as the roses," and danced with Casino Rose, Agate Eyes, and Cracker, a feisty crow with one leg, was named in many stories about the native acudenturist on the Naanabozho Express.

Grant Popper, the lawyer who once represented native sovereignty, was disbarred for land fraud on the reservation only months after he built a grand house on the south shore of Bad Medicine Lake. The second winter of his forced retirement he turned to gambling at the Ozaawaa Casino. He could think of nothing else at night but the sound of coins at the casino, and by the end of the year he lost his house, wife, everything. Popper, in fact, borrowed money from some of the natives he once represented in court. No one was really surprised because he always drank too much and never won many cases anyway. My cousins honored him as the first panhandler at the casino.

Popper tried to steal money from an old woman at a slot machine one afternoon. Ogin, a nickname that means both rosehip and tomato in *anishinaabe*, had just won fifty dollars in quarters, and as the machine spit out the coins, she caught a fat white hand in her purse. She shouted, *gimoodishkiiwinini*, a thief, and then turned to the crow on her shoulder. Cracker crowed, swooped, and pecked his hands. When the lawyer tried to smile, pretending that nothing had happened, she hit him in the mouth with a sack of quarters and broke his front teeth. The sack broke too, and as he searched for his teeth on the carpet he stole several coins. Ogin, and others, wacked the lawyer as he crawled out of the casino into the snow. That, more than anything, ended his career as a lawyer and gambler, but he won a signature denture for his wicked conduct.

There are several versions of how the old woman and the mongrels became dental assistants, but this is the true story. Once outside, the lawyer screamed with pain as the cold air rushed over the stubs of his broken teeth. He covered his mouth and marched in circles, a drunken white man at the entrance to a native casino.

Casino Rose and Agate Eyes circled the lawyer and barked once or twice, but the young mongrels were more curious than serious. Cracker crowed and bounced on the backs of the mongrels.

Popper heard the train at the casino station and must have considered the many stories about the native acudenturist, so he captured the two mongrels as payment for a partial denture. Gesture, who never trusted the lawyer because he wanted natives to sue the railroad for better dental care, created a goofy smile that amused everyone on the reservation. The first time he was allowed to return to the casino everyone laughed at his smile. Actually, the lawyer was rather pleased that his crooked smile won so much attention.

This, however, is a story about the mongrels not the lawyer. Ogin saved her coins but lost her lucky mongrels. Casino Rose and Agate Eyes were stolen as they waited outside the Ozaawaa Casino. Naturally, she worried about the mongrels, and sang love songs to honor their memory. Then, almost a year later, as she was singing in the dental chair on the train, the mongrels heard her voice. Casino Rose and Agate Eyes barked as they ran to find her in the parlor car. The mongrels leaped into the dental chair and licked her hands and nose.

Ogin, as usual, sang, "I am as beautiful as the roses." She was not, of course, beautiful in any sense of the word, but the song was a natural tease to cover her enormous nose. Casino Rose and Agate Eyes howled in tune, a great spiritual return.

The Naanabozho Express became a permanent home for the old woman, the crow, and two more mongrels. They lived on the train to the end of the line. Ogin assisted the acudenturist and entranced the patients with native love songs. Cracker rode on her shoulder. Casino Rose and Agate Eyes howled for everyone who sat in the dental chair, a mongrel tune in the natural motion of sovereignty. They left the train only to dance at the *debwe* festivals.

The truth festivals are cast in the autumn, but once we danced in the summer. Grandmother Wink had awakened from a dream of bears dancing in the autumn, so she beat the water drums. She was in her nineties then, round, almost silent, and a teaser of the seasons. We danced and never worried about the time or reason. Later, because of a storm, we almost changed the season of the festival. On the third night of the *debwe* that summer a tornado raised the Ozaawaa Casino. The winds twisted the slot machines at a great distance in the air, and thousands of coins rained over the heart dancers on the barony. Tune was in the dental chair at the time and his tricorn hat filled with bright new quarters. Naturally, the rain of coins became a sign of the times on the reservation. Two mission priests were out fishing when the rain of coins almost sank their boat in Bad Medicine Lake.

Gesture's dental chair was a wicked machine, but the *debwe* festival is such a pleasure that no one has ever had the heart to moan with acute pain. Grandmother Wink, however, is the only native elder on the barony whose teeth have never been repaired or replaced with a signature heart dance smile. Gesture, no doubt, would never have survived her poison breath. He even wore a gas mask as part of his military costume for the dances that summer, just in case she changed her mind about dentures. She does not believe in dentists, and certainly not in relatives who are acudenturists. As you know, she has always been suspicious of trains. She could not bear to see the vanishing point of the tracks in the distance.

The signature dentures soon became valuable collectibles, and several museum curators announced their intentions to buy a representative smile from each and every heart dance on the barony. Almost was certain that such a collection of native dentures would invite envy not humor.

China Browne was in Macao, her most recent exotic residence, and returned for the last few days of the festival. She was the public information director of the new Wanisin Elephant Casino, established and owned by our distant relative Griever de Hocus. The word *wanisin* means "get lost" in *anishinaabe*, and the name was accurate in more than one sense. Griever, you see, used the casino to liberate elephants.

China, as you know, was so named as a child because she was forever binding her feet with ribbons. At the festivals she bound her feet tightly with blue silk, and then she danced on the crescent as the thin cloth slowly unfurled. The mongrels barked and chased the waves of ancient silk. She danced for hours and the silk banners trailed her at a graceful distance, right down to the *madoodoo* with me. China is almost our favorite aunt, a fantastic dancer, and she has the most erotic lily feet in the world.

Grandmother Wink heard the name Griever de Hocus and rushed to remember the romance of the avian revolution on the reservation. Slyboots Browne graduated with honors in economics from Dartmouth College and returned to the barony to build airplanes, the celebrated Patronia Microlight. He had learned how to fly biplanes and trained many airborne native warriors who became the aces of the microlights. Griever, who was a teacher in the People's Republic of China, at the time, bought a microlight from Slyboots and was last seen in the air over Tai Shan Mountain and the Temple of Confucius with a blonde in the bucket seat, and on his shoulder that eternal rooster named Matteo Ricci.

"Griever vanished in thin air," said Wink.

"He landed in Macao," said China.

"That crazy rooster never could fly," said Wink.

"Griever convinced the government that a particular parcel of land near the cemetery was native and sovereign," said China. "You know he has a way with natural reason, and no one was really surprised when the government signed a treaty, so he started an incredible casino, and declared the sovereignty of his own reservation in Macao."

"We adopted that boy as one of our very own," said Wink.

"Actually, the sovereignty of elephants," said China.

"Microlights to elephants?"

"Naturally, the casino is not his real ambition, there is always more than the obvious in his stories," said China. "Griever started a circus along with the casino, and the secret of the circus is to rescue and liberate elephants, and other abused animals in the world."

Tune Browne was there in his tricorn hat, as always, and had his way with several animals. He wore a beaver breechclout and teased the mongrels, and then sat for hours between two foxes near the fire. My uncle sang, over and over in a nasal tone, "Two foxes facing each other, sitting between them."

Naturally, he was very pleased to hear that his nephew had been invited to start a similar *debwe* festival at the University of California. Tune was certain that academics could do much better if they only "learned how to masturbate more often with an animal rather than with models and paradigms in mind." He once lived in a native wickiup that he built with his own hands in the anthropology museum on campus, and he taught a seminar on "native wickiup meditation." Tune taught a tricky line of meditation, to be sure, but the moment he moved the seminar from the institutional wickiup to a public landfill, the new muse of refuse and waste lost his academic connections. The nomadic bark and brush was removed from the museum and the exhibition was closed.

Tune, however, was on the move. He unraveled the mystery of the "vanishing native pose" in ethnographic photographs, and then he vanished in the city. Tune was soon "discovered," as a newfound object, in a sense, by a curator of a photographic exhibition, and three years later he was named the Oshkiwiinag Professor of Simulations at the University of California, Santa Cruz.

Tune Browne is a teaser of the obvious, as you know, a natural inheritance of the barony. He once noted, for instance, that several native images had vanished on valuable photographs by Edward Curtis. He named these arcane escapes an "emulsion evanescence" and "postindian transmutation." For that, and his discovery of the disappeared poses, he was commissioned by three national museums to solve the mystery of the disappeared, the vanishing native images.

"Comic reversal of the obvious," said Almost.

"New creation stories," said Tune.

"Portrait genocide," said Ramona Reason, the curator of the national exhibition of native photographs by the celebrated pictorialist Edward Curtis. "We discovered, at first, and much to our horror, that three photographs had been stolen from the museum." She spread her fingers on the white marble counter, blue veins in the cold bone. "Later, of course, we learned that the situation was much worse, the very images of two warriors and one shaman in a bear skin had somehow vanished overnight from the untouched photographs."

"Alas, the vanishing race," said Almost.

"Those photographs were museum treasures," said Ramona.

"Discovered, no doubt, at an auction," said Tune.

"Worse, they were borrowed from private collections."

Tune teased the curator, her tastes in race, found objects, discoveries, and treasures, and told the museum directors that the first documented evidence of the vanishing native, or "emulsion evanescence," was in New Mexico.

"Naturally," said Ramona.

"The School of American Research in Santa Fe reported that the images of natives vanished in their collection of photographs," said Tune. "The insurance investigators were suspicious because the images of anthropologists in the same photographs were elevated, and in much sharper contrast once the natives were gone."

"Curtis never photographed anthropologists," said Ramona.

"The emulsion evanescence was an overnighter," said Tune. "The natives vanished in photographs with anthropologists at the same time that the museum director refused to return certain sacred objects to native communities."

"Nonsense," said Ramona.

"*Gegaa*," said Almost.

"Nothing is sacred here but the insurance."

"Emulsion evanescence is natural not causal," said Tune. "Should lightning crash twice in the same place that would be chance, and so native creation stories are never at once."

"Please show me some cause," said a senior museum director.

"The Karl May Museum near Dresden reported a similar incident on the same night that East German authorities erected the wall in Berlin," said Tune. "The images of natives vanished from snapshots and photographs in the entire museum collection."

"Wait a minute," said Ramona.

"Karl May vanished with utmost significance in his own stories of the warrior, and the natives, once captured and sold in emulsion, have now vanished in their own creation stories."

"Shadowy evidence," said Ramona.

"Edward Curtis lost his natives too," said Tune. "He lost the natives to save his own distance, and he erased the real, parasols, suspenders, hats, labels, and such from many of his photographs."

"Curtis retouched, so what?"

"The natives vanished in his pictures and left behind surreal clocks and other evidence of survivance, the remains of a culture," said Tune. "But the gaze of those behind the camera still haunts the pictures, the obscure presence of melancholy, and the epiphanies of a chemical civilization."

Tune Browne, Ramona Reason, and a radio reporter, waited in the shadows of the museum that night. They waited to witness the natural chance of creation, the postindian transmutation of emulsion, an actual disappearance.

"Professor Browne, why the focus on Curtis?"

"The camera creates an instance that never existed in native stories," Tune told the reporter. "The last and lost are not native poses but the stoical remembrance of the photographers who vanished with their own obsessions behind the camera."

"Curtis was an artist," said the reporter.

"Art is not a license of dominance," said Tune.

"One gaze invites another," said the reporter.

"Curtis, like other photographers with a melancholy gaze, discovered in the native other what they had not been able to find in themselves or their institutions, a simulation of silence."

"That picture moved," shouted the reporter. She leaned to the side and pointed at the photographic image of Chief Joseph. "He looks like he might vanish, but that would be the end of a great leader."

"The emulsion has no predicate, no racial real, no picture is the absence of the other," said Tune. "There is no ethnographic presence of natives in pictures, only an emulsion transmutation."

"The predators of tricky shadows," said the reporter.

"*Gegaa,*" said Almost.

"Susan Sontag wrote in her book *On Photography* that 'there is something predatory in the act of taking a picture,'" said Ramona. "To photograph people is to violate them, by seeing them as they never see themselves, by having knowledge of them they never have, it turns people into objects that can be symbolically possessed."

"'Photography evades us,' Roland Barthes wrote in *Camera Lucida*. 'Photography transformed subject into object, and even, one might say, into a museum object,'" said the reporter.

"Chief Joseph has vanished," said Tune.

"He was not insured," said Ramona.

"*Maanoo*," said Almost.

Almost was certain he could never start an academic *debwe* festival with the beat of water drums. Tune warned us that the sound of drums on campus would attract every culture cultist and muse of the waste within an hour of San Francisco Bay. Thousands of drum crazies would hear the beat in their blood and dance to be in touch with some obscure native spirit. The passionate search for spirits, no matter how earnest, would dominate the festival, and distract the heart dancers.

So, we decided to hold back the drums for a time and broadcast the *Academic Festival Overture* by Johannes Brahms. His composition, on the occasion of an honorary degree, was dedicated to the University of Breslau in Germany. More than a century later, his music was the native start of an actual academic festival in the Transethnic Situations Department at the University of California.

Almost first heard the *Academic Festival Overture* in the athletic center at Lake Forest College in Illinois. He taught tricky stories there for a year, his only formal teaching appointment, and then gladly returned to the bounty of the barony. The manager of the center, a psychology graduate, was convinced that such orchestral music spurred athletes to be more competitive, and moved the bored faculty "to be more active with their bodies." My cousin reported that the music roused at least one tetchy faculty member in the sauna.

James Atlas, in his review of *Auden: An American Friendship* by Charles Miller, mentions a monologue that reminded me of that tetchy professor. Miller cites a man who was "touched" by Auden. "He drew closer and touched me stealthily," said the man. Atlas considered this erudite situation, "Bad luck for Auden, running into his pitiless memorist. To cover his embarrassment, Auden launches into an incoherent monologue about Dostoyevsky and Kafka."

Almost was cornered in the athletic center by Milton Gore. The learned tease of the professor was the comic converse of the "pitiless memorist." We were alone in the sauna, and then the professor entered, aroused by the *Academic Festival Overture*. Gore "drew closer on the bench and overtly touched his own dick."

Almost lectured the literature professor on the color green, the native tones of green, and then told an ancestral *anishinaabe* story about an adventurous hunter. The native story, the professor learned, is the true source of the masterpiece *Sir Gawain and the Green Knight* by the obscure Pearl Poet.

"Green, native green on the run to the blues," said Almost. "The green of natural reason, motion, wind, rain, the warmer seasons, the sour green of fruit, wood, and nausea, and the verdure of the mighty natural dicks."

"Fairly, you're a scholar of tinct and greenery," said Gore. He moved closer to my cousin with his dick in hand. The bench was moist, and the heat seemed to turn the cedar into greenery. "Natives must have their natural way with colors."

"*Gaawiin*," said Almost.

"Chivalry is in the green," said Gore.

"*Gaawiin* became Sir Gawain in Middle English," lectured Almost. "The name *gaawiin* in *anishinaabe* means 'no,' and in the stories of the native hunter that name is a mighty negative."

"Sir *Gaawiin*, really," said Gore.

"*Gegaa*," said Almost.

"Show me," he said and moved an inch or two closer. He was more interested in my cousin than me. Gore leaned back, held his dick with both hands, and bounced on the bench with the music.

"Sir *Gaawiin* is a native hunter, as the tricky story has been told by the *anishinaabe* for more than a hundred generations. The hunter ignored the stories that *nookomis*, his grandmother, told about the demons, and set out from *gichiziibi*, the great river, to discover and tease the son of the evil gambler. Many days later, near *maazhi mashkiki*, Bad Medicine Lake, the hunter suddenly became nauseous and was overcome by a putrid stench."

"Obscure stories in the sauna?" asked Gore.

"*Gegaa*," said Almost.

"*Crambe repetita*," said Gore.

"Sir *Gaawiin* rested on the south shore of the lake, and no sooner had he started to dream when a shadow blocked the warmth of the sun," said my cousin. "There, looming over him, an enormous beast, was the son of the evil gambler. The wicked son was named *ozhaawashko inini* in *anishinaabe* stories. The name means "green man," and he carried a huge stone axe. The Green Man became the Green Knight in Middle English."

"Surely, there is more alliteration," said Gore.

"Sir *Gaawiin* was weakened by the stench of the green demon, but he had enough strength to swing his axe and wounded *ozhaawashko inini* on the thigh. He could reach no higher. Naturally, his blood was green, almost blue on the run."

First the mention of the green stench, and then the cut of the stone axe, the green blood, seemed to be heard not by the bored literature professor, but by his eager dick. He held his dick with both hands, bounced his head to the music, but the green story was a mighty distraction. My cousin could tease any dick to catch a wink over a tricky story in the greenery.

"Sir *Gaawiin* waited for the demon to respond, but instead he invited the bold hunter to strike as many blows as he wanted if he agreed to bear the same number of blows four seasons later. The hunter accepted the invitation and his first mighty blow of the axe cut off the beast's enormous *niinag*, or dick. As *ozhaawashko inini* leaned over to retrieve his bloody green *niinag*, the hunter struck another blow with his axe and severed the demon's huge green head. Green blood shot out of his neck and stained the trees.

"Sir *Gaawiin* moved back, bright and certain that he had defeated the son of the evil gambler. The hunter, however, was not so lucky, because *ozhaawashko inini* tucked his *niinag* under his arm, carried his green head by the hair, and lurched into the lake. The hunter ran to the shore and watched a dark green shadow move deep in the water.

"Later, *ozhaawashko inini* walked out of the lake on the other side, and with his head and *niinag* in hand, the green demon vanished in the woods," said my cousin. "That, of course, is no more than a start."

"The Green Chapel is much racier," said Gore. His dick was drowsy, the boast was out and the overture had ended, so he started his own stories. "Green lace, courage, and lusty knights on horseback arouse the mercy of statues, and raise the stone dicks. . . ."

"*Gegaa,*" said Almost.

"Listen, we can rise at the Round Table," said Gore.

"*Gaawiin,*" said Almost.

The *Academic Festival Overture* certainly would have been enough to announce the festival, as the composer was touched by student songs, a mischievous celebration at the time, but my cousin wanted much more a century later. So, to announce the festival he circled the corridors of the Transethnic Situations Department with his incredible bullroarer. Magically, the whir and roar of the carved willow instrument was a counterpoint to the orchestral music. The sound chased the lonesomes, the soul wanderers, and those cursed with envy, back to their haunts in the museums.

The academic festival started with a twist at the end of the regular nonsense of a departmental meeting. The faculty was about to vote on a motion to postpone the invitation to my cousin when he turned on the music and whirled his bullroarer. Some faculty members were stunned by the sound, and reached out to be reassured. Others smiled, loosened their clothes, and started to dance near the elevators. Soon, the entire faculty and staff were in the hallway ready to be enchanted and healed by the heart dance. Naturally, the inspiration of some dancers was not the pleasure of others, and that explains the departmental name, "transethnic situations."

"Almost everyone celebrates a true place in the shower," shouted Willy Trainor. The native literary critic raised his head to hold the sound of his last word, a nasal drone. The sound was a comical distraction. We had no idea why the shower was so important, and no one really cared about causes because it was the start of the heart dance. Willy waited for our attention and then slowly removed his shirt. He turned to one side in an awkward prance, the first dancer to be touched and done over by the willow bullroarer.

Willy's penis had been a very active but unseen member of the faculty for more than a decade. At last, his colleagues were more than curious to see what so many students had mentioned over the years in their stories. The faculty gathered around, mocked his poses, and taunted the vaunt-courier to remove the rest of his clothes. "Free the giant willy," chanted several students as they danced and teased him to reveal the most talked about dick in the history of transethnic situations.

"The morning shower is our best season, a warm creation place in a hand made world," he shouted, and once again held the sound of the last word as he removed his trousers. My cousin circled with his bullroarer, and soon the literary critic was down to his bright red undershorts. Willy's wide bare feet cracked a discordant tune on the polished floor. The crowd danced and roared even louder than the roar of the aerophone. Willy shivered as he pranced to the music.

The *Academic Festival Overture* announced the *debwe* festival, the sound of the bullroarer circled and teased the dancers. The students soon discovered the water drums hidden in a storage room. We could wait no longer to start the slow and steady beat. The sound of the drums in the distance raised the heat of the heart dancers.

Cozie Browne converted a seminar room into a parthenogenesis salon. She mounted the *oshkiwiinag*, the ancient crystal trickster that she recovered at a Girl Scout camp on the reservation, on a pedestal covered with crimson velvet. The salon was dark, and the museum light behind the crystal trickster created a mythic and numinous presence. Women who entered the salon were rushed with an erotic heat. In less time than it takes to get undressed, those women who chose to touch the *oshkiwiinag* conceived a child without the bruise or chance of a man. Naturally, there were many cautionary signs. For instance, "Do not touch unless you desire the instancy of conception." The signs were printed in nine languages and posted around the crystal trickster. Eleven women touched the trickster at the heart dance, and nine months later they delivered their babies.

The elevators delivered more faculty members from other departments in the building: cultural studies, philosophy, political science, anthropology, and the curious custodians of sociology. We beat the water drums louder and the sound buried the tick and snivel of social scientists on the sidelines. Naturally, the precious drum freaks arrived in search of a pure native presence. The freaks are much the same as wounded shamans who wander the earth with incomplete visions, and the mere mention of a heart dance is an instant invitation to the soul mongers. As usual the freaks wore too much leather, and too many polished stones and turkey feathers to be seen and heard without mockery. Curiously, they were drawn to the strut and shower philosophies of the academic stripteaser.

Willy Trainor's classes in native literatures, we learned later, were always crowded with drum freaks and wannabe shamans. Almost everyone returned to the end of the corridor and waited in a circle near the elevator to see if the hooded member of the faculty was ready to show his head and dance.

"My shower is a ghost dance," he sang and then lowered his undershorts. He spread his stout legs, raised his arms, and turned slowly in front of the elevators to show his bare body to the audience. Almost silenced the drums and bullroarer for a few minutes as a tribute. Willy turned once more in silence and the dancers moved closer to see the source of his vaunt. They leaned over in a natural motion, bowed to his crotch a few times, turned back to the circle, and then choked with humor. The faculty pointed at the actual size of his dick. At last, the students doubled over in wild laughter. There, the tiniest *niinag* core was hidden deep in pubic hair, shied, no doubt, by the demands of so many transethnic situations and academic seduction scenes. "My secret is an eternal shower," he droned to the last word. His unseen dick seemed to be aroused in the thicket.

"The dicks of color," shouted a graduate student.

"*Maanoo,*" said Almost.

The corridors were crowded with dancers by the third night of the festival. One by one over the course of the heart dance, office doors were propped open, nothing was closed, not even the toilets. The truth of the dance could not be contained, or denied, in the department.

A noted anthropologist who measures native stories as "mythicized psychopidgin" was heard mocking his own studies. The students mocked the faculty, the faculty mocked each other, and the administrators, the most tiresome of the dancers, double mocked their own weakness at the university. The heart dance was nothing but the truth at last.

Father Barry O'Connell, the generous and spirited professor of literature and history with a slight, sympathetic limp, and luscious tease, wore the handsome mask of William Apess, the Pequot missionary and activist in the Mashpee Revolt. Father Barry wore a scarlet cloak. He saved many students right there in the corridor with his humor, and wove into his conversations the thoughts of Apess. The violation of native "inherent rights," for instance, "by those to whom they had extended the hand of friendship, was not the only act of injustice which this oppressed and afflicted nation was called to suffer at the hands of their white neighbors, alas! They were subject to more intense and heart corroding affliction, that of having their daughters claimed by the conquerors, and however much subsequent efforts were made to soothe their sorrows, in this particular, they considered the glory of their nation as having departed."

"*Gegaa,*" said Almost.

Professor LaVonne Ruoff, the senior historian of native literatures, was there as a mask, and the author behind the mask said she was bored with academic retirement and more than eager to travel to a native heart dance. She, in turn, carried a mask of none other than the literary theorist and poet Paula Gunn Allen. Coincidentally, by the time the mask of the poet appeared in the corridor on the second night of the *debwe* there were already two other posers in the same name. Kenneth Lincoln, the author of *Native American Renaissance*, was there in a mask worn by a graduate student with a most convincing literary manner.

Later, the same student changed masks and appeared as the tough, generous, and humorous Paula Gunn Allen.

Ruoff, the poser in sturdy black shoes, danced and mocked the other postmodern poses of the literary theorist and poet, but no one paid much attention to the memorable double conversions until she came out of the toilet with an endless train of toilet paper. The coarse paper, caught in the waistband of her panties, unrolled in a long trail as she danced. We saw the train coming down the corridor and backed away, so as not to break the humor, and others danced to the side to avoid the toilet paper. The train almost circled the entire department before she turned and noticed the source of our humor.

"The essential academic dance," said the dean of situations.

"Coarse paper, a natural contrition," said a lecturer.

"Those damn tricksters, they follow me everywhere, right into the toilet and never miss a chance," said Ruoff. She towed that train of paper as the dancers circled and cheered the move. The drums were silent, and then the beat was hurried as she hauled in the paper. There, at the other end of the train, a graduate student carried another mask and pose of Paula Gunn Allen.

Ruoff wasted no time on academic countenance when it came to the pleasures of the heart dance. She posed a few minutes later in the dress uniform of an officer in the United States Navy. The students, touched by the presence of a naval uniform, mocked the officer with their salutes. Captain Ruoff shimmied in the corridor, a constant and unbroken mockery of the military.

Willis Regier, or the poser who wore his mask, was at her side as an adjutant officer. Regier was the director, at the time, of the University of Nebraska Press. The heart dancers continued to salute the naval mates, a comic scene at our heart dance. Regier told stories about their adventures at sea, the wild storms, the ruins of war, the shore leave, and the signature tattoos. The two masked posers revealed several floral tattoos on their arms, and the patterns were in the native tradition of *manidoominensikaan*, or beadwork. The bright patterns were, in turn, an imitation of nature and chintz trade cloth.

Kimberly Wiar, an acquisition editor at the University of Oklahoma Press, was at a conference in the area and thought she might contact a few authors at the *debwe* festival. She heard the naval stories as the elevator doors opened on the fifth floor. Wiar appeared as the obscure publisher Wanda Dénicher. She wore an enormous blond wig and fringed black leather jacket. Believe it or not, the beaded flower patterns on her jacket were the same, right down to the colors, as the tattoos on the naval mates. Naturally, they shared a common tradition of beaded imitations, and the three posers danced to the same tune for the rest of the festival.

Dénicher, in fact, was the publisher of *The Manabosho Curiosa*, the fifteenth-century monastic manuscript of sensual pleasures with animals. Almost said the manuscript was the most significant book she has ever published. Wanda has the instincts of a hunter, and, as a publisher, there are no sacred nests on her editorial watch. Later, when the demand for our blank books was more than we could produce by hand on the barony, she became the publisher and distributor of Wiigwaas Trade Books.

Wanda was pursued by many graduate students at the festival who wanted her to publish their dissertations. She answered every student and never missed a beat in the heart dance. "When a story moves me as yours does, there is no need to rob the nest, to consider publication too early, because your story, however noted by your professors, would be ruined by too much scrutiny, and my philosophy is never to aim at the praises or denials of ethnic essentialism or victimry." Somehow the eager students understood her arcane advice. She brushed back the mass of blond hair and shimmied in the corridor with the two naval mates.

Ishmael Reed arrived late to the heart dance. He wore sports earphones, bright colors as usual, in each of his three tricky appearances. The novelist was never without his radio earphones. His ruse as a celebrated feminist on the last night of the heart dance was very clever in orange earphones.

Ishmael first appeared as a black bear. The mohair creature suit was moldy, and so heavy and uncomfortable that he could not dance for more than a few minutes at a time, so he lumbered and roared in the corridor. Many students waited on the bear, and imitated the sound and motion of the animal, an original performance of nativism. They recited the names of the bear in other languages, *makwa*, ursus, bere, bruin, bar, oso, ours, koala, and more to overcome their fear and distance of the other.

"Black bears are hunted everywhere," said Ishmael.

"Not in my world," said a graduate student.

"Hunted everywhere but at the zoo," said Ishmael.

"One of my professors said bears masturbate."

"Watching bears is reckless eyeballing," said Ishmael.

"Bears scare me," a woman lecturer announced, and almost shouted the scare. She appeared as a man that night, dressed in a white canvas painter's shirt, necktie, leather trousers and jacket. She wore a huge welder's mask. The sound of her voice, however, was not convincing. The masculine pose was lost to fear and anxiety as she came out of the elevator and saw the bear.

"Bears scare you?"

"Naturally, one hug and you're dead," she said and then lighted a cigarette. She taught native philosophies and environmental studies in the department, and the students evaluated her as one of the best teachers on the campus, but her comments and smoke that night changed their views forever.

"Mosquitoes kill more people than bears, so why fear me?"

"The myth of the black beast," she said and blew smoke in his face.

"Smoke is more dangerous than a bear," said Almost.

Ishmael returned to the festival late the next night as a wolf, the mask and appearance of a gray timber wolf, and he wore the same orange earphones. Several students tried to howl when they saw him on the elevator. The wild sound, however, was not sincere.

"Ishmael, you're no wolf," said the third mask of Paula Gunn Allen.

"No one ever is," said Ishmael.

"Wolves are the natural masks of our desires," said Dénicher.

"Nothing's ever natural at the university," said Ishmael.

"Wolves dance in the distance," said Almost.

"The easy lopers are always the best dancers," said Ishmael. He set out to lope in the corridor, but could not get very far because of the crowds of heart dancers. Not only that, but there were three other masked wolves, and no one seemed to care very much about animals. However, later that night was another story.

Gloria Steinem made her appearance as a perfect mask on the third night of the festival. Ishmael's mimicry of her countenance was fantastic, and when she stepped out of the elevator the dancers applauded his feminist pose, a contradiction of pleasures in the class manners of white feminists.

Steinem carried a copy of the novel, *The Color Purple*, under her arm. Ishmael laughed under the mask, gestured in a courtly manner, and then sauntered down the corridor. Feminists in unusual costumes trailed her around the department, in and out of various offices, and at last the mask returned to the elevator. The feminist association was so moved by her appearance that the poser hardly mattered that night.

Alice Walker was there too, as a lovely mask worn by a secretary in the minority admissions center on campus. She appeared as the novelist with a shy black retriever on a short tether. She wore a sweat shirt with "born again pagan" printed on the front in purple letters. "I have relied on the fiercely sweet spirits of black men, and this is abundantly clear in my work," she told the mask of Steinem. "You really cannot step into the same river twice. Each time it is different, and so are you."

"Where did you read that?" asked Ishmael.

"In the *San Francisco Chronicle*," said the poser.

"Alice Walker told the truth," said a graduate student.

"Spielberg and the movie men told her stories," said Ishmael.

"Walker is a womanist not a feminist," said a lecturer.

"Then why *The Color Purple?*" asked Almost.

"Steinem does reckless eyeballing," said Ishmael.

"Where did you read that?" asked the mask of Walker.

"In my book *Writin' is Fightin'*," said Ishmael.

"You're no woman, you're a bear," said a white faculty feminist.

"Did you know that bears masturbate," said Almost.

"You're both misogynist bears," said the feminist.

"*Maanoo,*" said Almost.

"No black bear, whatever his class, is exempt from superstitions about black bears, a situation that causes anxiety," said Ishmael. "My disagreement with some feminists and womanists is that they have, out of ignorance or by design, promoted such myths in the media." He said that much and then danced in the stately manner of Gloria Steinem.

Renée Vivien arrived out of breath with her entire anthropology seminar. They climbed five flights of stairs to the heart dance because hundreds of people were waiting on the first floor for the elevator.

"We were in seminar and heard the heave of the water drums in the distance," said Renée. "Surely, you know better than anyone, the beat of the best native drums is a natural invitation to serious anthropology students."

"Serious culture cultists," said Almost.

"Whose culture?" asked Renée.

"*Maanoo,*" said Almost.

"Never mind," said Renée. She was so certain of her observations, the absolute anthropologist, that others at the heart dance were suspicious. Was her natural manner an unnatural pose, or was she sincere? Even her students were too certain of the beat that night. Together they were the absolute seminar, and with some humor.

Tune Browne lived and worked in a wickiup at the museum, as you know, and he told stories about almost every anthropologist on the campus. Renée, for instance, visited his wickiup many times. She wore very expensive pumps, but never in the museum. Late at night my cousin would hear the stealthy click of bones, the rush of clothes, and then she would serve the wine in his wickiup. Tune said she was "holosexual," but not a separatist.

"Renée loved to wear masks, and sex was absolute in a mask, an entire sensation, and not the mundane manners of gender," he told me. "She listened to me in the wickiup, and trusted me in the aesthetics of native stories."

Renée Vivien and the thirteen students in her seminar brought along face masks that were the likeness of many famous anthropologists, such as Alfred Kroeber, Ruth Benedict, Claude Lévi-Strauss, Clyde Kluckhohn, Victor Turner, and Margaret Mead. Renée wore the elegant mask of Clifford Geertz. Several students performed as Benedict and Mead, and there were three simultaneous appearances of Lévi-Strauss. An African graduate student wore the mask of Kroeber. Another graduate student, an older woman with a stainless steel neck brace, was the uneasy appearance of Kluckhohn.

Kluckhohn was never a heart dancer. He was a soul wanderer, a haunted man with a thick gray rubber grimace, who enticed the native students he cornered in the corridor to reveal their secrets about witchcraft. Many graduate students told him strange stories, but not about native witchery. Kluckhohn listened to their stories, and then, about every fifteen minutes, he rushed to the toilet and pretended to urinate so that he could consider his surveillance and make tiny notes of what he had heard. Likewise, the natives told stories about his prostatism and the wicked twist of his quinticultural heart.

"Poses of the culture cultists," said Almost.

"Many poses are the informants," said Kluckhohn.

"*Maanoo*," said Almost.

"Kluckhohn gave me a research job on the five cultures project, studying differential reactions of the cultures . . . to what were taken to be problems common to them all," said Clifford Geertz. Renée said he was wary of the "industrial social science aspects" of the research because he did not actually work with cultures in the Southwest, but considered fieldnotes at Harvard University. He wrote about his experiences in *After the Fact: Two Countries, Four Decades, One Anthropologist.*

"He read the tricky ruins of native sovereignty," said Almost.

"Those days anyway, the ideal of alone among the unknown, what has been called the 'my people' syndrome, was still very much alive, and there were depreciative murmurs to be heard about 'gas station anthropology' and 'meadow work rather than fieldwork,'" said Geertz.

"Give that man a panic hole on the meadow," said Almost.

"Aesthetic meadow work," said Geertz.

"*Maanoo*," said Almost.

"In any case, the question became moot when at the end of the summer yet another professor walked into my office in the Peabody Museum where I was blithely sorting Navajo ways of mourning from Zuni and both from Mormon, Texan, and Spanish American, never having myself so much as been to a funeral," said Geertz. "He said . . . 'We are forming a team to go to Indonesia. We need someone on religion and someone on kinship. Do you and your wife want to go?' I said, hardly knowing more than where Indonesia was, and that inexactly, 'Yes, we would.'"

Lévi-Strauss was cornered at the end of the corridor by native graduate students who were named the Ishi Underground. The seven students wore *trompe l'oeil* tee shirts of Russell Means as Chingachgook in *The Last of the Mohicans.* The tricky chief winked as the cotton stretched. "The family, that's what Indians, what Chingachgook is all about," was printed under his stoical pose. Actually, a student sold several tee shirts to the three posers of Lévi-Strauss.

The *debwe* heart dance was a constant source of humor, the poses were rich and ironic, and no one would ever be able to walk that corridor again without remembering with pleasure the seven nights of the festival. No one, in other words, was ever the same in the Transethnic Situations Department.

Lévi-Strauss, one, two, and three, Benedict, Kluckhohn, Mead, one, and two, Geertz, and Kroeber, wore the *trompe l'oeil* tee shirts. They held hands and danced in a wide circle near the elevators. The chief winked with the native students of the Ishi Underground. Almost said the natives and the masked anthropologists shared the same source of humor for the first time in the many faces of a "truly elastic warrior, the stretch cotton appearance of Russell Means." Victor Turner waited at the side of the dance circle. He noted the rituals and symbolic moves, and then, in turn, pouted as he read *Myth and Meaning* by Claude Lévi-Strauss.

"*Maanoo*," said Almost.

"People who are without writing have a fantastically precise knowledge of their environment and all their resources," said the first mask of

Lévi-Strauss. "All these things we have lost, but we did not lose them for nothing, we are now able to drive an automobile without being crushed at each moment, for example, or in the evening to turn on our television or radio."

"Give that man one of our blank books," said Almost.

"This implies a training of mental capacities which 'primitive' peoples don't have because they don't need them," continued the first Lévi-Strauss. "I feel that, with the potential they have, they could have changed the quality of their mind, but it would not be needed for the kind of life and relationship to nature that they have."

"Give that masked man a copy of *Tristes Tropiques*," said Almost.

"The critical issue, so far as concerns the anthropologist as author, works and lives, text-building, and so on, is the highly distinctive representation of 'being there' that *Tristes Tropiques* develops," said Geertz. "To put it brutally, but not inaccurately, Lévi-Strauss argues that the sort of immediate, in-person 'being there' one associates with the bulk of recent American and British anthropology is essentially impossible . . . it is either outright fraud or fatuous self-deception."

"The war of the masks at the heart dance," said Almost.

"At last we are the observers," said the Ishi Underground.

"You cannot develop all the mental capacities belonging to mankind all at once," continued the first Lévi-Strauss. "It is probably one of the many conclusions of anthropological research that, notwithstanding the cultural differences between the several parts of mankind, the human mind is everywhere one and the same and that it has the same capacities."

"Brutally accurate," said Almost.

"Since I was a child, I have been bothered by, let's call it the irrational, and have been trying to find an order behind what is given to us as disorder," said the second mask of Lévi-Strauss. The scene in the corridor was awesome, an extreme encounter of masks and manners. Russell Means winked and the rubber mouths of the posers puckered. "It so happens that I became an anthropologist, as a matter of fact not because I was interested in anthropology, but because I was trying to get out of philosophy."

"So, what does that mean?" asked the Ishi Underground.

"There is something very curious in semantics, that the word 'meaning' is probably, in the whole language, the word the meaning of which is the most difficult to find," said the third Lévi-Strauss. "What does 'to mean' mean?"

"A blank book," said Almost.

"Exactly, and what does the blank mean?"

"*Maanoo*," said Almost.

"Geertz, Lévi-Strauss, Kroeber, and the others, pose over here at the end of the corridor," said Thomas King. Hundreds of heart dancers posed in their masks, but the beat of the water drums was the soul of the festival. King, the photographer, and author of the tricky novel *Medicine River*, decorated the anthropologists with academic accoutrements that he carried in a "culture trunk." Geertz was pictured in a traditional cock feather headdress. Kroeber posed with five pocket watches. Benedict was decorated with dried chrysanthemums. Lévi-Strauss, one, two, and three, wore the black masks of the Lone Ranger. Victor Turner, the symbolic anthropologist, painted a red pentacle on his forehead. King, in turn, posed as Zorba the Greek.

"Man's 'imagination' and 'emotional' life is always and everywhere rich and complex," said Turner. "It is not a matter of different cognitive structures, but of an identical cognitive structure articulating wide diversities of cultural experience."

Alfred Kroeber wore a *trompe l'oeil* tee shirt, and as he lectured at the end of the corridor, the chief winked at every sentence. Naturally, we were very amused, but the humor was overcome by his observations. He said the *debwe* festival was quite similar to a festival that he had studied in colonial Africa. That comparison should have been an ironic moment, a trick of double humor, or more, but it was not. His comments were serious, and tedious in the academic sense of transethnic situations. Remember, the graduate student behind the mask was a graduate student from Africa.

"The N'zima people hold a 'holiday of reconciliation' once a year in Grand Bassam, Ivory Coast. The Abissa festival turns the old colonial capital into an exciting city of music and dance." Kroeber said the young men paint their faces, and wear masks too, and some men dress as women.

"You must mean *anishaa*, just for fun?" said Almost.

"The wild festival is a tradition, and the leader, Marcel Ezoua Aka, told me that there is no training for the Abissa, and we don't do any real planning either," said Kroeber. "Tradition is what guides us in our ceremony, but once it begins, it is the enthusiasm of the people that takes over."

"Were you ever there?" asked Almost.

"No, not really," said Kroeber.

"Virtually, of course," said Almost.

"Naturally," said Kroeber.

"So what is this about then?"

"The Abissa is one of the 'more raucous festivals' in the Ivory Coast, and 'its continued vibrancy is a hallmark of this entire region, where, despite galloping urbanism and the encroachment of Western ways of life, most people have clung stubbornly to some core of traditional values' that is an anchor in a sea of change," said Kroeber.

"Your enthusiasm has taken over," said Almost.

"Listen, Antoinette Aka said, 'As long as I am able to dance, I won't miss Abissa,'" said Kroeber. "She lives in France and returns home to be part of the festival. 'Every people has something they hold dear, and for us, this is our heart.'"

"Where did you hear that?"

"Where else but in the *New York Times*," said Kroeber.

"Has anyone ever teased you?" asked Almost.

"Why do you ask?"

"You seem tease resistant."

"Ishi teased me some, in the best humor," said Kroeber.

"He teased everyone with his wood duck stories," said Almost.

"He was a natural philosopher," said Kroeber.

"*Maanoo*," said Almost.

"In Bali, to be teased is to be accepted," said Geertz. "It was the turning point so far as our relationship to the community was concerned, and we were quite literally 'in.' The whole village opened up to us, probably more than it ever would have otherwise . . . and certainly very much faster."

"The deep cockfight tease, right?" asked Almost.

"By the time I left I had spent about as much time looking into cockfights as into witchcraft, irrigation, caste, and marriage," said Geertz. "Attending cockfights and participating in them is for the Balinese a kind of sentimental education."

"The tease of savagism and civilization," said Almost.

"Ishi was not sentimental, and that was true, it seems to me, because he was not at risk to win, and doubtless he heard more pleasure in myths and stories than in the bloody triumphs of a cockfight," said Kroeber.

"Ishi almost won," said Almost.

"Almost, indeed," said Kroeber.

"The cockfight is not the master key to Balinese life, any more than bullfighting is to Spanish," said Geertz. "What it says about that life is not unqualified nor even unchallenged by what other equally eloquent cultural statements say about it."

"Nor is *debwe* the master tradition," said Almost.

"Japanese arrange chrysanthemums and cast swords," said Geertz.

"The heart dance is the motion of sovereignty," said Almost.

"The intimacy of men with their cocks is more than metaphorical," said Geertz. "In identifying with his cock, the Balinese man is identifying not just with his ideal self, or even his penis, but also, and at the same time, with what he most fears, hates, and ambivalence being what it is, fascinated by . . . 'the powers of darkness.'"

"The *debwe* is the return to animals, masturbation with animals, not the resistance of other creatures," said Almost. "The cockfight is a dick war, and the conquest of the best cock is the cause of envy, but the heart dance is antienvy, the stories of natural reason, a striptease, and the motion of native sovereignty."

Umberto Eco arrived on the elevator twice worried about his *Travels in Hyperreality*. He appeared at the heart dance in two masks, as the novelist and semiotician, worn by Donald McQuade and Kathleen Moran who teach at the University of California, Berkeley. The masks were the advertisements of a "consumer society, a pose of absolute iconism." One mask said, "Disneyland is also a place of total passivity." Listen, the other mask said, a "sense of history allows an escape from the temptations of hyperreality." But elsewhere, "the frantic desire for the Almost Real arises only as a neurotic reaction to the vacuum of memories; the Absolute Fake is offspring of the unhappy awareness of a present without depth."

"*Maanoo*," said Almost.

Jean Baudrillard was the last heart dancer to arrive in mask and manner. Richard Hutson, the gentle literature professor, might have been the wise poser, but we were never sure who animated the simulation of the semiotician.

Baudrillard pranced in the corridor, touched the head of the crystal trickster several times, and then read out loud from *The Transparency of Evil*. Travel, travel, travel, he chanted, travel "was once a means of being elsewhere, or of being nowhere."

"Everywhere, the heart dancers," said Almost.

"Travel today 'is the only way we have of feeling that we are somewhere. At home, surrounded by information, by screens, I am no longer anywhere, but rather everywhere in the world at once, in the midst of a universal banality, a banality that is the same in every country.'"

"Baudrillard, sounds to me like you need to shout real soon into a panic hole," said my cousin. "You can bury the best banality of the universe and nourish a flower at the same time on the barony."

"Natives are the other, and in the 'symbolic universe there is no place for the otherness of difference,' not even the panic holes of the universe," said Baudrillard. He moved his head to the beat of the water drums. "Touch the word if you can and remember, 'neither animals, nor gods, nor the dead, are *other*. All are caught up in the same cycle. If you are outside the cycle, however, you do not even exist,' so name me a heart dance native."

"Dead voices are not the other," said Almost.

"Naturally, everyone 'wants their other. Everyone has an imperious need to put the other at their mercy, along with a heady urge to make the other last as long as possible so as to savour him.'"

"Museum natives without a pose," said Almost.

"Never dead in the cycle," said the mask of Baudrillard.

"*Maanoo*," said Almost.

5

Transethnic Commencements

 Almost Browne was invited by the student association to deliver the Transethnic Situations Department commencement lecture last summer in Ishi Auditorium at the University of California.

My cousin, as you know, has never been the obvious trace of our native ancestors. He shouts over panic holes, of course, but the line of his creation is obscure. He bears the memories of the barony, the rush of native generations, the tease of seasons and shadows, and the rue of heir and bone. These are the sources of his identities, a hotline healer with tricky stories.

The student association must have expected a traditional elder in leathers, feathers, and beads, because of their obvious mistrust and strained sincerity when we arrived at the cultural center on campus. Clearly, my cousin was not the native of their romance.

His traces are tricky, not tragic, and his stories are creation, not the hoe and strain of museum time. Even so, the turn and rise of his shadows over the wicked borderlines of civilization must be truer than a reservation. His natural ties are chance, anything but the treason of absolutes and victimry. The native stories that overturn the burdens of the *real* are his natural beam.

The student association wanted to hear tricky stories, to be sure, but they had no idea at the time that my cousin would turn their ceremonial invitation and transethnic poses into the anthropologetics of commencement.

Almost is an eternal brush of creation, more than the real, but never the lonesome testimonies of mere victimry. The fealties of his house and motion are heard in the native tease of the seasons, and always in the tricky solace of the barony.

The Ishi Underground and other graduate students heard his wild lecture on reservation casinos at a recent economic ventures conference. The lectern was a slot machine and he lectured over the constant play of numbers and cherries. Naturally, he won every time he made a significant point to the audience about gaming and native sovereignty. The student association was more than eager to nominate a controversial commencement speaker.

Tricksterese, his wise banter on cultural envy and "testcross sovereignty," or the sovereignty of native traces and natural motions, aroused the students at the time, but his otherwise obscure tone, contradictions, and ironic manners at the commencement ceremonies were too much to bear in one hour, as he was bound to tease the very sacred denials of transethnic dominance and nationalism at the university.

Ishi Auditorium was named in honor of that obscure other, the native other who had been humanely secured in a museum, as the last of his tribe, by the anthropologist Alfred Kroeber at the University of California.

Almost wanted me to listen to his lecture at a distance, in the back row of the auditorium. A couple, handsomely dressed for the occasion, sat next to me. The man wore a new suit. He told me that he and his wife were once refugees, and that their daughter was the first in their ancient families to be educated, to earn a university degree. Families must be proud everywhere at graduation. There, by chance, we were the heirs who had overcome the cruelties of dominance and the contradictions of nationalism. The horrors of war and genocide were in their near memories, as the massacres of natives were in mine, but not a trace of that past was heard in the back row. Our presence that morning at commencement was an assurance of survivance, not victimry.

Almost gave me the final copy of his lecture when we arrived on campus earlier in the week. We worked together on the ideas of his presentation, considered several sources, and then a secretary recorded and printed his practice lecture. He seldom writes, as you know, and rarely ever considers a written narrative. My cousin would rather tease the silent printed words into an actual oral performance, and he wanted to tease me in that way at the commencement.

The Vietnamese couple next to me could not, at first, appreciate my cousin's native humor and tricky stories. Later, when the students resisted the obscure notions in his lecture, the couple was clearly troubled. They were pleased, nonetheless, to hear that my cousin said much more than he had actually written. Almost was always more eloquent in sound than in the silence of written words.

The Vietnamese man turned and told me that his new name was much the same, more than the words. His breath was scented with mint. "Gio Nom, my nickname here, not my real country name," he said as he printed his name in capital letters next to the name of his daughter on the program. "My name mean *south wind*, my freedom name." They were honored, of course, by the achievements of their daughter, and, at the same time, justly moved by the references my cousin so casually made to a constitutional democracy.

Almost was not so honored by the faculty of historians, literary theorists, social scientists, and others. They were curious, to be sure, and wary, but that common attitude soon turned to cynicism, accusations, and aesthetic evasions when he announced that academic evidence was "nothing more than a euphemism for anthropologism and the colonial dominance over native memories and stories."

The "erstwhile transethnic identities," he shouted, "are fake because we are tried, yes, *tried*, and feathered by the racial evidence of invented cultures, and the tricky trash, you heard me, tricky *trash*, of transethnic nationalism and anthropologetics." He coined such words as anthropologism, anthropologetics, and tricky trash, to underscore his notion that the practices of cultural anthropology were, as he said at commencement, "colonial doctrines, and the deistic rue of dominance."

Almost could not see the seven faculty members seated in a row behind him on stage. Later he told me they were mere circus crows, "their sickle feathers trimmed to suit the metal chairs." Nearly every sentence in his lecture caused some bodily response in the faculty, a twitch, a frown, a turn, a murmur, and at least the sound of their shoes on the hardwood stage. The natural motions, as it turned out, to escape from his lecture and the ceremonies.

"Listen to that trash," said a sociologist to a historian.

"What, the rue?" said the historian on stage.

"Who is this clown, a television evangelist?"

"The student's choice," said the historian.

"Choice, indeed, he sounds like an aborted anthropologist."

"Surely, no more than an invented native."

"Not really, he's the choice of the students to get even with the faculty," said the sociologist. "He might crow their sermon, but not on my time." Slowly he removed his gown and hood, folded them into a neat bundle, and then walked out at the back of the stage.

Almost was always in motion, his natural fealty, and seldom troubled by death, departures, or the turn of seasons. Not much academic ever worried him either, but he pretended otherwise in some of his stories. Natives, he said, "are almost always in constant motion, even the spirit after death, and that's what native sovereignty means, motion, motion, motion, not the curses and causes of manifest manners at universities."

The very moment that he raised his arms over the podium, and opened his wide mouth over the microphone that morning in the auditorium, only a few students could remember, without evasions or apologies, why on earth he had ever been invited to lecture at the commencement ceremonies. Even the couple next to me had their doubts until he mentioned native sovereignty and the "tricky motion of constitutional democracies."

Almost leaned closer to the microphone. He was in constant motion at the podium, an assurance of his own sovereignty. The faculty was trained to listen, but they were more practiced at other academic maneuvers, and made wry faces as they sat at the back of the stage in borrowed nests, circus crows in their black gowns, velvet hoods, and bright ribbons. The students, who were once his promoters, shunned the very sound of his voice early in the lecture. Not that he was a terrible speaker, almost never less than the turn of a memorable contradiction. He was timely, and the tone of his voice was rich and dramatic, but he turned and traced words and sentences in such an ironic manner, his tease of survivance, that no one could be sure what he meant. No one was ever sure of the native tease, or that tricksterese ever meant anything, anytime, anyway.

Almost teased the measures of civilization and the inventions of the native other, the abstruse other of dominance, as the extremes in his tricky stories. Besides, he said, "manners are more extreme at universities." Those students on the committee who dared to stand by their nomination, and that out of mere courtesy, did not understand extremes either, but in the end many students, and most of their parents, wanted to learn how to stand and deliver a lecture in native tricksterese.

The Ishi Underground, an association of native students, insisted that his lecture was a learned satire, and for that, unwise, given the trans-ethnic manners of the audience, but they too were taken with the notion and motion of native survivance. Nonetheless, his notions were evaded at the time, and since then his words have been twisted, revised, and terminated in hundreds of extreme comments and criticism at the university. The faculty never understood why he was invited in the first place, but no one ever forgot that he was there.

Almost was embraced, hissed, and shunned, in turns, because of his obscure theories and conceit of transethnic histories, and, more than anything else, because of the ironies he meant in the title of his lecture, "transethnic derivatives." The students started their hissy fit when he said commencement gowns were "colonial drag, the happy hour of transethnic medievalism, ecclesiastical evidence of a dead letter degree in mere mimicry."

"How does he write that?" said Gio Nom.

"That's native tricksterese, an oral performance." He bowed his head and seemed to measure each word as he listened to me. "As you can see, there's nothing like that here in the manuscript, mostly because he seldom ever writes anything." The Vietnamese couple was astonished, at first, that he could create a lecture on his feet, and pretend that it was written. Later, they admired the practice and were pleased to follow the text and hear how he teased the printed words to dance on stage.

"Almost, darn good man on his feet," said Gio Nom.

The transethnic faculty, moved by situational politics, shouted at the speaker and demanded that he explain what he meant by his hostile ironies, such as "colonial drag" and "happy hour." Seven faculty members were seated on stage at the beginning of the ceremonies, and at the end the metal chairs were empty, but for one. The ceremonies that year were memorable, to say the least, but more bent with ironies than the customary manners of such events. Since then the provocations of the faculty, the fickle rage of the students, and the dismay of parents, have been established as something of a transethnic tradition. Almost is remembered, in spite of everything, as the prime mover of the new agonistic commencement ceremonies at the University of California.

"The American Revolution, that celebrated war of independence, was not the *first*, but the *second* revolution on this continent," shouted Almost. His mouth touched the microphone closer than a rock singer, so close that he might have swallowed it with a sudden gasp for air. He raised his arms and turned his hands in tune with his words, each finger a gesture of tricksterese. His voice vibrated in the metal chairs on stage and rushed to every hidden corner, every secret pocket of silence in the auditorium. "These are the comparative chronicles of sovereignty, the motion and historical contradictions of our time, the everlasting traces of our resistance in a constitutional democracy."

"What constitution you talking about?" shouted a student.

"The end of colonial drag," said Almost.

"Man, get tuned to the movement," said the student.

"Transethnic nationalism?" said Almost.

"What kind of native, native, native are you?" said another student. She moved to the aisle at the side of the auditorium. Her black gown was decorated with ribbons, feathers, and beads.

"The kind that never turns the wit of shamans, shamans, shamans into academic manners, manners, manners," said Almost. He chanted the words. "The kind of native that teases the transethnic mutants of nationalism."

"Indian peoples always talk for their communities, so where are you from to talk about shamanism and colonial constitutions anyway?" asked the native student.

"Almost everywhere," said Almost.

"Mister, you better come from somewhere."

"More than once a tricky reservation."

"Constitutions are white reservations, and that's not our tradition," she said and folded her arms over the beads and ribbons. The audience turned to the aisle and praised the native student. "So, what's your native name?"

"Almost," said Almost.

"You're no Indian," said the native student.

"Almost Yosemite," said Almost.

"You're a white man."

"Almost," said Almost.

"Almost nothing," said the student.

"Almost true," said Almost.

"Who gave you that name?" asked the student.

"The *first* revolution was native, native, native," he shouted into the microphone. The power of his voice silenced the students. "The *first* was a war of independence from colonial domination and the rush of missionaries, and that was launched almost a century before the *second* historical revolution of the thirteen colonies and the formation of the United States."

"That's not our history, never," said another student. Others raised their hands and clenched their fists to support the statement of resistance, and several students in the front row moved to the back of the auditorium.

"The southwestern natives initiated the *first* united revolution on August 10, 1680, and defeated the Spanish Kingdom of New Mexico." Almost paused, brushed back his hair, and waited to hear the response of the audience. The students did not resist, so he continued. "Marc Simmons, in the introduction to *The Pueblo Revolt*, wrote that 'this dramatic episode represented one of the bloodiest defeats ever experienced by Spain in her overseas empire,' so that was the *first* revolution on this continent. 'And, as historians are accustomed to say, it was the first successful battle for independence fought against a European colonial power in what was to become the United States.'"

"So what?" a student shouted from the back of the auditorium.

"So what, indeed," said one faculty member to another seated on stage. "The Spanish and Indians both lost their land in the end." Nearby, several other faculty members murmured and nodded their heads in agreement.

"Che Guevara, he was a true warrior," shouted a student.

"Che was a transethnic conquistador," said Almost.

"Che fought for the natives."

"Che was a tourist," said Almost.

"Almost, you're a fascist, man," shouted another student.

"Che wrote in his travel journal that 'Cuzco invites you to don armour and, astride a sturdy powerful steed, cleave a path through the defenceless flesh of a flock of native indians whose human wall crumbles and falls under the four hooves of the galloping beast.'"

"Che, who is this man?" asked Gio Nom.

"Ernesto Guevara, he was trained as a medical doctor in Argentina." He leaned closer to listen. "Later he became a revolutionary leader and one of the most important comrades of Fidel Castro in Cuba."

"Where is he now?"

"Che was executed in Bolivia."

"No, no, here," said Gio Nom. He pointed to the manuscript and followed the written lecture with his finger, but could not locate many of the words that he heard.

"Almost never wrote that in his lecture." He loaned me his pen to print the names. "No, he probably just read the new translation of Che's journal, *The Motorcycle Diaries*, about his trip around South America." Gio Nom wrote the title on the side of the program.

"The unities of that native revolution, and others since then, are the origin histories of survivance in this nation," shouted Almost. He turned from the podium and waved to the faculty who were seated on stage. The faculty, in turn, waved back, tiny, hesitant motions, as cautious children might wave to strangers. The audience laughed and then mocked the childlike gestures of the faculty. "Whatever the course of sovereignty, then and now, native resistance has been contrived as an aesthetic extreme, as either incertitude, necromancy, or mere victimry." The students hissed the last words in his lecture.

"Man, get real somewhere," shouted a student.

"Hissed again, what about this time?"

The hiss increased and rushed to the thick stage curtains.

"What word, what's the hiss word now?"

The hiss circled the auditorium in harsh and uncertain waves.

"Incertitude, is that the hiss word?" shouted Almost.

The hiss seemed to weaken.

"Necromancy?"

The hiss heaved, rose louder, and became a demon wave.

"Victimry, how about pity, and tragic victimry?"

The demon hiss reached extreme overtones. The hisses circled, an enemy wave, and rushed every ear in the auditorium, but the intensities could not be sustained without some trace of humor. The hiss bounced, wavered, and at last weakened, and then the students laughed at their own performance.

"The victims have it over the necromancers," said Almost.

"Never, never, never," chanted students at the back.

"Why the students do that?" asked Gio Nom.

"No one knows what causes these academic hissy fits."

"So much to hear," said Gio Nom. He was troubled by the want of manners, and, at the same time, he seemed to be amused by the hiss play. He spoke in another language to his wife about the students.

"Stay out of those word museums," warned Almost. His mood turned more serious, cautionary, and the audience was silent. The students were uncertain and looked to each other for an explanation.

"So, who are you, the tricky curator?" said a student in the first row. No one was sure what he meant by "word museums," but it had to be an ironic storehouse of native stories. A double irony because he teased the very words that created the museums. The faculty on stage raised their hands, shrugged their shoulders in casual doubt, and then laughed, artfully.

"The museums that bear our bones and stories," shouted Almost.

"No bones here," said Gio Nom.

"Bravo, bravo," shouted Ishmael Reed. The novelist, who wore sports earphones, had arrived late and was standing at the back of the auditorium. As the audience turned to see who had shouted such bravos of approval he walked down the center aisle toward the stage. Many children, the brothers and sisters, sons and daughters of the graduates, trailed him and said their bravos in the aisle.

"Tricksterese is the best street talk anybody ever heard at the university," said Reed. "We've heard too much from the tattlers, rattlers, and race talkers in backlighted museums, bank lobbies, and network news." The children danced in the aisles, they were amused by his gestures, tangled gray hair, and bright orange earphones.

"The converse histories of dominance rather than native survivance have been secured in museums and at universities by several generations of academic masters, and no one ever hissed about that," shouted Almost.

"Masters, who uses such a word?" said a woman in cultural studies.

"Who, indeed," said a political scientist on stage.

"I mean, the word is right out of the ruins of colonialism, the essence of dominance, at best an anachronism," she said and tapped the heels of her shoes on the hardwood floor. "Who does he think he is, a candidate for the senate?" She closed her backpack and left the stage.

Almost turned and saw one faculty member leave as another arrived. Ishmael walked on stage and sat in the empty chair next to a visiting faculty member. The children waved to him from the aisles. The audience was amused, and even the faculty that left waved to the children.

"Now that's a civilized way to bear commencement," said Maisie Peel, a visiting scholar from the University of Kent at Canterbury. "Please, what's on the orange radio?"

"O. J. Simpson trial," said Reed.

"Americans are so demonstrative about crime," said Peel.

"What was that?" said Reed.

"Natives are forever studied, invented as abstruse cultures, and then embodied in motion pictures as the simulated burdens of civilization," said Almost. "These adversities became more grievous and caused a turn in the notions, courses, and literary canons at universities, but the treacheries and dominance of anthropologism, the obsessive, unmerciful studies of natives by social scientists, have not been overturned in comparative transethnic studies at this great university."

That much brought the students to their feet in anger, because most students, transethnic or not, were eager consumers of native feathers, leathers, arrowheads, crystals, baskets, turquoise, photographs, and the passive manners of mother earth. The students raised their arms to protest the speaker, and black gowns spread out like sails with their gestures. Columns of students marched in the aisles and chanted "natives are not, not, not unmerciful, never, never, never."

Several faculty members removed their hoods and walked out of the back of the stage. No one was sure, then or now, what word or notion so tormented the students and bored the faculty. One faculty member in education suggested that the students had no sense of what such words as necromancy meant and, rather than show their ignorance at the moment of their baccalaureates, the students protested, a common academic cover story.

"Listen, every study, even comparative masturbation, is unmerciful, think about that under your medieval gowns," said Almost. Naturally, masturbation was another tricky story. Nine students threw their mortarboards at the speaker. He ducked eight, caught one, and wore it on the back of his head.

Almost raised his hands in prayer, a mock pose, and then he laughed at the students. He took the microphone in hand and walked back and forth on stage, as an evangelist might, but he pointed and laughed at the students in the front rows of the auditorium. Then he paused and shouted at them, "see, these must be the merciful students who have never masturbated."

"Almost, darn good on his feet," said Gio Nom.

"Even better with his hands."

The parents and relatives of the graduates were seated in the back rows of the auditorium. They were bothered by demonstrations and the mere mention of sex at commencement, and concerned, no doubt, that their children be seen as scholars not troublemakers. Most of the students were the first graduates in their families, and their parents probably considered manners a wiser measure of an education than demonstrations. The parents convinced most of the students to return to their seats, but a few students shouted their way out of the auditorium and never returned to the commencement ceremonies.

"Doctor Browne," said a parent standing in the back row.

"Almost, please."

"Doctor Almost, please forgive the disruptions and kindly continue your speech," said the parent. He wore a dark suit and tie. Two children waited at his side and looked up to him when he spoke. "Many of us have never been at a university before and we would like to hear what you have to say, even though some of us don't understand what you are saying."

"Listen too hard, nothing makes sense," said Almost.

"Almost, you got that right," said a political scientist. He walked out at the back of the stage as the others had done earlier. He stooped over and ducked his head to avoid notice on the way out, but the front of his gown caught under the toe of his shoe and he stumbled into the curtains.

Almost laughed and returned to the podium. The faculty on stage watched his every move, and they were much more critical in the end than the students. He wore no socks or tie, his shirt was too large, and his sports coat was stained on the sleeves and torn at the back. Unhurried, he turned over several pages of his lecture notes in search of his last words, and then continued his performance.

"Johannes Fabian wrote in *Time and the Other* that 'anthropology's alliance with the forces of oppression is neither a simple or recent one,' not simple or recent in transethnic studies either," said Almost. "Transethnic studies is no exception to that oppression because the 'relationships between anthropology and its object are inevitably political,' and the 'production of knowledge occurs in a public forum,' such as this one, right here, the parents, students, and the last of the just faculty on stage."

Almost paused to hear the hisses, but he seemed surprised, as the faculty and students were silent. So, he hissed at them and then continued. "Fabian, you know, argued as everyone must, that 'among the historical conditions under which our discipline emerged and which affected its growth and differentiation were the rise of capitalism and its colonial-imperialist expansion into the very societies which became the target of our inquiries.' So, the historical alliance with anthropology and the social sciences is evermore political in transethnic studies, and you might say, that this graduation ceremony is another statement of that dominance."

"What does he mean?" asked Gio Nom.

"Almost means anthropology is the natural enemy of natives, an idea we worked out years ago with student anthropologists on the reservation, but this may be the best place to tease the profession."

Professor Simon Macbeth, the senior cultural anthropologist, one of the faculty members on stage, removed his black gown and walked toward the podium. A blush blotched his bald head and his face was double creased with concern. His shoes squeaked, and the moment of his authoritarian manner was lost to humor. Almost turned to the squeak and saluted the anthropologist.

"Browne, must you malign everyone to make your point?" said Macbeth. His wide mouth stretched back over his dark teeth, over the microphone, and his cheeks shivered as he spoke. "This is not the time to criticize the good work we have done to bring transethnic studies into the real world of the social sciences."

"Have you ever been in the military?" asked Almost.

"Have you ever been a professor?" countered Macbeth.

"Never, but we both know how to salute."

"Fabian is not relevant," said Macbeth.

"So, he's a squeaky name?" said Almost.

"He never wrote about ethnic studies anyway."

"You mean, he never mentioned *your* name?"

"Almost, is that a traditional name?" asked Macbeth.

"*Maanoo,*" said Almost.

"Nickname, or is that a surname?"

"Fabian wrote about the expansion of anthropologism, about the tragic curse of anthropologetics, and he almost wrote about your squeaky shoes and the end of natives in the social sciences," said Almost.

"Never mind the insults, nothing you've said makes any sense, and that's my major objection, not that you were the student's choice, with no credentials, not even a traditional name, but that you think you can tear down what we have taken so many years to build," said the anthropologist.

"Does that mean dominance?"

"Someone must preserve native traditions and the standards of research, and the best of our alliance, as students, faculty, and parents, demonstrates how wrong you are," said Macbeth.

"*Maanoo,*" said Almost.

"The students shout at you, they shout for your silence and absence, and because of you the faculty, for the first time in our history, has walked out on our commencement," shouted Macbeth.

"*Maanoo,*" said Almost.

"You're no native," said Macbeth. His manner weakened, a pathetic pose over the microphone. The audience was never on his side, and the students were more critical of his dominance than they were of the obscure traces of survivance in my cousin's tricky stories.

"Anthropology's on the ropes," said Almost.

"We *are* the ropes," said Macbeth.

"Macbeth, you can say that again."

"I have never, in more than thirty years of teaching, been so humiliated and angry at a graduation ceremony," said the anthropologist. "You may have the right to speak at graduation, but you will never have the right to my attention as a listener."

"So, what are you saying then?" asked Almost.

"You should be silenced," said Macbeth. He waved his arms, and the sudden motion tossed his gown over his face. The students laughed, and with that he marched to the back of the stage and vanished between the curtains. His shoes squeaked in the distance.

"Not a good man, that anthropologist," said Gio Nom.

"The Transethnic Situations Department at the University of California inherited, in a curious sense, a new narrative enactment of that agonistic abstraction of two historical revolutions," said Almost. "Three centuries later the misnomers and contradictions of independence are redoubled in an academic union of learned natives, of newcomers, socialists, separatists, cultural essentialists, narcissists, anarchists, and even those trustily shriven with aesthetic victimry."

"No shriven word here," said Gio Nom.

"No trustily either." We searched for the other words in the manuscript. "So, he's on his feet again." Gio Nom carefully printed the new words in the margins.

"Now wait a minute," said the native historian Ranald MacDonald. He might have been the namesake of an adventurous ancestor, the first native teacher of English in Japan. MacDonald, however, said he was "almost Japanese." He was seated on stage between Ishmael Reed, the novelist who had just published *Japanese by Spring*, and Maisie Peel, the visiting transfeminist interpreter of language poetry from the University of Kent at Canterbury.

"Who said that?" mocked Almost.

"You know nothing about our department," said MacDonald.

"Doctor Almost, surely you could deliver the separatists without misrepresenting the pleasure of narcissists," said Peel. She leaned back as she spoke, as if her thin and tired voice would have a greater, more dramatic range. "Narcissism is a classical pose, a national tradition, and, might we mention here, that separatism has always been safer in sex than politics."

"Tricksterese, either way," said Reed.

"Not much at the end of the day," said Almost.

"Exactly my point," said MacDonald.

"What are your aesthetics situations?" asked Almost.

"What are your sources?"

"*Maanoo*," said Almost.

"What was that?"

"The same as you, never mind," said Almost.

"Do you boys know the gender of your sources?" asked Peel.

"Really, does a narcissist care?" asked MacDonald.

"That's too easy," said Almost.

"Calm down boys, gender has never been transethnic," said Peel.

"You never mention anarchists," said MacDonald.

"Native creation is tricky, not anarchy," said Almost.

"Transethnic situations have no gender," said Peel.

"The Transethnic Situations Department was constituted at the time of civil rights activism, the peace movement, ethnic nominalism, and radical turns of racial consciousness in the late sixties," chanted Almost. "At that very moment of social transformation this new academic enterprise embraced four ethnic programs of study in an uncommon political and academic union, a national congruence of transethnic situations."

"Congruence, what are you on about?" shouted Peel.

"Are we at the end of the day?" asked MacDonald.

"Transethnic manners of dominance," said Almost.

"Naturally, and this is a transethnic double date," said Peel.

"*Maanoo*," said Almost.

"Almost stop?" asked Gio Nom.

"No, not really, when you see that smile he won't be silent for long." We turned to the manuscript. "He was about to say, 'that enterprise is a crucial advance in conservative academic conventions.'"

"His words are big," said Gio Nom.

"Not so big, not in his ordinary tricky stories."

"Since then the academic missions and contradictions of transethnic studies have widened in a new graduate studies program, but comparative practices are never certain, as the transethnic narratives, subjects, objects, theories, and methodologies, are seldom comparable, maybe *never* comparable, because ethnic similarities are transethnic redactions, rather than wiser studies of distinctions and extremes," said Almost. "Listen, transethnic theories must transcend the diversities of native cultures, erase the natives of that first revolution on this continent."

"What are you getting at?" asked MacDonald.

"The empires have returned as transethnic studies," said Almost.

"That's trickster talk, right?"

"*Maanoo*," said Almost.

"What he mean?" asked Gio Nom.

"*Maanoo*, never mind, an academic tease." My whisper seemed too loud, as the audience waited in silence. "Faculty members evade most action, they take cover in theory and aesthetics, and then, later, everyone takes the credit for the origin if something works out."

"Transethnic history never ends," said MacDonald.

"Native American Studies resisted the empires of transethnic studies," shouted Almost. He paused, looked back to the faculty on stage, and then continued his lecture. "This was not a revolution, but a resistance that later proved to be a wiser academic course than transethnic separatism or the rush to new empires."

"The Spanish Empire, is that your ironic double date?" asked MacDonald. The veins in his neck bulged as he leaned forward in his chair, a thin and angular figure. "Surely not, because the remains of empires, double or not, are never ironic."

"The aesthetic empires are over," said Almost.

"Then why the play of resistance?"

"Natives bear the eternal traces of empires."

"That's arguable," said MacDonald.

"Almost, enough with the empires," said Peel. She crossed her legs, and wagged one shoe as she lectured. "The British Empire is the only real empire, and we should fear to say as much in ethnic company."

"Ethnic unities were mere poses," said Almost.

"Once more, you've gone too far," said MacDonald. "Your notions are hostile, not rhetorical, and the students were right to protest your lecture." He gathered his books and walked down the center aisle. Several graduate students followed him out the back of the auditorium.

"They escape their own resistance," said Almost.

"MacDonald said it right," said Peel. "When he leaves, we both leave." She minced down the aisle in red pumps, waved to students on the way, and then, at the back of the auditorium, she turned and shouted, "Almost, double dare you to walk out with me!"

"You bear too much empire," shouted Almost.

"Empires are double dates," said Peel.

"Native American Studies has always had a wider eclectic mission than transethnic nationalism, and more, more, more," said Almost.

"More indeed, and you might have mentioned film studies," said

Jason Frame. He taught comparative race and ethnicity in commercial motion pictures. He loved students, hated the faculty, and was never hesitant to say so at meetings. His film classes were very popular, as were the high grades he gave to students, and so he attracted more football players than any other faculty member on campus.

Ishmael Reed and Jason Frame were the last two faculty members on stage, seated at opposite ends of the row of metal chairs. Reed tuned his earphones to the trial and listened to the lecture at the same time. Frame read his mail and heard little of the lecture.

"Native American Studies is comparative by reason of cultural differences not because of transethnic similarities," said Almost. "This eclectic presentation of diverse histories has been reduced by anthropologism and those who use natives as transethnic scapegoats, because 'anthropology as the study of cultural difference can be productive only if difference is drawn into the arena of dialectical contradiction,' wrote Johannes Fabian."

"Almost Fabian, now there's a union," said Frame.

"*Maanoo*," said Almost.

"Man, they both talk fantastic tricksterese," said Reed.

"How much was he paid for this lecture?"

"Twenty thousand, at least," said Reed.

"That's criminal," said Frame.

"Native American communities are the very origin histories of the Americas," shouted Almost. "The resistance of natives is survivance over the dominance of colonial discoveries and anthropologism, and so, the basic academic mission of native studies is inherent and sovereign in the sense of the *first* revolution on this continent."

"Native survivance, the amen of tricksterese," said Reed.

"Browne's a canvas evangelist," said Frame.

"Who are you, the *film noir* separatist?" said Reed.

"Ishmael, you're great, but what's with the earphones?"

"O. J. Simpson trial, what else?"

"Native American studies programs were established at many colleges and universities in the past two decades," said Almost. "However, few of these new programs survived anthropologism and the rise of new empires of transethnic studies."

"New empires are nonsense," said Frame.

"Transethnic studies and situations became a new measure of dominance," said Almost. "For instance, the notions of aesthetic borderlands would erase the presence, resistance, and traditional histories of native communities. The first native revolution that overturned the cross and crown would be twice silenced in transethnic borderlands."

"Twice silenced, now that's rich gossip," said Frame.

"Jean Baudrillard wrote in *The Transparency of Evil* that today travel 'is the only way we have of feeling that we are somewhere.' That notion of a borderland as 'somewhere' is the transethnic simulation of native territories and resistance."

"Surely, he cries at movies," said Frame.

"The representations of native cultural differences are obscured as the other in anthropologism and transethnic studies. The natural reason and contradictions of the native are transposed, but the simulations of the exotic other are redoubled in museums and motion pictures, the natives and their narratives are erased on transethnic borderlands at universities."

"Right on brother," shouted a student.

"In the 'symbolic universe there is no place for the otherness of difference. Neither animals, nor gods, nor the dead, are other. All are caught up in the same cycle. If you are outside the cycle, however, you do not even exist,' wrote Baudrillard. 'Everyone wants their other,' and natives are the others in the new empire of transethnic anthropologetics. 'Everyone has an imperious need to put the other at their mercy, along with a heady urge to make the other last as long as possible so as to savour him.' And this 'other is the locus of what escapes us, and the way whereby we escape from ourselves.' The other 'is what allows me not to repeat myself for ever' he wrote in the *Transparency of Evil*."

"We can only hope *he's* not repeatable," said Frame.

"Who, Baudrillard?" asked Reed.

"Almost, and he probably invented Baudrillard as his other, but who can understand either of them?" said Frame. "Look at the students, can you believe it, now they pretend to understand, when only a few minutes ago they were ready to hiss him out of the auditorium."

"You might repeat yourself forever," said Reed.

"Surrounded by tricky information, of course," said Frame.

"Almost Baudrillard," said Reed.

"They're both evangelists," said Frame.

"Baudrillard argues that the simulation of the other is a great game, and 'racial otherness survives everything: conquest, racialism, extermination, the virus of difference, the psychodrama of alienation. On the one hand, the Other is always-already dead; on the other hand, the

Other is indestructible.' The native other is the aesthetic victim of anthropologetics and transethnic studies."

"The listeners are the victims," said Frame.

"Man, you should have left with the others," said Reed.

"Almost suckered by an evangelist."

"You've got some documentary in mind, right?"

"The rise of anthropologetics is a banal encore of the other," shouted Almost. "The episodes of the other are reduced to transethnic situations, the mere revisions of native resistance, and the causes of separatism."

"What does that mean?" asked Gio Nom.

"Don't know, but that's what he wrote right here."

"They talk behind his back," said Gio Nom.

"Almost calls it academic shunnery."

"He's not filmic, but he has an eerie gospel," said Frame.

"You're an eerie scripture," said Reed.

"The basic theoretical maneuvers are not resistance but a mere academic presence," said Almost. "Whatever were the ethnic burdens of academic programs founded on the politics of racial resistance are now the banal virtues of transethnic situations."

"Theoretical rubbish," said Frame.

"Perhaps, in a literary sense, an ethnic presence in transethnic situations is an unmeant comedy," continued Almost. "Not a tragedy, but a comedy of ethnic posers and their incessant desire for academic recognition, compensation, and aesthetic salvation at the university."

"Listen, that's tricky academic street talk," said Reed.

"Reed, look around you, the chairs are empty for a good reason," said Frame. "That's not a pose or mere academic shunnery."

"So, what keeps you on stage?"

"Fear and pity, and a good tragic end," said Frame.

"Not good, because 'tragedies end badly,' wrote George Steiner in *The Death of Tragedy*," said Almost. "Listen, 'the tragic personage is broken by forces which can neither be fully understood nor overcome by rational prudence. This again is crucial. Where the causes of disaster are temporal, where the conflict can be resolved through technical or social means, we may have serious drama, but not tragedy,' because 'tragedy is irreparable. It cannot lead to just and material compensation for past suffering,' and so, the other side of native victimry is survivance."

"Governor Wilson should hear this," said Frame.

"Why, because he ends badly?" asked Reed.

"Trash politics never ends, that's bad enough," said Frame.

"They miss the comedy for the victimry," said Reed.

"Comedies are derived from tragedies, a sublime chance and contradiction at universities that search for causation," said Almost. "Politicians are the real comedies, and their aims are the powers of nonsense, the imitations of action, and they are seldom, if ever, heard as tragic stories, because there is nothing to fear but expediencies."

"Almost, he is on his feet more here," said Gio Nom.

"Right, he overturned his own lecture."

"Tricky native stories are natural comedies, the traces of chance that bear no end, no imitations, because stories are the start, the creation," said Almost. "So, here we are on the run at commencement, a repeat of the other in black gowns, a faux comedy, and the real pieties are in academic shunnery, the causal imitations of the faculty."

"Evangelists are everywhere," said Frame.

"You've had enough, right?" said Reed.

"Right, too much," he said and walked out the back of the stage.

"Now, my last thought at this commencement is from Walter Kerr," said Almost. "He wrote in *Tragedy and Comedy* that 'comedy is relief, it is the rest of the bitter truth, a holy impropriety. . . . Why should tragedy have more of a future than comedy? And why should comedy be happy enough without one?' The natural reason, of course, is that tricky stories are the credence of native motion and survivance, and tragedy is the imitation of an aesthetic action, the transethnic twist of victimry."

"Almost turn around on his feet," said Gio Nom.

"Completely different from the manuscript."

"Why faculty leave?" asked Gio Nom.

"Arrogance, they pretend to listen and repeat themselves."

"No good to leave stage," said Gio Nom.

"Reed's the only one who stayed."

"Doctor Almost, the faculty has abandoned you," said a student.

"Not really, they hate me too much," said Almost.

"But they're gone," the student shouted.

"Hold on," said Reed. He tuned his earphones and moved to the podium. "This is tricksterese, man, and the people who walked out the back of the stage are nothing but shunners, they're afraid to hear another story."

"There is a trace of the empire in those empty metal chairs, the pitiful absence of a faculty on the run," said Almost. He turned and shouted the names of the absent faculty. The students were hesitant to laugh, at first, but then they cheered the absence of each honorific name, the academic doctors, Macbeth, MacDonald, Peel, Frame. Almost shouted other names too, Reagan, Wilson, Packwood, Thatcher, Churchill, and the students cheered the faux comedies, but turned silent when they heard the name Che Guevara.

"Professor Maisie Peel, Peel, Peel," the students chanted over and over. Maisie Peel must have heard her name shouted at a great distance on campus, because she was the only faculty member who returned to the auditorium. No one noticed her until she minced down the aisle to the stage.

"Almost certainly got us thinking, didn't he," said Peel.

"Peel, is that a nickname?" asked a student.

"Peel is my mother's name, a great name of the empire."

"What empire?"

"You better read your history," said Peel.

"Professor Reed, what's on the radio?" asked another student.

"O. J. Simpson trial, man," said Reed. He leaned over the podium, raised one earphone to the microphone, and broadcast the voices of defense counsel F. Lee Bailey and police detective Mark Fuhrman.

"Almost worry about faculty?" asked Gio Nom.

"Maybe, but not much, ask him yourself."

"Doctor Almost," said Gio Nom. He stood in the aisle with his arms straight at his sides. He enunciated each word, but the broadcast of the trial had distracted the audience.

Reed saw the man in the aisle and moved away from the microphone, raised his hands, and silenced the audience. The students wanted to hear more of the trial, but then they turned to Gio Nom. "Please continue, your question was lost for a moment," said Reed.

"Faculty gone, what do they fear?" asked Gio Nom.

"They fear chance and stories that have no end, but you know, they'd be here if their pay was based on their attendance at graduation," said Almost. "So, what grade would you give them for their time on the stage?"

"No graduation," said Gio Nom.

"Incomplete," a student shouted and then everyone broke into wild laughter. "Fail the faculty, no pass, no pass, no pass," the students chanted in turn. Then, in a fever, the students threw off their gowns and danced in the aisles. They declared that moment of resistance their commencement.

"Wait a minute," shouted Reed. He turned to the side and tuned his earphones close to the microphone. "Listen, F. Lee Bailey just asked Mark Fuhrman if he ever uttered the word *nigger* in the past ten years."

The students hissed and the sound rushed and circled the auditorium once more, an eerie echo created by hundreds of hissers. The students started another mutant hiss, and the sound was in constant motion. They covered their mouths, and then their ears, but the echo resounded in flesh and bone. The children were frightened and ran out of the auditorium. Soon the parents and students threw their gowns aside and rushed to leave the ceremonies.

"My God, what on earth is happening?" shouted Peel.

"The hisses created a mutant other," said Almost.

"What, a commencement shaman?"

"Yes, the rush of native creation," said Almost.

"Sounds more like a great white noise."

"Creation is here and we are the others," said Almost.

"That's nothing but trickster nonsense," said Peel.

"Listen, that hiss is a thousand native shamans."

"Almost, get real," said Peel.

"The other is the real," said Almost.

"You're a weird shaman."

"This has happened four times before," said Almost.

"Stop it, now you're spooking me," pleaded Peel.

"Once at the worst of the great flood, the second time was at a native dance at a mission near the ocean, but the rush of that creation sound was told only by native women," said Almost.

Almost waited at the podium and turned his head to the motion of the hiss in the auditorium. He leaned in one direction, and then another. "Listen, you can hear the rush of creation."

Peel stood alone in the center aisle. She was on her way out of the auditorium a second time, and then turned back to the stage. Suddenly, she stood on her toes, in her red pumps, and tried to raise her voice over the wild hiss. "Almost, you only named two mutant creations, what were the others?"

"Santa Cruz mountains, seven years ago," said Almost.

"So what?" shouted Peel.

"The Santa Cruz creation rushed down from the mountains to the university," said Almost. "The hiss lasted for several years there, and suddenly, no one knows why, the hiss was gone, but the university has never been the same since."

"So, where is the last one?" asked Peel.

"Secret," said Almost.

"Secret nonsense," said Peel. She waved her hands and shook her head in disbelief over the creation stories. "You finally chased everyone away from the graduation," she said. "Now that was quite a trick, and a story to remember." She smiled, removed her shoes, and pranced out of the auditorium.

Gio Nom waited with his daughter at the back of the auditorium. At first he was troubled by the demonstrations of the students, and the absence of the faculty, but in time, as he heard the creation of a lecture, he was moved by the performance. He might have been the only parent there who heard the native creation stories.

Almost walked down the aisles and gathered as many commencement gowns and hoods as he could carry. He packed several bundles into trunks and mailed them back to the barony. He was never paid for his lecture because he would not reveal his address or social security number to anyone. The truth is, he does not have a number, and his home is the back seat of a station wagon.

Reed tuned his earphones to the broadcast of the trial. He was the last faculty to arrive at commencement that morning, and he was the last to leave the sound of creation stories in Ishi Auditorium. "Survivance, now that's a tricky creation story."

6

Glossolalia Hermits

Almost was on his merry way to visit the Glossolalia Hermits on Ghost Island, or *jiibay minis* in *anishinaabe*, near the international border in Lake Namakan. The native glossolalists are forever in a trance over the music of words, no matter the season, the contradictions, or the tone of native stories.

Many people avoid the island, and the official state maps of the border lakes are clearly marked with a simple warning to boaters, "Beware of Wild Voices on Ghost Island." Truly, the native hermits are enchanted, and there is no reason to be worried about native ecstasies at any time.

Contrary to the cautionary advice on the maps, the notice on the island, printed on an enormous billboard at the end of the dock, invites visitors to "Share the Natural Gift of Tongues."

Almost visits the Glossolalia Hermits, a community of nine men and thirteen women, at least four times a year, at the end of every season, to walk and talk backwards on the island, and to liberate the dead words of institutional memories. "Politicians wound our creation stories with dead bolt causes, and then they leave our words out back for dead, abandon our stories with no motion, no presence, no memories," my cousin once told a boater who dared to dock one afternoon at Ghost Island. "So, fast talk loosens our memories, and sometimes the world makes more sense backwards in stories."

Last autumn we carried smoked salmon, blue chicken, chocolate crickets, olive bread, and wine to the island for a feast with the solitary glossolalists. We ate and the conversations were rushed, to be sure. The tongues rushed with the sound of waves over the island stones, words creaked and moaned with the dock, as my cousin announced a few dead letter words, such as "privileged information" and "risk management" and "dicks of color." The tongues were wild over the sounds, "ivi form isk emana rolo skid," and then the sounds were voiced in musical tones, "gegaa itinirosked tamionirp degament foscoicks rolo colo rolo colo seekivi."

The Glossolalia Hermits have been on Ghost Island since the creation of stones, the seasons, and natives. Some doubters wonder if there is some strange energy in the stones on the island, an energy that evermore twists tongues. There is no real resistance to the twist, trance, and paradise of glossolalia. My father told me the glossolalists are touched by a native passion, the ecstatic voices of shamans, and the original oral tongues of bears and humans.

Almost was in a rapture of tongues when a water patrol officer circled the island, and, with a bullhorn, he shouted my cousin's name several times. The glossolalists were enchanted by the sound as the name wavered on the wind. They chanted variations of his name, "am amos, gegaa, wabnew mo, bone, ownamost, gegaa."

"Who are you?" shouted Almost.

"International water patrol."

"Dock, and have some salmon and tongue."

"Not today," shouted the officer.

"Why not?"

"The President of the United States wants to talk with you right now," the officer shouted as he raised a radio telephone in one hand. His voice wavered over the bullhorn. The glossolalists turned the sound of his voice into a chorus of tongues. Their tongues were so spirited that we never worried, at first, or even wondered why a water patrol deputy would bear a message from the President of the United States.

"Come ashore," shouted Almost.

"Not a chance."

"Once more, why not?"

"My tongue is loose enough," said the officer.

"He's right, not a chance," my cousin said to me.

"President Nixon is on the line."

"The Great Pumpkin would come ashore," shouted Almost.

"Who?"

"The man on the line."

"Come out to the end of the dock," shouted the officer.

"*Gegaa* notion resipresinon non non none," said my cousin. We poured more wine and then walked out to the end of the dock to meet the deputy. The sun rushed to the shore on the waves. The glossolalists were there, but no one said a word as the patrol boat moved closer. The deputy was nervous and would not allow me to tie his boat to the dock. He handed the radio telephone to my cousin, sucked his tongue in silence, and then reversed the engines.

"Mister President," said Almost.

"Almost Browne?"

"*Gegaa*, almost," said Almost.

"Where are you?" asked President Nixon.

"Listen, hear that glossolalia choir on the dock."

"*Gegaa* am amos mo bone oxinotion," chanted the glossolalists.

"What was that?" asked Nixon.

"Native tongues."

"Never mind, wait there for the helicopter."

"*Maanoo*," said Almost.

"No, military."

"Why a helicopter?" asked Almost.

"Presidential," said Nixon.

"Where are you?" asked Almost.

"Never mind." Soon a pontoon helicopter landed near the dock, and a few hours later my cousin was on his way to the capital in Washington. President Nixon scheduled a short meeting the next afternoon in the White House. Almost called that night to tell me a few stories about their conversation.

Almost told me he bought an inexpensive miniature tape recorder at the airport and secretly recorded about eighteen minutes of conversation with the president. That muted, scratchy tape turned out to be the only record of the session. We amplified the voice of the president at one of our *debwe* festivals at the barony. My cousin had no idea at the time that every conversation was recorded in the Oval Office.

The Supreme Court, as you know, rejected the claims of executive privilege and ordered the president to turn over to the special prosecutor the secret tape recordings of telephone conversations and meetings in the White House. So, we were worried for a time about that decision. Almost was there and might have become the focus of a congressional investigation, but the very conversation my cousin had with the president had been erased. Those few minutes of erasure were the traces of political conspiracies.

Almost, you see, had the only tape recording of that incredible conversation in the Oval Office. About eighteen and a half minutes of crucial presidential history was our secret. We never were sure what to do, and so we did nothing but listen for more than twenty years. Luckily, when we played the recording at the *debwe* no one believed it was the voice of the president. That conversation with my cousin was, in fact, evidence that the president was directly involved in covert actions, conspiracies, and the abuse of executive authority. The president might have been convicted of the obstruction of justice. Tulip was convinced that he was involved in an earlier conspiracy that resulted in the assassination of President John Kennedy.

Eternal Flame transcribed the only tape recording of the lost eighteen minutes of presidential deception and subversion. The scratchy conversation was played so many times we could recite almost every word of the president. Almost provided descriptive comments to the conversation.

"Where did you come from?" asked the president.

"Ghost Island," said Almost.

"That must be your reservation, is that right?"

"No, but close enough," said Almost.

"Now, let me say this right away, that we gave your people, what was it, about sixty thousand dollars to leave town, and at the time we asked nothing more than loyalty, but now the country needs you more than it ever has in the past," said the president.

"Manhattan?" asked Almost.

"Sixty thousand god damn dollars for nothing, and what we want now is your loyalty and nothing less than a revolution, and your people should be good at that, and that's what my advisors say, get the Indians to do the hard work, because they live a hard life," said the president.

"Sixty thousand for what?"

"My old man lived a hard life too, he worked hard and never had much, and that lemon ranch never amounted to much in the end, but he was a great man," said the president. His voice wavered and then he turned to the window.

"What town was that again?" asked Almost.

"Whittier, California."

"No, the sixty thousand dollar town."

"The Bureau of Indian Affairs," said the president. "Your people took over that building right before the election, not a good time to stage a fucking stunt like that, and we had a hell of a time trying to blame that on some son of a bitch in the Democratic Party." He leaned back in his chair and rested his feet on the desk. He wiped the sweat from under his nose.

"So, that was your money?"

"You know, we worked hard in those days," said the president.

"Quakers are hard workers," said Almost.

"You know, my mother was always a saint."

"Follow the money," said Almost.

"Your people got the god damn money," said the president.

"Indians are not Quakers."

"You know, your people are the true revolutionaries."

"The American Indian Movement is not a revolution," said Almost.

"Someone better work for that money," said the president.

"So, why are we here?"

"I want to say this right now, you're the man."

"*Gegaa*," said Almost.

"The country needs you now," said the president.

"*Maanoo*," said Almost.

"Whatever you need to get the job done."

"What's the job?"

"Revolution," said the president.

"Right on brother," said Almost.

"A new voice heard across the world," said the president.

"Mister President, you name the reservation."

"I was a low man on the totem pole once, on the labor committee." The president turned in his chair, and then walked slowly to the window. First he folded his arms on his chest, and then he shoved his hands into his pants pockets and touched his head on the window frame. "John Kennedy was on the labor committee, we were both on the bottom once, but his kind always had money and the connections, everything came easy for them."

"Northwest coast natives?"

"Listen, we want your people to launch the revolution."

"You talking guns or stories?" asked Almost.

"Whatever it takes," said the president.

"Should we spin the globe?"

"What the hell are you talking about?" shouted the president.

"Where is the revolution?"

"Cuba, for Chrisake!"

"So, what do you have in mind?" asked Almost.

"Overthrow that son of a bitch," said the president.

"Fidel Castro's saying the same thing."

"No, he's saying, that 'capitalist son of a bitch,'" said the president.

"Now there's a story," said Almost.

"This is the business of the people goddamnit, so you get your people in line and get this job done, this is a revolution that will make our country great again, and your people can redeem themselves, they can have the credit for the overthrow of that commie bastard," said the president.

"Why me?"

"Indians got the money, so this is pay back time."

"Mister President, fuck the money."

"That's the spirit, my people were right about you."

"Would you sign one of my blank books?"

"Now that's funny, my people said you were a comic."

"So, where do we start?" asked Almost.

"Indians, you people have always been revolutionaries."

"Quakers are better than natives, hands down."

"Maybe you have something there," said Nixon.

"Castro's become a capitalist, the tourist dollar is back on the streets, the natives are building casinos on the island, and the revolution is a marvelous adventure," said Almost. "Cuba's the land of venture capital, so what's in this revolution for me?"

"My people never mentioned the casinos," said the president.

"Your people are more talk than chance."

"I want to say this, you can have your own casino."

"Native stakes are higher than you might think," said Almost.

"You know, you would make a damn fine vice president."

"That's much better than an average chance."

"Vice President Almost Browne," said the president.

"Now there's a nickname," said Almost.

"Do you like the sound of the vice presidency?"

"Almost the president," said Almost.

"Listen, you get your people to overthrow Castro, take Cuba, and declare some sort of Indian sovereignty over the island, and for that, my friend, you will become my next vice president," said the president. "Don't forget, Columbus discovered Cuba and your people have the absolute right to liberate Cuba."

"How about your covert people?"

"We stand behind you, of course," said the president.

"Spiro Agnew, does he get his own casino?"

"He's about to leave with a serious tax problem," said the president.

"Almost another treaty," said Almost.

"More than almost, you deliver a revolution in Cuba, and the vice presidency is yours," said the president. He was standing at the side of his desk with his hands in his pockets. His cheeks trembled, and his black eyes chased the silence. "Kennedy failed, but we've got the Indians on our side, and you know, this is a true story."

"So, is this a regular day in the presidency?"

"You know, I want to say this right now, we could call this a comedy of errors," said the president. "Revolutions are like that, nothing ever turns out the way it was planned, and when it happens that way, it might as well have been a comedy."

"Treaties and comedies never end," said Almost.

"You know, there may be some instances that you, and some of your people, may be ahead of us," said the president. "But there are other times that we are ahead of you, and that's the way it goes, but who writes the history?"

"You know, my people were right about you," said Almost.

"We had a hard life," said the president.

"No, they said you're a discreet poker player," said Almost.

"You know, my father never showed his hand."

"Sir, your next appointment is here," said H. R. Haldeman.

"Who's out there?" asked the president.

"Henry Kissinger."

"He's probably got his shorts twisted again," said the president.

"I never wear shorts," said Almost.

"You know, you both come from the lost tribes."

"Almost lost, and the rest is a true history," said Almost.

7

Hotline Healers

Native stories, as you know, are the slaves of our remembrance. Maybe stories better our traditions and ordinary lies. No, our stories are the slaves of the ancient ones whose lies would otherwise never be remembered in translations. Either way, the word slaves, or the aesthetic shadows of my cousin's stories, are the new hotlines to the animals.

Almost created a hotline to native healers, a widespread nine hundred number in touch with healers close to animals. "Once we were hunters, closer to the natural stories of the animals," my cousin said in a radio advertisement. "Now, you can be as close to the animals as a hunter, as close as your telephone."

Almost, with a federal economic development grant, provided hundreds of cellular telephones to the very best story tellers on reservations and elsewhere in native communities, and even to a few people who spent their entire lives in casinos. He once told federal auditors that "native gamblers are some of the most imaginative healers on the hotline."

Many of our relatives were connected as hotline cellular healers at the barony. Grandmother Wink told stories about the *madoodoo* on the winter hotline. Shadow Box heard the shouters, so he built a cradle to hold the cellular telephone over a special hotline panic hole. Many people called and shouted for a few minutes. One summer there were four hotline panic holes to hear the shouters. Eternal Flame heard confessions on the hotline at the Patronia Scapehouse. My father even told a few erotic animal stories on the clerisy hotline. Actually, most of the hotline healers were closer to wild stories than to secretive creatures or the constant brunt and mundane breath of real beasts.

"The hotline healers are natives with the best stories," Almost told a reporter for the *San Francisco Chronicle*. "Would you make a long distance telephone call to a real farmer and expect to be healed by a livestock report?"

"Exactly, the hotlines are animal stories?" asked the reporter.

"Listen, we are the true healers."

"Then, the real animals are dinner?"

"We get most of our calls right after dinner," said Almost.

"After dinner hotline confessions?" asked the reporter.

"Listen, stories are the *real* starts, the best native starts, not the slavish end of our nature with the barrows and hogs, and the end has never been more than another start," said Almost. "That double twist of silence, the tease of chance, is another hotline creation in stories."

"Everything you say is a double twist," said the reporter.

"Wise men tease the obvious," said my cousin. He teased the newspaper reporter, but there was no blood of humor, no twist of chance, no waves of memory. Almost told me he would rather chase the *wiindigoo*, the *anishinaabe* winter cannibal monster, than hear the dead voices of journalists. So, he often walked away with a tricky smile and left me with the ruins of a conversation.

Almost lived to tease native stories. Stories were his start, his slaves, his name, his animal business, and the hotlines soon became one of our great success stories on the barony. Last month, for instance, more than a thousand lonesomes dialed our nine hundred number for a conversation with a native in touch with the animals. Yes, *lonesomes*, those who have lost their stories and natural memories of nature. Hundreds of natives are out in the wild this very moment with cellular telephones, eager to serve their stories. This hotline presence of animals is a new consciousness, and our native stories have not been this close and vital for more than a century.

Almost must hear the natural sounds of animals to be alive, and that's how our hotlines got started last year. Everyone knows that native bear stories are needed to tame the lonesome beasts in the cities. We listen to nine hundred stories several times a day. My cousin listens to bear stories in the morning on the hotline, stories told by a woman who lives alone with bears in the mountains. Truly, she roams and roars with the bears on the hotline.

You can hear beavers and hold your breath, listen to your heart beat under water, and no doubt you can be closer to beavers on the hotline than to your own families. The hotline wolves run with you at night in the cities, in memories and stories.

Anyone can connect with the animals in their natural seasons on the hotlines. Summer on the river stones, and the crack of beaver tails. Autumn is the mortal tease of our memories. Winter, the rush and score of wolves at the treelines. Not even the *wiindigoo* breaks the traces of the scent of spring. The meadow is our hotline to the seasons, and no one is ever alone there with the animals. We are always in motion with the river otters, and with the crows on the distant roads. Come closer, we are almost close enough to hear the breath of bears and the ancient lies in the rain. Our breath is wild in the cedar.

The stories of animals and the ancient ones are the cures in our dreams and native memories. Even the silence of animals is a trace of nature in our stories. That silence of creation, the rise of natural breath, the uncertain wisps of memory that turn to sound, a sneeze, the distance of a whispered name, wait to be heard in our stories.

Almost said his names are the traces of silence, not the museum notions of our "warrantable native ancestors." Traces are the wind, not the seasons, the sound of wind in the summer birch, the scent of hooves, and the slow bounce of crows on the winter wires, those eternal wires. The animals on the hotlines are the creation, the start not the end of civilization.

Naturally, native stories ended our silence. We listened over and over again, and now we are the ones to hear animals on the hotlines. Once the names were sounded out, and the silence broken, we turned our stories around in memories to bear the silence of our own creation. The stories about our start are a new native season.

Panda Radio, a late night radio talk show, was the first national station to broadcast some of our hotline healers. That particular show was based on conversations with creature companions. Almost and most of our relatives would never answer to television, and that's the truth, because the animals on the hotlines are stories to be *heard* not seen in some electronic zoo. Our memories are the traces of nature not the cold wash of dickered pixels, or the coarse animations on a screen. Besides, stories start in silence not in the notions that are translated on picture calendars. Our memories are the sound of animals, and the animals are heard in nature on the hotlines.

Panda Man, the host of the radio talk show, was a mighty man of sound in spite of his absolute silence in the morning. He told me that nature, not stories, is the source of silence, and "the real world is no more than an advertisement." He is, nonetheless, very serious about natives and their associations with animals. "Who could be natural without animal stories?" asked Panda Man.

Naturally, he believes that we have a corner on creature companions with our hotlines. His notion of silence is twisted, unnatural, but, to his credit, he believes that sound is more creative than mere pictures. "Pictures are silence, sound is the *real* real," he announces at the start of his radio shows. "Pictures are poached and puny without a host."

Panda Radio, one of the most popular late night radio shows, invited me and my cousin to answer questions on the air. The actual radio studio was located in Chicago, a few blocks from the Newberry Library. Almost had accepted an invitation to lecture on tricky stories at a native gender conference and, at the same time, he signed several copies of our best edition of blank books for Frederick Hoxie, a historian and administrator at the library.

So, we were in the city anyway and could not resist an invitation to tease a few listeners on talk radio. We had crossdressed for the gender conference and decided to continue the same poses. No one at the radio station had any idea who we were at the time, so we declared new radio identities and nicknames. My name that night became an elaborate radioactive story. Almost posed as my shy sister, and the most he ever said that night was *gegaa* and *maanoo* on the air.

Panda Man introduced our nine hundred hotlines on radio and then started out by asking me to explain the meaning of my radioactive nickname. Earlier, we told him that every native has several nicknames, and one of my name stories was more active than the others. I was evasive, of course, and told the radio audience, with certain pauses, about a dream that had followed me for many years around the country. He turned and raised his hand several times over the microphone, but he could not break that trace of silence in my stories. I doubled the twist of my stories that night with tricky poses and he was mine for a time on talk radio. Dreams are like that, you know, the listeners become the stories, no matter their resistance.

"I am alone and hungry in a strange place, a rather common dream scene, but wait until you hear the rest," I told the listeners of late night Panda Radio. "I walk into a building looking for food and, no doubt, some contact with people. I open a metal door, enter a large room, and discover that the floor is covered with body parts, a horrible scene.

Heads, arms, eyes, hands, internal organs, cover the entire area from wall to wall. I turn in horror to escape but my body does not move, my feet are not mine in the dream. My body does not hear my story. I try to shout but my voice is caught in silence. I strain to be heard by someone, anyone."

Silence, and the radio host missed his cue. "Then, at last, the silence is broken and my shout is heard, not by someone who could save me, but by the body parts on the floor. Bloody heads turn toward me and wave, eyes open and wink, arms rise, fingers point, mouths move a mute salutation. I shout louder and louder to be heard, to be real, and then, at last, awaken in the stories of my own dream. Since then the severed heads, the mouths, eyes, and hands have returned in many dreams.

"I must be the catchword in the ancient stories of diseases and native death. I am their stories, awakened as their past in my own dreams. Later, in the same dream that now follows me everywhere, the bodies are cut into tiny parts, and dead animals are beside them, some without hair or claws. In my most recent dreams the body parts are hideous mutations, giant eyes that open to my shouts, the moist dark eyes of an unbelievable distance and silence, and short blue arms that slither and bounce, and miniature hands that reach out to pinch me. I wait in the dream to be pinched, and wonder if that touch is our creation. Those hands, my hands, the fingers had no nails. Those hands that pinched me were the stories of the ancient ones. I must be the voice of their silence in my dreams."

"Death is never silence," said a radio listener.

"Plutonium, is that your nickname?" asked the host of the radio show. Panda Man was nervous, he stared at me for several minutes in silence before he shouted my name three times, as if he had entered the stories of my horrible dream to rescue me. I learned later that the silence between my stories and his shout was not noticed by the radio listeners. They, too, had awakened in the stories.

"One of many reservation nicknames."

"Born and raised on a reservation?"

"*Gegaa*," said Almost.

"You bet, and native nicknames were our tradition."

"The pleasure is mine." The host leaned closer to the microphone, an unnatural radio intimacy, and asked me the name of my natal reservation. I knew he had some native romance in mind, a place of great nostalgia and tragic suffering, and then he would be ever so wise and sensitive to ask me how it was to survive starvation and genocide with a clean smile, or some such notion of eternal victimry. Naturally, he had no idea that my response would be so ironic, and match so perfectly his moronic notions of native identity. How could he ever understand that there were no answers to the romantic summons, the dominance of tragedies, and the taut histories of victimry?

"What reservation?"

"The Hanford Reservation in Washington."

"Hanford?" Panda Man whispered the name, uncertain of the ironies, and then he leaned back from the microphone. His nostalgic prey had become a trickster and the intimacy ended right there on the air, and in silence. The host had been deceived by his own romance of native land-scapes and traditions. He missed the obvious, the *real* victimry.

"Yes, the nuclear reservation."

"Our listeners must wonder how that can be true."

"My father was a technical assistant to an arms research physicist, and so we lived on several nuclear reservations and sites over the years. My father worked at Savannah River, the Pantex Plant on the Texas Panhandle, Rocky Flats in Nevada, Los Alamos National Laboratory, and the Oak Ridge Reservation in Tennessee. Nuclear or not, my father practiced real native traditions, and in the summer we always visited our relatives on the *other* reservation, so now you can understand the nature of my radioactive nickname."

"Not really," he said in a tone and manner that reminded me of our social distance, a commercial radio voice of the night and a contradiction in native stories. The host seemed to be concerned that he might be poisoned by the mere sound of my nickname, as his sense of the real was trained so close to the microphone. The questions he asked soon turned to ironies, and so my name was in need of a tricky story change right then and there on the air.

"Plutonia is my *real* nickname."

"Traditional, to be sure," he insisted at a distance.

"Naturally, but an active distance."

"Plutonium, then, is the element of your name?"

"*Maanoo*," said my cousin. He watched the radio host closely and mocked his every move in silence, the wave of his hands and the strain of his mouth over the microphone. The host could not hear ironies and he could not see mimicry.

"Plutonia, from plutonian not plutonium," I said twice with my mouth close to the microphone. "Plutonian, the cause of my traditional nickname is not some transuranic element, but the underworld, the trace of that great natural distance."

That story of my *new* nickname was a lie, of course, but at the time, live on a talk radio show, it was my way to counter his late night radio lies. His manner, no doubt, was manifest, a sense of cultural dominance, and he used an unseen audience to true his distance. What a treat, then, to be a radio show discoverer of unusual native names and places. My new name would be the everlasting stories of the hotlines.

"Plutonia, then," he said to the microphone.

"I am a native child, born on a nuclear reservation, and nothing since then has ever been the same, click, click, click, click. Listen, my grand-mother was great with stories and she told me that we were the heirs of that ancient and mysterious Noongom Nuclear Tribe."

The host, once more, moved closer to the microphone. He ran his eyes over me and told the listeners about my clothes, the turn of my hair, my eyes and hand gestures. He was interested in our hotlines, of course, that's why he invited me to talk on the show, but for a time he could not get past the color of my eyes. First, he wanted my name, and then he wanted to own my eyes. My eyes are turquoise, not brown, and he told the radio audience several times, "There is clearly something radioactive about your gaze."

"Get it, click, click, click, click?"

"Naturally," he said and watched my eyes.

"Every time my grandmother visited us on *our* reservation she would say that, 'click, click, click, click,' a mock measure of radiation. She con-vinced me as a child that we were nuclear natives of the most ancient traditions. I suppose she was right in a strange way, we are active heirs of the water and the stone. Many native origin stories haul humans right out of the hotbed of the earth. Imagine that, we are the natives of a ra-dioactive mother earth?

"I never doubted my identity until other students laughed at me in school. We were native, my families are from the woodland, that much is clear, but that stupid label of the nuclear tribe stuck to me like pitch pine for a long time. Still does, as you can hear right here. That was a critical lesson then, humor is a hotline healer not a cultural curse."

"*Gegaa*," said Almost.

"Panda Radio listeners are eager to hear the voice of nature and the real animals on your hotlines," said the host of Panda Radio. "Now, are your hotlines ready for a little stimulation?" The host flashed several pictures of animals in front of me, a panda bear at a zoo, two wolves on a snowy rise, and a pack of hyenas with bright eyes in a night scene. For some strange reason he must have thought the pictures would inspire me to chant a hotline mantra.

"What's with the hyenas?"

"Poached pictures of random animals, thought they might stimulate your hotlines and amuse our listeners," he said and flashed the pictures a second time. "How about the panda, do you have a direct hotline number to the pandas?"

"I am a true healer with many numbers, and people know at least that much about me." I whispered close to the microphone. My dupery and insecurities would have been too obvious in a louder voice. "We were never poachers." He flashed several other pictures of native hunters posed over dead deer and bear. "Panda Radio is the poacher, because you never even see the game in the pictures." He threw his head back and laughed, but he was hearty only to the microphone. "Grandmother Wink taught me how to tease animals and birds, and how to heal with animal stories and bird visions."

"Wink?"

"My grandmother's nickname."

"She must have been your voice of the panda?"

"What panda?"

"Panda Radio, the sound of true creature companions."

"I lived with my grandmother for thirty years and we traveled and healed, but my stories and visions died with my grandmother." Once more the host moved closer to the microphone and waved the panda picture. My pose was worrisome, as you know, because my grandmother might find out that she had been buried in a story on talk radio. On the other hand, she would have teased me with even trickier stories. So, the course of my new nickname meandered over talk radio waves. "My power to heal was gone, my stories were dead, and the animals were lonesome and avoided the desperate squeeze of my own imagination."

"Panda Radio is here to bear your story."

"The very people who were once healed by my stories turned against me, and their humor might have broken the silence, the desperation, but the wicked rumors convinced them that my nickname and stories were evil, that my name had poisoned the memories of the animals."

"Plutonia, our listeners thank you so much for that intimate confession," said the host. "But now, we must break for a special message from one of our sponsors, the Las Vegas Magic Zoo, the first virtual reality animal garden where the pandas are more at home away from home, an unusual experience with animal companions for the entire family."

"Mister Panda Man, are you serious, a virtual garden?" I would have said more about the virtual zoo but the engineer cut our microphones when the commercial was aired. The host leaned back and laughed, he was unconcerned and seemed rather pleased to silence me for the moment.

"Panda Radio, my friend, is a virtual companion in sound," said the host. "The truth of our time on the earth, and one of your hotlines, to be sure, is in the sound not the poached pictures." He leaned forward, framed my face with his hands, stared into my eyes for a long time, and then turned away in laughter. "Wow, those radioactive eyes are serious hotlines!"

"Panda Man, are you a virtual hotliner?"

"Virtual or not, wild animals are oxymorons."

"Where?"

"Panda Radio, naturally," said the host.

"Not in my stories."

"Even your stories could be companion advertisements," said the host. He cocked his ear to hear the end of the commercial, the simulated sound of animals in an urban forest, the moan of traffic and wild bleat of horns. Two virtual bears brushed close to the microphone, beaver smacked their tails on water, and loons chuckled over the tack and clack of casino machines at the Las Vegas Magic Zoo.

"Panda Radio is back on the air with our hotline healer lady, a creature with the natural connection to the way we once were in sound," said the host. "Our listeners know that the sounds of animals are the true companions of our time."

"Have you ever touched an animal?"

"Hirsute animal?" He cocked his head, the pose of a weasel at the microphone, and his thin fingers roamed on the table, over the thick brown felt. The matted fibers might have been one of his companions.

"Have you ever pushed your fingers into the warm hair of an animal in summer, and breathed so close to an animal that you were in the same shadow of air?" I watched his fingers turn under and rest on the table. "So close that you can tease the heat of creation, the touch that heals, that rush of stories in the heart." Panda Man was aroused, he turned twice around in his chair, and then motioned to the studio engineer.

"Now to the animal hotlines," said the host.

"What animal should we hear first?"

"Chimpanzees," said the host.

"There are no chimpanzees on reservations."

"Why not?"

"Chimpanzees are in laboratories."

"So, why not call one?"

"Chimpanzees, as you know, are human."

"So are bears," said the host.

"You mean, bears masturbate?"

"I was thinking more about healing," said the host.

"Masturbation is healing. . . ."

"Not on my radio show," said the host at a distance.

"Panda Radio listeners must have something to say out there, so why not invite them to call in and tell us about their experiences with zoo bears and chimpanzees?" Panda Man tried to trick me but in the end he was tricked by his own late night radio listeners.

"My friends, we would like to hear from those of you who have had experiences with chimpanzees," the host announced. "I mean, of course, experiences as companions." Panda Man gestured to the studio engineer to screen the telephone calls, and in seconds many listeners had called the station with stories about their experiences.

"Laguna Beach, you're on the air," said the host.

"My sister once taught chimps how to write love letters."

"Written to whom?"

"Why, to anybody, she wrote for a greeting card company."

"What about the chimpanzees?"

"You know, they did the love messages, the chimpanzees were the real healers, and my sister got the credit," said the listener. "I mean, she worked hard to train them, and they were really great for the card business."

"Please, share a chimpanzee love letter," said the host.

"My star is in your triangle," said the listener.

"What does that mean?"

"Chimpanzees wrote symbolic love messages."

"Panda Radio is on your side, true love's in a triangle," said the host. He waved his hands and moved to the next listener on the line. More than a dozen lights blinked on the telephone console, each light an eager listener with a story about an experience with chimpanzees. "You're on the air, where are you from?"

"El Monte, and we live in an interstate trailer park."

"Do chimpanzees live in your park?"

"I should say not, monkeys spread diseases."

"Thank you, and now on to our next caller," said the host.

"Panda Radio?"

"Yes, you're on the air, and from where?"

"Berkeley," said the caller.

"Do you have chimpanzees as companions?"

"Yes, my baby sitters were chimps."

"Baby sitters, in what sense?" asked the host.

"My mother was a research assistant at the university and my baby sitters were truly chimpanzees." Her voice was loud and clear over the sound of trucks and construction equipment in the background. "The chimps learned how to write and cared for me at the same time."

"Surely you were not in the same cages with chimpanzees?"

"Yes, of course, the chimps were my parents for more than a decade, and they worried about me as any parent would under the circumstances." She shouted to be heard over the sounds of heavy machinery and construction.

"Where is your telephone located?"

"On my ear," she shouted.

"I mean, where are you calling from?" asked the host.

"Interstate 580."

"You're on the highway?"

"I control traffic at a highway construction site," she explained.

"Fantastic, so back to your baby sitters," said the host.

"Yes, my experiences were family not research, and chimpanzees taught me how to write with abstract symbols, how to love, and how to fly, hold on. . . ." Her voice was lost in the roar of machines and diesel trucks.

"Berkeley, are you there?"

"Yes, that was a load for the earthquake."

"You said, before the trucks roared over your voice, that chimpanzees taught you how to love and fly," said the host. "Now, love is one thing, but consider me slow on this point, so please, in simple sentences, explain how chimps could teach you how to fly."

"That was easy," she said over a cellular telephone.

"Listen, children jump off garage roofs and try to fly, a natural rite of passage, to be sure, but chimpanzees as flying instructors is a bit much to believe, even if they were your baby sitters," said the host.

"Chimps have much more imagination. . . ."

"Than what?" shouted the host.

"More imaginative than the average human, but most people would never know this because they were never raised by chimps," she said. "I climbed with the best of them in the cages, and then learned how to fly."

"Right, and they taught you how to love?" asked the host.

"Naturally, and how to read symbols."

"So, can chimpanzees write love notes for greeting cards?"

"Absolutely, we exchanged birthday messages."

"Give me an example," said the host.

"My cone holds your circle, triangle, and star."

"Panda Radio, your companion in sound, will take a short break to hear another message about the Las Vegas Magic Zoo." The virtual garden beasts roared in the advertisement and then their sounds were modulated into comments on the humans at the zoo, a wild reversal of the participant observer from the inside of the cages. Commonly, the animals noticed the flesh and bones of humans more than their manners and clothes. Over the lust of a lion the radio host turned to me and roared, a comment on the recent callers and their stories.

"Panda Radio is back on the air, and now with great anticipation we turn to the animal hotlines," said the host. "Plutonia, who is our first animal hotliner?" Once more his fingers were poised on the felt table.

"Ghost Island," said Almost.

"No, but close to the international border." I dialed an earnest beaver family near the woodland lakes area on the border. The line was busy. So, the host aired another advertisement. Later the beaver connection was broken as the host announced that a "persuasive listener was on the wire."

"Panda Radio, you're on the air."

"I don't normally call talk shows," said the listener.

"Few people do," said the host.

"Besides, we are on vacation," said the listener. "I could not, however, let pass the earlier comments about the language abilities of chimpanzees, in particular, the notion that chimps can learn how to read and write."

"Sir, where are you from?"

"Monterey, at the moment, but that should not be important."

"What's your experience with chimpanzees?"

"My research activities in animal behavior would not support the notion that chimps demonstrate an innate capacity for human languages," said the listener. "Moreover, much of what has been noticed is mere chimp mimicry."

"Monterey, are you saying that chimps are incapable of love?"

"Love is inscrutable, and chimps are not poets."

"Then what are you saying about love?" asked the host.

"Nothing, but the language that expresses the poetry of love is not innate to chimpanzees," said the listener. "Animals are smart, some are wise mimics, but humans have inherited the capacity for language."

"Would you say that some animals can outwit humans?"

"Indeed, and some chimps are better mimics," said the listener. "However, there is no evidence that mimicry makes a history or literature of chimpanzees, no matter the poetic inspiration of the cage."

"How about flying?" asked the host.

"Yes, that was an intriguing story by one of your listeners, and her experiences cannot be denied, of course, but to attribute the intentions of chimps to teach flying is an invitation to another critique," said the listener.

"Fly that by our listeners again?"

"*Maanoo*," said Almost.

"True, children are eager to fly, and from garage roofs, as one of your listeners mentioned, but imagination is not the same as the evolution of arms and feathered wings, and to learn flying from a chimp is magical, the great imagination of an artist."

"Monterey, who are you?" asked the host.

"Never mind, we are on vacation," said the listener.

"*Gegaa*," said Almost.

"Panda Radio has a turn to fly, but not before we hear from the Pet Core, one of our most imaginative sponsors in the business of natural pet foods and grooming products," said the host. Panda Man mocked the advertisement, as it was aired, by brushing his blond hair with a cat brush.

The host turned to me and the hotlines once more. I decided to try the avian hotlines, our new connections, because there had been so much talk about flying. I called Father Berasimo, our natural bald eagle man at Lake Namakan. Berasimo never was a priest, but, for reasons he has never been able to understand, others insist on the title. He lives in a shrouded cabin near Ghost Island.

"Panda Radio, you're on the air."

"Franz Kafka here at the World Trade Center," said Berasimo. "I just woke up in the smart feathers of an urban falcon." Berasimo always pretends to be someone else when he answers the cellular hotline. Last week he pretended to be Eleanor Roosevelt in the Salvation Army.

"Kafka, are you there?" shouted the host.

"Your there is my here," said Berasimo.

"Where might that be?"

"The orthodox slipstream, who are you?"

"You're on the air," said the host.

"Never, not out here," said Berasimo.

"What's happening out there?" asked Panda Man.

"The black flies are vicious."

"Tell our listeners about the bald eagles?"

"Right, the eagles invented these flies," said Berasimo.

"How is that?" asked the host.

"Humans, you see, were taking too many fish."

"What about the bald eagles," said the host.

"Listen, for one thing, bald eagles are not really bald."

"Do you get many calls on your hotline?"

"Not many, the flies are miserable," said Berasimo.

"Panda Radio, your companion in sound, will be back with another hotline in a moment, after more natural grooming advice from Pet Core." Panda Man was not pleased with the bald eagle man and insisted that we try the beaver family once more. The hotline was busy, but by the end of the advertisement we made the connection.

"Panda Radio, you're on the air," said the host.

"Yes, are you hotlining the beaver?"

"Maybe, where are you at the moment?"

"Fortuna," said the beaver man.

"California?" asked the host.

"North Dakota, and the black flies are horrible."

"I thought you were with a beaver family?"

"I am, but the rest was a tricky story," said the beaver man.

"Who trains the hotliners?" asked the host.

"Nobody but the best beavers."

"What have you learned?" asked the host.

"That black flies are wicked," said the beaver man.

"The hotliners are natural teachers, as natural as the animals and birds of their imagination," I said with my mouth close to the microphone. Panda Man frowned and then trotted his fingers over the felt table.

"Where have the beaver gone?" asked the host.

"Nowhere," said the beaver man.

"Then raise your head and say the beaver are at their dam."

"The beaver are at their dam."

"More, our listeners want to hear more."

"Panda man, the black flies are thick and mean. . . ."

"Who is this?"

"Beaver man on the hotline."

"You sound like the bald eagle man to me," said the host.

"That was on the other hotline," said Berasimo. "The black flies chased the beaver out, the children are in the city, separated from their beaver parents who moved farther north with the bears, and so on, but here we are on the hotline with the flies." The host cut the beaver connection and turned to the bear on the hotline. The bear man answered with a roar.

"Panda Radio, you're on the air mister bear man."

"No panda would survive here."

"So, what's your hotline story?" asked the host.

"Last night a bear broke through the glass door of my cabin, chased me into the loft," said the bear man. "The bear tore open the cans and containers with his bare claws and ate everything, including the sardines and chocolate."

"Now that's what our listeners want to hear."

"Who said that?" asked the bear man.

"Panda Radio, your companion in natural sound," said the host.

"The only thing natural about a bear is human."

"What does that mean?"

"Would pandas steal my food?" asked the bear man.

"Never," said the host.

"Right, humans are the thieves."

"So, what's the point about the pandas?"

"Bears steal, bears are human," said the bear man.

"That's crazy glue logic," said the host.

"Bears masturbate, bears are human."

"Hotline, indeed, but too much heat," said Panda Man.

"Listen, right now the glass door and screen are broken, bits of food, flour, and rice cover the floor and my sleeping bag, and the cabin is swarming with many generations of black flies," said the bear man.

"What is this, the hotline of black flies?" asked the host.

"Mister Panda Man, when you hotline nature, you get black flies, because the black flies were here at the crack of creation," said the bear man. "Black flies are on the other end of every real hotline in the world."

"Wait, you said that eagles invented the flies."

"That was a lie."

"You're the fly," shouted the host.

"No, this is the bear hotline."

"You're the same fly as the eagle and beaver."

"No, the black flies are the same, the bald eagles are in their nests, the beavers have moved to the cities with the raccoons, possums, and bears, and this is a natural hotline that pays me more than enough to live in the woodland with traditional black flies," said the eagle, beaver, and bear man. Father Berasimo disguises his voice and answers several hotlines at once.

"What's with the black flies?"

"Flies are the natural advertisements of nature."

"Leave it to the flies," said the host.

"Black flies at the Las Vegas Magic Zoo," said Berasimo.

"Panda Radio is a natural companion, flies are a nuisance, and our listeners must be ready to swat you and your flies right out of the air," said the host of Panda Radio. "Get those black flies off the hotlines."

"Flies are the true companions of nature."

"Say something about bears or you're dead on the air."

"Bears masturbate," said Berasimo.

"Naturally, and flies pray," said the host.

"I built a large privy this summer because the bears sit there at dusk and read my magazines," said Berasimo. "The bears come by to read the magazines and masturbate, and there are two bears in my new privy right now," shouted Berasimo.

"Panda Radio, that's it for the animal hotlines."

"Wait, wait, we're about to hear a black bear." I pushed my microphone around the table, closer to the Panda Man. The studio engineer waited to cut the hotline to the bear. "Wait, this is live, a real bear on the hotline, no more flies."

"*Gegaa*," said Almost.

"Once more on the hotlines," said the host.

"Listen, you can hear the hot breath of two bears in the privy," said the bear man out of breath. "My voice is a harsh whisper as we move closer to the hotline outhouse. Crows crack the air, and you can hear the leaves brush the cellular telephone," he said in a whisper on the air to millions of listeners late that night on talk radio. "There, you can hear two young bears masturbating over my gun and glamour magazines."

"Not on the air," said the host of Panda Radio. "This is a family station and our advertisers do not condone such behavior with animal companions." He motioned to the studio engineer to cut the line. Father Berasimo was the last of the animal healers we heard on the hotlines that night.

8

Body Counts

 Almost gave our cousin a bright copper penny as a reward for the many dog fleas she had captured on the bellies of the mongrels. Liberty, the second granddaughter of our cousin Ginseng, crushed the parasites with an awesome concentration that afternoon. She flattened their hard bodies on the train window with the rim of the new coin, and then insisted that she deserved at least "one cent a flea." The window held the tiny traces of body counts.

"Lord, dog fleas are tricky warriors, worth a whole lot more than an ordinary penny, you can ask the mongrels," he said. Almost turned the sense of the pennywise stories around, a natural tease, but she was persistent about the payment. He was almost never insincere, but no one could ever be sure.

"Mongrels don't talk, you know," said Liberty.

"Pure Gumption told you that lie, right?"

"No, they don't talk that way," she said and crushed several more fleas. Then she counted the traces on the window and waited to be paid in pennies. We teased her about the count. For every flea she caught, three more feasted on that secure meadow out of reach on the back of every mongrel.

"Listen, mongrels are always hiding their lucky fleas," said Almost. He scratched the mongrels with another bright new coin. "Once the fleas even got me to confess my otherwise life as a mongrel, a mongrel who drove cars, so you better watch what you say about my cousins the fleas."

Liberty ignored his inane warning, as usual, and carefully stacked the dead fleas in a bottle cap. Then she raised her head and smiled, as if she understood his "otherwise life stories," and insisted, then and there, on a body count payment.

Almost told her many other mongrel stories but she would not be distracted from her mission to the mongrels. Naturally, he assured her that the bright penny was worth much more than "a hundred fleas dead or alive."

Liberty counted three times the dead fleas. The penny payment was stingy, you might think at first, but not as the start of a tricky story. Almost tried many other evasions, but she was determined to be paid for the body count. At last he told her that one of the intaglio copper words was "incorrect" and, because of that, the coin could be worth more than a "meadow load of warrior fleas on the back of a lame mongrel."

"Don't talk to me that way," said Liberty.

"Listen, fleas fought in the wars with the mongrels," said Almost.

"That's dumb, fleas don't fight," said Liberty.

"Dogs were truck drivers behind the lines and the fleas went along, so they deserve some of the glory," he said. Almost, once again, turned the stories around to the time he trained mongrels to drive trucks and cars. He said there were three situations that brought about the discovery that ordinary, reservation mongrels, could drive. First, everyone has seen dogs move into the driver's seat in parked cars, and pretend they were driving. "You know the tricky manner, the dogs never turn to look you straight in the eye, because you might notice he has a domestic dog face."

Almost said the second situation was that two mongrels from the barony, Ritzy and Cranberry, stole his car, the first one he ever owned, the one he made out of stray parts from other junk cars. The mongrels were stopped by the highway patrol twice in the same day, but no one worried much about a car with barony license plates. "Ritzy told the officer he was on his way to his grandmother's wake in the city."

"Stop that, dogs don't talk," said Liberty.

"Think what you want, but you better not say that at the dog pound," said Almost. The mongrels, he told our cousin as a secret, were in the city for several days. "First, they ate two hamburgers each with fries at the Doggie Diner."

"They wouldn't do that," said Liberty.

"Ritzy then treated Cranberry to an afternoon at a wild cat village in a junk yard near the river," said Almost. "The two of them chased cats from one dead car to another, and everybody had a great time that afternoon."

"You made that up," said Liberty.

"*Gegaa*, and then the cats sat on cars and negotiated a truce with the mongrels at the junk yard, because, more than anything in the world, they wanted to learn how to drive a car," said Almost.

"Cats don't want to drive," said Liberty.

"Don't be so sure, cats always act superior to dogs, they never had any reason not to think they were better, but then the barony mongrels learned how to drive and left the cats behind forever," said Almost.

"That's really dumb," said Liberty.

"Tricky, but almost true," said Almost.

"What did they do?" asked Liberty.

"See, you know how cats act around dogs," said Almost. "Cranberry invited the cats on a grand tour, as many cats as could sit in the back of the car, and they drove to the stadium and then to the university, down the river road, over the bridges, almost every place in the city."

"Stop that, cats don't ride in cars," said Liberty.

"Junk yard cats live in cars," said Almost.

"No, no, no, they never, never did that," said Liberty.

"Listen to what they did next," said Almost. "Ritzy, as you know, is a very smart mongrel, he can drive anywhere in the city, and the next stop was at the Society for Prevention of Cruelty to Animals."

"I was there once with my mother," said Liberty.

"Cranberry opened the big door and nineteen cats rushed inside, and caused a great commotion in the pet prison," said Almost. "Everybody was running around, some of the children started to laugh and joined the chase, and others were scared and ducked behind their parents."

"Why would they be so scared?" asked Liberty.

"The cats, you see, were taking orders from the mongrels, and that seemed strange to the children, but everything happened so fast that no one really had time to worry very much," said Almost.

"What did they do to the cats?" asked Liberty.

"Nothing, the cats were great warriors, they ran around and chased each other, so the mongrels could open the cages and liberate the prisoners without a casualty," said Almost. "The dogs leaped in great circles and barked for freedom, and the cats waited and waved their paws through the wire until they were freed and ran around with the other cats."

"Ritzy likes cats, doesn't he," said Liberty.

"The car was crowded with cats and dogs," said Almost. "The dogs stuck their heads out the window and barked at everybody on the street, and some of the cats ran under the seats so as not to be seen with dogs."

"Did they come back to the barony?" asked Liberty.

"Not right away, because most of the freed cats wanted to live in the junk yard and learn how to drive like the dogs," said Almost. "The dogs went everywhere, you know how they are when they have a new scent of the world."

"Did they find children?" said Liberty.

"Ritzy drove them to the parks in the best mongrel neighborhoods, and most of the liberated dogs adopted children and went home with them," said Almost. "Ritzy and Cranberry took down their addresses and they write to each other during dog days in the summer, when Sirius, the Dog Star, rises and sets over the barony."

"That's really nice," said Liberty.

"Even the cats bark at night on dog days," said Almost.

"They do not," said Liberty.

"You caught me that time," said Almost.

"Did the dogs come home?" asked Liberty.

"Ritzy drove around the city for a few more days, they took in a few good restaurants, had a few picnics near the river, and then he gave the car to the junk yard cats so they could learn how to drive," said Almost.

"How did he get back?" asked Liberty.

"Ritzy and Cranberry took the bus home," said Almost.

"Bus rides are fun."

"They sat in the back by the windows."

"What happened when they got home?" asked Liberty.

"Ritzy helped me teach other mongrels to drive, as payment for the car he stole, and we even established a limousine service on the barony."

"Ritzy's not here," said Liberty.

"He moved to New Mexico," said Almost.

The third situation that convinced my cousin that ordinary dogs could drive was the chance of history in New Mexico. The White sisters, Amelia and Martha, owned valuable property in the old Armenta Spanish Land Grant that would become the School of American Research in Santa Fe. Amelia, the bold and eccentric daughter of Horace White, once the editor of the *Chicago Tribune*, served as a nursing assistant in the Great War. Later, she became a prominent breeder of Afghan hounds and Irish wolfhounds. The dogs were trained to be warriors, learned how to drive, and served in Dogs for Defense during the Second World

War. Many of these warriors were buried with honors and markers at the School of American Research.

Almost was on a lecture tour when he first heard these stories and visited the memorial dog cemetery. He walked between the markers, heard the memories of the first canine warriors, the daring dogs who learned how to drive. These dogs overcame the boundary of their pedigree, and bested their ancestors, but they were never as tricky and bright as the mongrels on the barony.

The Animosh Driving School was established a few months later when my cousin returned to the barony. As part of their driver training, the mongrels had to chauffeur native elders to and from their friends and relatives, and to the missions and medical center. The drivers were never any trouble, although every now and then one of the mongrels would savor a lusty scent and run wild for a few days. Actually, the mongrels were much more reliable as drivers than humans.

Hawk, a black mongrel with short legs, a gentle manner, and a great smile, was hired as a chauffeur by the priest at the mission. The nuns fitted him in very nice clerical clothes, so at services he was dressed like a miniature priest. Naturally, we worried that he might be the first mongrel to bear the sacraments, take communion, and become an altar dog.

Almost designed a beaded hat for the drivers so that the public could identify the graduates of the Animosh Driving School. The mongrel chauffeurs were featured in a newspaper story, and after that there were hundreds of inquiries to hire mongrel chauffeurs. Slyboots, our cousin who studied economics, negotiated the contracts to be sure the drivers would be provided with a fair salary, comfortable accommodations, and at least one free day a week. Now and then in the next two years there were other newspaper and magazine stories about the mongrel drivers in the city. Some were hired by rich families, and others were truck drivers for construction companies. Schoolchildren wanted mongrels as their bus drivers, but we could not convince the insurance company to cover mongrel drivers. Everything was going along just fine, but then a group of righteous animal protection activists marched around the barony and demanded the end of "pet exploitation" at the Animosh Driving School.

"Dogs have always been waiting behind the wheel to drive, and they want to be seen as human, that's why they domesticated humans so long ago," said Almost.

"Don't patronize us with anthropomorphism," said an activist.

"What does that mean?"

"You know what it means," said another animal activist.

"Listen, don't be stupid about mongrels, they must drive, they must be chauffeurs, because this is a situation of punctuated equilibrium in the stories of evolution," said Almost.

My cousin could remember the most obscure ideas and theories, and this one came from a lecture by Stephen Jay Gould. The situation was serious, of course, but we could not hold back our humor when he came out with "punctuated equilibrium." He told us later that the words mean exactly what the mongrels have done as drivers, "an episodic swerve, a merge in nature, rather than the idea that evolution is a gradual change." Those two words stunned the animal activists, but they soon suspended their knowledge of evolution and continued their beastly protest.

"Dog chauffeurs is the same as animal brutality, no different than slavery," chanted the animal activists as they marched around the scapehouse and the crescent. The leaders shouted with bullhorns that we were "animal abusers, and murderers."

"Pets are slaves, mongrel drivers are free," said Almost.

"Driving a car is not freedom," shouted an animal activist.

"They travel and see the world," said Almost.

"Dogs are pets, not menial servants," said the activist.

"Mongrels behind the wheel are not servants," said Almost.

"Dogs are exploited as chauffeurs and treated like humans with low wages, and worst of all, the dogs are exposed to extreme conditions of polluted air and the stress of driving in heavy traffic," said another animal activist.

"How did you get here?" asked Almost.

"I would sacrifice my life to save an animal," said an activist.

"Now that's a good story," said Almost.

"Don't threaten me like you abuse your dogs," said the activist.

"Have you ever gone crazy?" asked Almost.

"What are you talking about?"

"Listen, your mouth is more stress than rush hour traffic," said Almost. He raised his hands, turned to the activists, and shouted the names of each mongrel driver. Then he laughed in a high pitched voice, the humor of a hotline healer, and returned to the back seat of his station wagon. A few minutes later my cousin was on the crescent with his willow bullroarer. He whirled it overhead and the roar aroused every mongrel on the reservation.

Hawk heard the roar, and as he raced back to the barony in the priest's limousine he stopped many times along the way to pick up other graduates of the Animosh Driving School. Soon there were hundreds of mongrels bouncing behind the bullroarer. The animal activists were aroused by the sound and ran with the mongrels. They circled each other and then danced on the road. The activists were entranced by the bullroarer, and my cousin teased them with the sound into the lonesome cedar that night, a great distance from the barony.

Almost started a great fire for the activists in a clearing. They sang many happy camp songs and bonded with nature around the fire. Later that night we decided to scare the activists, so we wore masks and shouted at a distance in the cedar. Then we chanted *anishaa* in *anishinaabe*, over and over. The word means "just for fun, or no real purpose," but the tone of our chant could have been heard as ironic and demonic. The activists heard demons not native ironies.

The activists were tired and very worried in the morning, but they were not yet ready to leave the barony. So, we brought our grandmother to breathe a few words on the animal rights activists. She huffed and puffed on everyone in the camp. Many students were sickened and overcome by the wicked reek of her ordinary salutations. They loaded their cars in haste as the mongrels arrived to chase them out of the barony.

Hawk trailed the activists for a few miles in the priest's limousine, and then raced ahead to wait for them at the reservation border. He wore his black clerical clothes, a white surplice, and stood in the center of the road with an enormous wooden crucifix. At first, at a distance, the activists must have seen a miniature priest. Then, when they could make out the obvious features of a mongrel, the priest's chauffeur with a crucifix, they were hysterical and drove into the weeds at the shoulder of the road. Hawk barked *anishaa*, *anishaa*, and waved the crucifix at the activists.

The animal activists never returned to the barony. Two years later, however, the same coalition of animal rights activists convinced the legislature to vote on a law that made it a crime to use a pet or domestic animal as a chauffeur in the state. At the time the legislature was debating the issue, many mongrel drivers circled the state capitol and honked horns in protest.

Hawk, unfortunately, was involved in a minor accident at the capital, and when the insurance company learned that the mission had hired a mongrel to chauffeur the priest, the agent canceled the automobile policy. The accident probably convinced the legislature to vote against mongrel drivers.

The Animosh Driving School was closed that summer. Curly, the last graduate, became a simulated chauffeur and race car driver. Soon, the retired mongrel drivers turned to the video arcades and simulated driving machines. Once again many mongrels posed as drivers, but this time they told mighty stories about the enlightenment on the barony.

Hawk and several other mongrels were on the move and could not turn back their punctuated equilibrium. They were bored with driving anyway, so they decided to become aviators. The new state law said nothing about mongrel aviation. Slyboots had once built microlight airplanes on the barony and he had never abandoned his vision of an airborne revolution. He taught flying to many natives and was not easily convinced that mongrels would be good pilots. They were very good, of course, and you can imagine how startled some people were when they saw a dog with a white scarf flying a microlight over the lakes and around the barony.

Almost is motion, and survivance is his best creation story.

Pure Gumption and Admire moaned and then turned over to sun their bellies. Chicken Lips rested his chin on the arm of the dental chair. Casino Rose and Agate Eyes were the new conductors on the train to the barony. They made the rounds of the seats, sniffed shoes, crotches, and sleeves, and then licked the back of every hand, but they were always close to their master the acudenturist in the parlor car. The other mongrels sat in the window seats and barked at the wind, at airplanes, and other creatures near the tracks.

Hawk circled the train in his microlight and the mongrels barked with pride, a mongrel chauffeur became the first aviator on the barony. The mission priest had hired the mongrel as his pilot rather than his driver. As they flew closer to the train we could hardly tell them apart. The priest was a small man, and he wore the same collar and black clothes as the mongrel. Hawk had a short nose, but his ears were much too long and hairy to be a priest. They both wore long white scarves, and they were magnificent creatures in the air. The two of them could start a new religion of motion, and we would have become their first converts, no doubt about that at the barony.

The Naanabozho Express rounded a curve and ran closer to the river. The sun turned and waved over the seats on the train. The curve, near a lonesome rise of ancestral cedar, was no more than an hour to the station near the barony.

Grandmother Wink insisted that we gamble with her for the day at the Ozaawaa Casino. She won several hundred dollars at blackjack, and was ripe with simple humor, so we tried once more to trick her into the dental chair on the return trip to the barony. A few extractions would have cured her breath, and the rest would have been a signature smile.

"Never, never, no one touches my mouth, not even a railroad relative," our grandmother shouted. We turned aside and ducked as her rotten breath passed over our heads. "False teeth, nothing doing, only a fool is tricked with a false smile," said Wink. She teased the mongrels with her breath, held their ears and blew into their faces. Casino Rose closed her teary eyes and then sneezed. Wink won at the casino, we were convinced, only because of the wicked stench of her breath over the blackjack table.

"She speaks the truth," said Shadow Box.

"False teeth never hurt anybody," said Ginseng.

"My ghost teeth never hurt either," said Wink.

Liberty was almost five years old at the time and never forgot the stories of the pennywise parasites and ghost teeth. Since then she has learned how to count with a sweet vengeance. The continuous stories of that coin, otherwise the measure and body count of dog fleas, are the traces of a tricky bond at the barony.

Naturally, at the time, our cousin checked every word on the penny several times in the dictionary. She was determined to catch her older cousins at something. Liberty was literal in the extreme, and for the money, to be sure. She worried in turn about *e pluribus unum*, but not the other words on the bright coin, and remembers to this day that her tricky older cousin never made clear what he meant by an "incorrect" word on the coin. She wrote to him several times about the "penny words," but that seemed to make matters worse, because he almost never writes letters to anyone, not even to his mother. Finally, he sent her a blank book many years later with the signature of a tricky author.

Almost signed the name of Isaac Singer. He dictated and asked me to write a short note to our cousin who was, by that time, studying at the University of Colorado. "My last words to you over the years were frozen in those great blue islands of winter, on the way to the sea, and then the lake ice cracked overnight, and we were caught in the wild stories of the ice woman, so treasure that bright penny." That summer she asked him to translate his note in the blank book, but he brushed aside her concerns with more stories about warrior moths, the artistic splendor of spiders, and the acoustic harmony of black flies on the barony.

"The mongrels never forget anything, and so they saved hundreds of fleas for you to catch," he said, but she was much too literal to be amused by more mongrel stories. At last he told her that one of the words on the coin was not authentic, and not even considered trustworthy.

"Listen," he said, "I'll give you seven casino dollars for that new penny if you promise the mongrels never to ask me again about the worth of fleas." Liberty refused, of course, because she had decided by then that the coin might be rare and valuable. Even so she could not understand what he meant by trustworthy. The more obscure his stories became the more she treasured the tricky trash of that bright penny.

Almost tried many times that summer to trick her out of the coin, to end the flea stories and return the trick but she would not be double tricked, not then, and certainly not as a college student. She would not be the brunt of another trickster story. My cousin, you see, was born literal, an absolute fault and fate of the barony. Liberty demanded to know, for instance, the precise meaning of nicknames, and, as the names were not recorded in dictionaries, she was a naive and bothersome listener. She demanded the absolute meaning of metaphorical names, even obscure native words, and would hear nothing less than a definition that was hard and fast. Consequently, she was the black hole of irony and ambiguity. We teased her about the "metaphor terminators" that were stuck in her ears. No one, you can be sure, was taken by surprise when she became a student of anthropology.

Liberty earned three nicknames that summer of the bright penny. Crusher, Verby, and Beebig, or *bibig*, the *anishinaabe* word for flea. Verby for being so verbal and verbose, and the nickname seemed to be the truest literal trace of her observant and tiresome nature. She searched for her nickname in the dictionary, and decided that it was derived from verbena, an aromatic tree. That deserved another nickname, but she was much too literal to hear the tease.

Liberty polished that coin so many times over the years that Abraham Lincoln lost his cheekbones and beard. Seventeen years later she turned that penny and her naive traces of the literal into an academic profession. She returned as a cultural anthropologist to interview native storiers, the best trickster story tellers on several woodland reservations, for a graduate course at the university.

Liberty was a memorable character, an "authentic fleabite," said one native storier who would not be interviewed. The stories she recorded were literal, right out of the tricky tank of the obvious. She was told stories that she could not bear to hear, a literal treason, and that became

the truth and terminal trash of her research. At the time the native storiers she interviewed wondered what could be more than tricky trash in
cultural anthropology.

Liberty heard several versions of her own penny stories, and, at the
same time, every trickster wanted to buy the bright coin. She was wary
of their interest and worried about the value of the penny, but not for
long. The worth of the coin was in the story, of course, and that could
have been the very reversal of found objects in a material culture. At last
she turned the value around and announced that she would give that
bright penny to the first person who could name the word that was not
authentic or trustworthy on the coin. Liberty tried to return the stories
in a contest with tricksters, but the tease of trickster stories was unbearable. She would never be otherwise and leaned on the literal notions of
culture.

"No returns on stories," said Almost.

"Mine is a penny," said Liberty.

"Nothing is authentic, no matter how bright," said Almost.

Almost was born in native motion and ever since he has teased the
truth to better his chances. Truly, he was born in the back of a hatch-
back. Over the years, as you know, his friends have called him just about
everything, *gegaa*, roughly, nearly, not quite, on the edge, almost otherwise. Chance is almost his own best story.

Chance is almost his source of natural reason. So, a few weeks before
that crucial beauty contest, he told me that "beauty is chancy trash, the
crossover of chance and history, and that's a true story." Later he insisted that "chancy beauty is the absolute truth, believe it or not, and
death too, truer than empathy, and cultural trash is almost truer than
death."

Almost turned most of his stories to beauty contests one summer. At
the time, we never thought much about the way he posed and smiled as
he told his stories. "Beauty is theater, the tricky talk of the truth," he
said, "the chancy trash of body counts," and then he recited the *anishinaabe* dream song, "I am as beautiful as the roses." Chancy trash could
have become one of his nicknames that summer.

Almost is a storier, a trickster of chance, a native philosopher who
celebrates the common and, at the same time, denies the obvious in stories. "The absolute measure of beauty is the double talk of the truth,
and the more the truer is chancy trash," he said and cocked his head almost to his shoulder.

"Stories are chance, my beauty chance, so leave no stones unturned, almost none." Almost would leave almost anything to chance that summer, but not beauty contests. There, in the stories of body count beauty, he drew the line in his stories.

Almost insisted that we attend an annual pageant. "For the beauty stories and chancy trash," he said, and so we sat in the back row out of sight. Almost had a chance in mind, to be sure, but we had no idea what his interests in the contest might be at the time. Liberty double tricked the trickster and returned that precious bright penny at a beauty contest.

God was invoked that spring evening in the auditorium as the supreme patron of chancy beauty, the provider of students, and as the absolute preserver of native traditions and cultures at the University of Oklahoma. Doubtless, the invocation warned the tricksters, ecstatics, and academic shamans in the audience to show both hands and hold their tongues. The pageant ceremonies were embraced at every turn by monotheism, the very measure and authority of tricky beauty, and no one was troubled in the slightest by the contest.

Richard Van Horn, who was then the president of the University of Oklahoma, laid down the comic authority of the pageant entourage a few months earlier when he announced, without a hint or trace of irony, his concern about a "better learning environment" on campus. He asked the students to be more friendly toward minorities. "Saying hello to minority students on campus," he wrote, "will help to create a better living and learning environment for all."

Natives were not named, and for no obvious reason, but such salutations were comic reversals. The racial pause and other conceits, academic manners and courtesies, were natural in the presence of beauty contestants. The pageant was indeed a learning environment.

"Say Hello, OU President Urges," was the headline on the front page of the *Daily Oklahoman* in Oklahoma City. The following day the same newspaper published an unsigned editorial about the president's salutation that accredited a modest instance of a tricky story. "Some have chuckled at OU President Richard Van Horn's modest suggestion for students to 'Say hello to minority students' on campus. That's a gesture, but he's on track. Respect. Diversity. Dialogue. These create an environment in which learning can occur. The words describe values which are not black, white, Hispanic, or Asian, but American." Natives were not mentioned in the capital or in the generic first string names of diversity, but natives certainly were given as much time for a beauty pageant as those racial and ethnic categories mentioned in the editorial.

The Third Annual Miss Indian Pageant was held in Meacham Auditorium at the University of Oklahoma. The invocation was a solemn summons to be in the presence of a supernatural tutelary. God created students in that pose of a pageant service and preserved amenable native cultures, but no one said amen.

The invocation was followed by a native honor song, and then the introduction of the contestants who were decorated in ceremonial leathers, feathers, and beads. Three of the four contestants were escorted across the stage by men who wore dark business suits. The women wore moccasins, the men wingtip shoes. One contestant was escorted by a man in traditional native vestments.

The contestants were Roxana Johnson, a sophomore majoring in French, and representing the Choctaw and Sioux Nations; Deborah Reed, a junior majoring in radio, television and film, and representing the Cherokee Nation; Hankie Poappybitty, a senior majoring in psychology, and representing the Kiowa, Caddo, and Comanche Nations; and Donna GoingSnake, a sophomore majoring in public administration, and representing the Cherokee Nation.

Considerations of traditional and modern talent were followed by impromptu questions, the farewell address of the past winner of the pageant, the presentation of awards, and then the very popular traditional stroll. The talents of each candidate were praised by enthusiastic admirers in the audience.

God was named in both the traditional and modern presentations of native talent. One contestant performed the Indian sign language dance to the Lord's Prayer. Shawn Emmerson, Miss Black at the University of Oklahoma, attended the Miss Indian Pageant.

Bird Runningwater, a staff reporter for *The Oklahoma Daily*, wrote that the Tahlequah sophomore who represented the Cherokee Nation was crowned Miss Indian at the University of Oklahoma. "Donna GoingSnake was crowned before an audience" of more than one hundred "as part of American Indian Heritage Week."

Runningwater continued her newspaper story that GoingSnake "won the modern talent competition singing, 'My God is Real.' Her traditional talent performance of 'At the Cross,' in her native Cherokee language, was also judged the winner. . . . Other competitions in the pageant included personal interviews, impromptu questions and essays describing why the contestants wanted to represent the Indian students" at the University of Oklahoma.

"GoingSnake said the title would give her a chance to serve as 'a liaison to the university . . . to actively promote American Indian awareness" on the campus. "She would encourage American Indian events, concerns, and issues through direct contact with the student government, faculty and staff, she said. The contributions and positive qualities of American Indian students to the campus should be highlighted to achieve the goal of cultural diversity."

Runningwater noted that as Miss Indian, GoingSnake received as prizes a tuition fee waiver, a beaded crown, a sash with her name and title, and a shawl with the emblem of the American Indian Student Association.

Almost is almost the master of tricky stories, and he was very tricky when he persuaded me to become one of the judges at a recent Indian Princess Pageant. The annual ceremonies rise to the insignificance of contested beauty, the trivial cause of racial entitlements, and chancy entertainments.

Liberty studied tricksters, as you know, and she also studied the influences of religion on social and cultural functions, such as beauty contests. Almost would have been the perfect judge, as he could turn the otherwise earnest presentation into tricky stories, and without pity. Our anthropologist cousin could have counted him twice, the trickster and the judge of beauty, in her studies. We should have tricked him right back to take my place that night, but he vanished a few weeks before the pageant.

There were four final contestants at the pageant that year, as there had been at the previous annual ceremonies. As usual the invocation was followed by an honor song, and then the presentation of traditional and modern talent.

Liberty was at the back of the auditorium, an escape distance that she learned as a child on the barony. The judges were seated in the first row, close to the stage. My eyes were at the level of the contestant's shoes, and my mind was in flight, an escape from the churchly poses and the scent of leather.

The contestants wore leather dresses and moccasins with decorative beads. The men who presented them to the audience were dressed, as usual, in dark suits. The contestants, it would seem, were more traditional than the native men at hand. The men, no doubt, were on their way to riches in the business world, and the pageant women were trained to serve the aesthetic manner of native traditions.

This was the first pageant that erased the "miss" in favor of "princess" in the title and welcomed older women to become contestants. Many native women were inspired by their children, who were students, to return to the campus. Many older women entered the new pageant, and two survived as contestants. The older women were concerned about ageism, to be sure, but no one was troubled by the gender separation of wingtips and moccasins.

The contestants were Tunny Taaner, a sophomore in virtual communications, who represented the new urban Cherokee Circle of Ancestors; Bee Thanks God, a senior in content instruction and administration, who represented the remnant Choctaw; Penny Birdwind, a senior in native animations and simulations, who represented the Kickapoo Border Nation. Haidee Casino Mason, the last contestant, was a sophomore in museum management, and she represented, for the first time, the very prosperous native Casino Nations. Bee Thanks God and Penny Birdwind were celebrated in the pageant program as the "maternal" and "more mature" contestants.

The judges scored the presentation of each contestant on a scale of one to ten, but in the end we avoided the scores because we were so moved by the lip-synch performance of the popular song "Fever" by Peggy Lee.

Penny Birdwind was not a winner of the traditional talent, the sign language dance to the "Lord's Prayer," a very popular dance at the pageant, because her performance was a rather graceless gesture of "Our Father." However, when she moved her mature mouth around "Fever," we were convinced that she would wear the beaded crown that year as Indian Princess of the University of Oklahoma.

I get a fever . . .

Peggy Lee's voice echoed with a fever in the auditorium, *fever in the morning* . . . Penny, dressed in a very tight white cocktail dress, decorated with hundreds of bright bent pennies, danced between the curtains on stage, and moved her sensuous mouth to the music.

Captain Smith and Pocahontas had a very mad affair . . .

Penny turned and leaned closer to the judges in the front row of the auditorium. She lip-synched with a lusty motion that aroused the young men in wingtips and more than one beauty judge. Only then, when she opened her mouth in a particular way, and the slit in the dress revealed her thigh, did my sexual responses turn to humor. My heart rushed with the music, and the recognition of two familiar gold teeth and a signature scar on her right thigh.

Penny was my cousin, no doubt about that. The judges had been tricked by their own fever over a trickster in a tight white dress and red gloves. Almost conceived of his lip-synch performance long before he tricked me into being one of the judges at the pageant. The judges deserved to be tricked, we decided later, because we were our own measure of tricky stories. We were at the scene of a cultural tease. The fever was the tricky story.

Almost winked at me and the other judges near the end of his performance. We winked back, of course, but the beauty judges never learned that the talented woman in the white dress was my cousin, almost a woman that night at the chancy pageant.

Almost registered as a student at the university when he learned that older women would be eligible for the first time as contestants. He, and then she, was a mere name and picture, and whatever virtues of gender she might have lacked as a contestant, such as thick thighs, rough hands, and a strange voice, were overlooked with sympathy, as these were the first older contestants in the new Indian Princess Pageant.

Winona Beaverman reported in the local newspaper that more than a hundred people attended the pageant and were "moved by the 'Fever' of Penny Birdwind who was crowned the Indian Princess at the annual pageant last night at the University of Oklahoma.

"Penny wore a bent penny jingle dress and danced to a popular song in red platform shoes, after a very impressive performance of the 'Lord's Prayer.' The judges were impressed with other performances by the contestants, such as the spirituals and ecstatic liturgies in native tongues, but the natural sound of the bright coins on her dress, and the emotional power of her rendition of 'Fever,' convinced the judges to crown Penny Birdwind, the first mature princess to be so honored since the pageant began nine years ago.

"The Kickapoo Border Nation senior received the usual fee waiver, the traditional shawl, and a crown of beaded red roses. Penny lip-synched the 'Lord's Prayer' when the judges announced their decision that she was Indian Princess. The audience joined in the silent gestures and lip-synched along with the winner of the pageant. The fever music was the talk of the reception, but no one could remember if the Indian Princess ever uttered a sound during the evening. One judge said she lip-synched her way through the entire ceremony.

"Penny said in a written statement that she would return to the reservation when she graduated and practice lip-synching operas with her favorite anthropologists. Penny, in a characteristic gesture, gave her white dress decorated with a hundred bright pennies to Liberty Browne.

"Liberty, a cultural anthropologist, in turn, gave to Penny a bright copper penny which she said was worth hundreds of dollars because there was one word missing on the coin," wrote Beaverman.

Peggy Lee's recorded voice filled the auditorium one more time, and the entire audience lip-synched the lyrics to "Fever." She sang, we danced, and then everybody got a tricky native fever that night.

Fever, you know, started long, long ago, as a native tease.

9

Naanabozho Express

Lake Namakan never hides the reason of our seasons. The wind hardens snow to the bone, a natural cerement over the cedar ruins, and hushed currents rush under the ice to weaken the reach of winter and silence.

Overnight, you can hear our ancestors in the birch, and the chase of wise crows. Higher, and at a distance, bald eagles brace their nests once more with fresh wisps of white pine, the elusive censers of the summer.

Silence is never natural in creation. Listen, storms are on the rise, rivers cut the stones to the ancient heartlines. "Memories are precise, and my brush of the seasons covers the barony," said my cousin. "Tricky stories are the tease and currents of creation, the natural reason of our motion and sovereignty."

Gesture is our great uncle, as you know, a man of motion and precise memories, an esteemed acudenturist, and the founder of the first native railroad on the continent. He was born on an island near the international border at the same time the timber wolves hunted alone. He teases chance and creation in the same way as my cousin, and they both shout into panic holes.

Henry Ford established a modern assembly line to build automobiles in the summer that my great uncle was born. That industrial gesture and the coincidence of his railroad adventures as an acudenturist are cause to mention the course of natural reason in tricky stories.

Lake Namakan, the tack of seasons in our memories, the bounce of crows and timber wolves, the chance creation of the barony, and the revolution in the manufacture of automobiles were obscure connections to my great uncle, a common vision of motion and native sovereignty.

Gesture reasoned, as he probed a carious lesion in a molar, that the assurance of native sovereignty was not a crown decoration of discoveries and treaties, but a state of natural motion. He shouts at the crows, as his father had done from the water tower on the reservation, that stories of motion are native sovereignty, never the dead voices and cultural documents of invented histories.

Almost shouts at motion in the same way as his great uncle and other relatives. He shouts at the crows and mongrels from the water tower, and he climbs the highest trees to shout at the eagles. He shouts at the natural motion of the river with the same vision of native sovereignty. My great uncle and cousin tease the obvious and shout at silence. At one time or another both of them have said, "Native shouts are natural motion."

Gesture told me that tricky stories come out of the heart, not the mouth. "My heart hears the silence in stones, the heartlines, but my teeth might be false. Wimpy smiles, you see, never cover false teeth or dead stories, that's why my teeth are never the same." His words warmed the air and brushed my cheek as he leaned over me in the dental chair. He smiled as he leaned, but never showed his teeth. Later, he showed me his crowns, and the many models of original and hued false teeth.

Gesture, as you know, is an acudenturist in natural motion, an acute denturist with a singular practice on his very own railroad. The dental chair is located at the end of the train, at the back of the luxurious parlor car. The train had been designed for a rich banker who traveled on weekends to his country estate near Lake Namakan.

The banker, by chance of an abscessed tooth and a wild storm on the lake, gave his entire private railroad to our great uncle, the acudenturist, and created an endowment to sustain the operation of the train on the reservation.

Gesture was born on Wanaki Island in Lake Namakan. He could have been a child of the wind and timber wolves. The otters heard his stories on the stones in the spring, and he was more elusive in the brush than cedar waxwings. The islands were heard in his stories of the seasons, and seen in the bright and everlasting flight of native memories. The shamans visit his father on the island twice a year, in summer and winter, to hear the stones and tricky stories.

Ashigan, his father, was born near the border on Ghost Island. Six years later his family was removed from the island by treaty and sent to a reservation, and once there the unscrupulous federal agents ordered him to leave forever the White Earth Reservation. The second removal order was a paradox, as he was banished back to the very island his family had lived on eleven years earlier. The story is a double removal, and the cause was ironic. He shouted that the United States Indian Agent should be removed for crimes against native sovereignty, and held the agent hostage in a rain barrel on the water tower. Ashigan told his son that "one removal must beget another in a stolen nest." Many years later the agent was actually removed for incompetence.

Ashigan shouted out the names of the criminal agents and told tricky stories on native sovereignty several times a day for three weeks on the water tower. Some people listened under the tower, others laughed and waited for the agents to shoot him down. He was a scarce silhouette at that elevation, smaller for his age than anyone in his family, but his mouth was enormous, and his loud voice had been hired more than once to announce the circus and wild west shows. He was no more than seventeen at the time of the second removal and had earned the nickname "big mouth bass," or *ashigan* in *anishinaabe*, for his stories about the heinous incursions, assaults, larcenies, and murders on the reservation by the federal government.

Ashigan moved to the border islands and never mentioned the removal, the wicked agents, the twisted mouths of missionaries, or those native emissaries who had weakened his revolution on the water tower.

Wanaki Island became his sacred stone, and the avian shadows his natural solace, but he never shouted about anything ever again. At last, in his eighties, he returned to the reservation with his son, at the controls of their own train. He said the native railroad, *ishkodewidaabaan*, or "fire car" in translation, was his "island in motion." Luster, his younger brother, remained on the reservation, as you know, and became the Baron of Patronia.

Since then native people with terminal teeth, some of them with abscesses bigger than the one drained on the rich banker, drank wild rice wine in the lounge and watched the landscape rush past the great curved windows. They waited in the sovereignty of the parlor car to have their teeth repaired by their very own native acudenturist.

"So, lucky for you this is not heart surgery," he said and then leaned over me, the side of his thick hand on my right cheekbone. Lucky indeed, were my very thoughts, but my heart was in my molars not my stories that day. The silence was ironic. No one else has ever had permission to enter my mouth with various instruments, inflict pain, and then ask me questions that were not answerable. No silence could be more sorely heard than my mute responses to the intrusions of an acudenturist, my great uncle.

Gesture poked and scratched with a dental probe at the ancient silver in my molars. Closer, his breath was slow, warm, and seductively sweet with a trace of clove and commodity peanut butter. The leather chair clicked, a clinical sound, leaned to the side, and shivered as the train rounded a curve near the river and the barony. "Loose here, and there, there, there, can you feel that?" He pounded on my molars and we nodded in silence on the curve. Then, with a straight chisel he scraped the rough edges of the silver. The bits of metal, the cold instruments, and his warm bare fingers in my mouth, had the same taste.

"Native sovereignty is motion, stories straight to the heartlines, not the mere sentences of scripture, not the cruelty of dead words, or the shame of who we might have been if only our language had been written," he said, and we nodded as the train leaned in the other direction. "Museums iced our impermanence, and the cold donors measured our sovereignty in the dead voices of their own cultures." He snorted and then explained that he would not be able to use an anesthetic because he was an acudenturist, "not a drugstore doctor." The silver was already too loose in my molars to wait on a licensed dentist at the public health hospital.

"Instead, here are some scents of the seasons on the islands," he said and turned a narrow cone toward my face. The rush of air was moist and cool, and the first scent was a thunderstorm, then wet wool, a bear in the cedar, and later the essence of sex, but that must have come from generations of sweat on the leather chairs in the parlor car.

We nodded in silence and he turned the dental chair from the curved windows and the landscape to the power instruments. The other patients in the lounge seemed to turn with me. The instruments at that moment were more critical than the rush of birch and white pine. He started the mechanical dental engine. The drill was archaic, but the sound of the drive cables created a sense of contentment, the solace of an acudenturist in his own tricky stories. He drilled and cleaned the lesion, and then pounded real gold into the central grooves of my molars.

"Now, you are truly worth more than you were last night on the reservation, and we are both in motion and still free," said my great uncle as he turned the chair back toward the curved windows. The sun was blocked by huge clouds out of the west. Colors turned, the river darkened and shivered.

Gesture never hides the natural reason of a storm on the islands at Lake Namakan. He waits on the massive stones for a burst of creation. The wind bends in the birch, roars over the water, and thunder crashes in the distance. He told me that the most natural death in the world is to be struck by lightning, "a crash of light and a name turns to thunderstone."

Ashigan and his son were healed by the power of the west wind, the rush of water over the massive stones, by thunder and lightning. Gesture is always a child when he faces a storm, and it was a ferocious thunderstorm over the islands that changed his life forever. Indeed, he was out in the wild wind, but he was struck by a banker, not by lightning in the end.

Cameron Williams, the rich banker, was out in a canoe that very afternoon, a chance to show his grandson the bald eagles near the international border. The banker had no sense of natural reason and, distracted by the rise of the eagles on the wind, he drifted on the rough water over the border and was lost in the many bays and islands on Lake Namakan.

Gesture saw a canoe turn over on the waves near Wanaki Island. The banker was lucky that such a native man would stand in a storm and watch the lake catch the wind. The canoe tumbled on the waves, and then he saw the blue face of a child in the water, the faces that haunted him in dreams, the blue faces beneath the ice near the mouth of the river. The ancient blue ancestors of native stories. He tied a rope to the tree and swam out to the canoe. The lightning hissed overhead, and the wicked water pitched and tumbled on the wind. The child was ashen, blue around his eyes and mouth, and his ancient blue hands were closed on a miniature plastic paddle. The banker trembled, he was too scared to shout, but he held onto the canoe.

Gesture tied the rope to the canoe and towed the banker and his grandson to shore. Cameron tried to smile as the waves rushed over them and lightning crashed in the trees on the shore. Later, the child recovered near the fire, but the banker weakened, his eyes were swollen and lost the bright trace of his confidence. The thunderstorm passed overnight, but the wind howled and the waves crashed on the stones for several more days. They could never paddle against the high waves.

Cameron was weakened because he had a canine abscess that distended his right cheek and ear, and closed one eye. The swollen banker was delirious on the second night. He cursed women and the weather for his condition, and then he started to wheeze, his breath was slower, strained, and his thin hands turned inward to the silence.

Gesture could hear the rage of last stories in the old man. The lake was thunderous, and the waves were too high for a canoe, so he decided to operate on the banker, then and there on the island, and drain the abscess. That night he built a small sweat lodge and warmed the old man near the heated stones, and moistened his swollen mouth with willow bark soaked in hot water. The next morning he moved the banker out to the boulders on the shore, turned his head to the sun, and told the child to hold his swollen mouth open with a chunk of driftwood. The child did as he was told in silence. Then, my great uncle told me, he wound a thin copper wire several times around the base of the canine, and with a wooden lever, braced in the seam of a stone, he wrenched the poison tooth from his mouth.

Purulence and marbled blood oozed out around the tooth, ran down his chin and neck, and stained the boulder. Then pure putrid mucus gushed from the hole of the abscessed canine. He choked and gurgled, but in minutes he could see. His swollen eye opened and he turned to his side on the boulder and moaned as the infection drained from his head. The child cried over the color of the pus and blood, and then he gathered water and washed the poison from the boulder.

Later, the child touched the dark hollow abscess with his fingers. That afternoon the banker laughed and said his sense of navigation was "not much better than Columbus." Perched on the warm stones he told stories about his childhood, and took great pleasure in his missing tooth, the natural imperfection of his perfect smile and weathered face.

Gesture paddled the banker and the child in their canoe back to their vacation home on the luxurious western reach of the lake, a great distance on the other side of the border. The water was calm in the narrows, and the sun bounced over the scant waves. The eagles teased the wind and then circled closer and skimmed the shallow water near the shoreline.

Cameron told me that he was a descendant of John Williams, a minister at the turn of the eighteenth century in Deerfield, Massachusetts. His family was captured one winter night, and his daughter was touched by the natives. She never returned home. Eunice Williams renounced the dominance of her puritanical father and married a native man, and that historical document could not be denied by enervation. Twelve generations later the banker is an heir to that crossblood union of Puritans and Kahnawakes in Canada.

Cameron had invited me to travel with him back to the islands to visit my great uncle. He was silent in the limousine to the airport, and barely gestured as we flew in his private jet over the lakes and landed at an airport near his vacation home. Another pilot met us there with a pontoon plane and we flew close to the peaks of red pines, circled the many islands, and then landed on a calm sheltered bay near Wanaki Island.

Gesture should have been there to meet the seaplane. How could he not hear the engines, and how often does company arrive by air? There was no dock on the island so we waded over the massive boulders to shore.

"We were caught in a vicious storm and rolled over right out there," said the banker. "And here, on this very boulder, a stranger saved my life, and he asked nothing for his trouble."

Gesture was reading in his cabin, a precise response to the curiosities and uncommon praise of a banker. Not even his mongrels were moved to denounce our presence on their island. "Me and my mongrels never challenge bears or humans," he told me later. My uncle reminded me that it had been more than ten years since my last visit to the island.

"I tried many times to picture what your house looked like, but my memory of that time is lost to a fever," said the banker. The mongrels sniffed his boots and ankles and sneezed several times.

High Rise, the white mongrel with the short pointed ears, moaned and rolled over at the feet of the banker. He rubbed his wet jowls on his boots. Cameron reached down with one hand to touch his head, to push him aside, but the mongrel moaned louder and licked his hand.

Poster Girl, the mottled brown mongrel that looked like a cat, was very excited by the scent of the banker and the moans of High Rise. She barked and ran around the banker in tiny circles. Her nails clicked on the wooden floor, an ecstatic dance. Cameron pretended to be amused by the mongrels.

"High Rise must have a nose for bankers," said Cameron.

"Maybe, he goes for the scent of mint," said Gesture.

"Really, from the executive carpets."

"You see, even mongrels have rich tastes," said Gesture.

"Gesture, could we get down to some business?"

"You mean the mongrels?"

"Would you like a paid scholarship to dental school?"

"Dental school?" asked Gesture.

"Yes, an even chance to turn a mere instinct into a real profession, and you could be the very first dentist in your entire tribe," said the banker. His manner was earnest, he owed my great uncle his life, but the invitation was an obscure pose of dominance.

"You flew way out here to send me to dental school?"

"A measure of my respect," said Cameron.

"The measure is mine," said Gesture. He pointed to the books stacked near the wooden bench and the mongrels moved in that direction. There were several novels and a book on dental care and hygiene. "You see, out here we are denturists with no natural reason to be dentists, our teeth are never the same, but denturists never turn mouths into museums."

"You saved my life," pleaded Cameron.

"Maybe," said Gesture.

"You owe me the courtesy to recognize my everlasting debt to you," said Cameron. "My grandson admires you more than anyone else in the family right now, he thinks you are the chief and dentist of the islands."

"You had the abscess, not me."

"You are an original," said Cameron. He moved to the bench and read the titles of books in several stacks. High Rise nosed his ankles, and Poster Girl posed beside him on the bench. There were several new novels by native authors, Louis Owens, Gordon Henry, Betty Louise Bell, Louise Erdrich, Thomas King, and Randome Browne, and older novels by Franz Kafka, Herman Melville, and Yasunari Kawabata. He was distracted by a rare book, the *Manabosho Curiosa*, the very first native manuscript published in the middle of the seventeenth century.

"Gesture, this curiosa is a very rare book."

"Poster Girl is our best healer."

"So, what does she heal?"

"You name it, and she heals."

"Listen, what do *you* want?"

"Want is nothing, what do you have?" asked Gesture.

High Rise raised her head at the tone of their voices. He was aroused by their shouts. Poster Girl waited on the bench at the side of the banker. Cameron seemed to be more interested in the *Manabosho Curiosa*, than in the stories of the mongrel healers at his side.

"Basically, it comes down to this," said Cameron. He laid the curiosa on the stack of books, leaped from the bench, and turned to the window. "What would you accept that would make me feel better about my debt to you?"

"Make me an offer," said Gesture.

"Come with me and see," shouted Cameron. He turned and marched across the room to the door. The mongrels followed him out to the boulders. He ordered the pilot to make room for one more passenger.

"Would you consider a scholarship to study at the university?" asked Cameron. The pontoon plane bounced several times and then lifted slowly from the water. The mongrels barked and bounced on the boulders in the distance.

"Why the university?"

"Say, to study literature," said Cameron.

"I already do that," said Gesture.

"Anthropology then."

"Anthropology studies me."

"You have a point there," said Cameron.

"Natural reason is the story."

"You could be a pilot, and have your own business on the lakes," said Cameron. The plane circled the islands near the border. The late sun shivered in wide columns on the rich blue water.

"Do you have a railroad?" asked Gesture.

"Yes, my own private line."

"Give me that, and we have a deal," said my uncle. He was certain about a railroad and gestured with his lips toward the shoreline. Bald eagles turned over on their shadows, over and over on Lake Namakan.

"Great idea, the first tribal railroad in the history of the nation," said Cameron. He raised his hands and shouted the pleasure of an agreement. "Did you hear that mister tribal acudenturist, this is the return of the noble train."

The Naanabozho Express, a luxurious seven coach train, lurched that summer out of the Ozaawaa Casino Station on the White Earth Reservation. The train roared into the sacred cedar near the river on that first run, circled the reservation, stopped at seven stations, and returned to the casino at no cost to native passengers. My cousin has been on board ever since.

Gesture, our great uncle, the acudenturist of the tricky express, fixed and fitted teeth in the parlor car, and soon the train provided other services to natives, but none of this in the end would please the wicked and wily reservation politicians. They were envious and decided the railroad should be taxed as any service on the reservation.

Gesture tried to negotiate with the politicians, but they were debased by casino cash, and could not reason that a free railroad on the reservation was a natural performance of sovereignty. Grievously, the politicians then announced a tax on the national mobile native art exhibition that was scheduled to open on the train. My great uncle would no longer tolerate the corruption of the politicians.

The Naanabozho Express was named an "island in motion" in the summer of the third year of services on the reservation. Gesture dedicated the train the "native state of survivance" in honor of his father. Ashigan, as you know, shouted out against the corruption of the agents on the reservation, and the train would continue his shout of native sovereignty. The tricky express made one last run to the White House in Washington.

10

Crystal Trickster

 Cozie Browne once heard that the warm west wind was lost, an ominous situation to consider that winter on the barony. She heard the crows too, and rushed outside to warn the birch near the river. She shouted to the wind, but the ice waited in silence, hardhearted over the blue mire. The cedar waxwings were uncertain, so late the turn of seasons that year.

Notice of the lost wind was delivered by her cousin who lived in a cold basement in the city. He was not a true cousin, not even a native cousin, but that was never a concern as he was a visitor on the reservation in the summer. Cozie was seven years old at the time and enticed by his urbane manners. The mere mention of cities, that sense of distance, and wicked tease of advertisements, created new seasons in her stories. She could hear the tease in music, but heard tricky stories with a cold ear. He was older and wiser about obscure native traditions and convinced her that he could hear the secrets of nature on the weave and wander of the wind.

We were never worried, as his stories were not tricky.

Cozie was a new cousin, and that was evermore on the barony. She had been abandoned as an infant in a brown sack in one of the telephone booths behind the Last Lecture. Her parents, one or both, delivered a final lecture in the tavern, no doubt, and then took up new identities without a child. My father and our relatives embraced the infant at once, and she became an ecstatic presence on the barony.

Cozie was born in the summer at the same time that the first nuclear powered submarine sailed under fifty feet of polar ice. We teased her more than anyone, it seemed, because we wanted her to be at home in our stories. The wind touched her head at birth with an ovate bunch of blond hair, a sign that native elders were reborn in their children. She learned to hear the bald eagles and to carry a sprig of white pine. She mourned in the presence of spirits, not humans, and no one but shamans dared cross her trail to the fire.

Tricky stories tease a native presence, a chance to be heard in more than one place. She was heard in the city and at the barony. Otherwise, unseen, she might have shivered in silence over the poses and insinuations of natural reason. She soon learned that shouts and tricky stories tease the absence not the presence of a warm wind in winter.

Cozie earned four memorable nicknames in the natural service of the seasons. One name at birth, the second was shortened and secular, and much later she secured two more names as the first night nurse at the public health hospital on the White Earth Reservation.

Gesture named our new cousin *minomaate*, a native word that means a good smell, like "something burning" in the language of the *anishinaabe*. The shorter version of her name was *mino*, a word that means "good," and that was translated as "cozy" by the missionaries.

Cozie told "good stories," but never answered to the name *minwaajimo*, the word printed on a tavern coaster found with her in that telephone booth behind the Last Lecture. The two time release nicknames, the first such postindian names on the reservation, were given when she became the night nurse.

Cozie is her heartline name, a trace to the ancestors, but the two other nicknames are essential in the stories of those who heard the seasons and were healed by *oshkiwiinag*, the crystal trickster in the dead of night.

She is touched by the sound of the night wind, the distance of shadows, that presence of creation as the dew rises, and the natural ecstasies of ancient rivers. Later, she is morose as the sun haunts the ruins of the night in her memories. She hears the tricksters of creation overnight, never in the bright light.

Sour is her nickname at first light, and later, seen closer to the sunset, she is summoned as Burn. The dawn and sunset determine the mood and manner of her timeworn names in the hospital on the reservation. The doctors examined her many times but could not explain the condition.

Eternal Flame told me that the sensitivity to the sun was "primal, the memory of that bright sun on the morning she was found in the telephone booth." Almost teases the obvious, and his mother too, "so, she goes for the night and not the sun, and some men are worried about the dark."

Sour in the morning. Burn as the night nurse.

Cozie told me she was summoned one early morning to the hospital. "Some sort of emergency," the director said on the telephone. She was not pleased, but there was a reported medical crisis on the reservation at Camp Wikidin, a Girl Scout center near Bad Medicine Lake. The scouts had been ravished and were rumored to be in "posttraumatic ecstasies."

"To be sure, the bitter light of day is on me," she said and leaned over his polished desk for instructions. Sour covered her eyes and than asked him to close the blinds behind his desk.

"Sour, you know we would never bother you in the morning, but it might cloud over and rain, so we thought you could bear partial light and examine the campers," said the director. "Who else could answer the emergency?" He closed the blinds very slowly.

"Heat rash?"

"No, more serious," said the director.

"Poison ivy?"

"No, more serious than that, it seems."

"Hornets in the shower," said Sour.

"No, more serious, some sort of ecstatic hysteria brought on by something they ate, some allergic reaction, or whatever," said the director. "The camp leader said it might have something to do with the discovery of a statue."

"What statue?"

"No, no, this is not that myth of the trickster who transformed all the tribal women one summer in ancient memory," he said and then raised his hands to resist the rest of the story. "No, no, this is not one of those trickster diseases, these are young white girl scouts from the city."

"Why not?"

"No, the trickster of that story was made out of crystal."

"The *oshkiwiinag*, and plenty more," said Sour.

"Right, hundreds of women were pregnant that summer."

"My grandmother told me those stories."

"Never mind, get out to the camp," said the director.

"My great uncle said the crystal trickster was a man and a woman at a circus that summer, and somehow, *oshkiwiinag* teased the population to double in one year on the reservation," said Sour.

Sour packed a medical case with calamine, ammonia, baking soda, various antihistamines, and epinephrine. She drove the shortest route over unpaved backroads to the Girl Scout camp. The road was on the way to the barony.

Cozie promised to take me along on any emergencies that might sound like shamanic ecstasies. We were both convinced that shamans were touched as much as they chose their ecstatic states. That touch could be a connection to the stories once told about the *oshkiwiinag* trickster. So, she picked me up at the barony. The first giant drops of rain burst in the loose sand, and the black flies wavered in the slipstream. Splendid foliage leaned over the road, a natural arbor that reduced the light north of Bad Medicine Lake.

Camp Wikidin was established on stolen tribal land, a sweetheart concession to the Girl Scouts. The summer camp was on land once ascribed to natives in treaties that created the White Earth Reservation.

Almost waited at the treeline near the cabins. He waved with both hands, as we turned into the camp, and then ran behind the car. He was there, as we were, to hear the stories of a most unusual situation on the reservation. My cousin was certain the scouts were touched by the natural heat of crystal.

Cozie told me that at first she thought the scouts might be allergic to the reservation. The camp director and two anxious assistant scout leaders were waiting in the parking lot.

"This thing is sexual," shouted one leader. Her cheeks were swollen and bright red, her gestures were uncertain, and she watched the shadows at the treeline in the distance.

"*Gegaa,*" said Almost.

"Wait a minute," said Sour.

"Really, some kind of sexual thing," she insisted.

"No, no, stand back and let me park the car."

"Dark windows," said the other leader.

"The cruel sun," said Sour.

"Allergic?" asked the camp director.

"No, just hate what the bright light does to faces and the play of shadows," said Sour. "So, now about that sexual thing, where are the girls who need some medical attention?"

"We locked the girls in the main cabin to protect them for now," said the camp director. "We thought it best, as they had the very same symptoms."

"Why?" asked Sour.

"Because, this thing *could* be sexual," said the director.

"Do you mean a man?"

"Something very sinister has happened here," said the leader.

"*Maanoo*," said Almost.

"Doctor Sour . . ."

"Nurse Cozie Browne," said Sour.

"Good enough for now," said the camp director. She was not aware of me or my cousin. That pleased me, of course, as my interests were in the stories of a tricky heat not in the poses of medical authority.

"Nurse Browne, we thought you would be a doctor."

"Perhaps you need a rich surgeon from the city," said Sour.

"*Maanoo*," said Almost.

"Never mind, it's just that we've been touched by something very strange overnight," said the camp director. She turned toward the nurse, her face was narrowed by one wide crease down the center of her forehead. She turned the loose wedding ring on her finger. She was worried, but did not seem to be frightened. "Something that *could* be sexual, but we cannot believe our own words."

The assistants were closer to panic than the director. Their hands were unclean and trembled out of control. The assistant with the big red cheeks chewed on her knuckles. She could not determine if the "sexual thing" was the beginning or the end of her career as a girl scout leader.

Sour moaned at the last turn to the main cabin. The wild campers were at the windows, their bright red faces pressed on the panes. Their sensuous bodies had overheated the building, and a wave of moist warm air rushed out when the director unlocked the door.

"Crystal heat," said Almost.

"Nonsense," said the camp director.

"Heat is the word," said Sour. She examined every camper in a private office, soothed the girls with gentle stories about nature, images of lilacs, pet animals, and garden birds. Most of the campers were shied by the heat of their own bodies. They told stories about their dreams, the unnatural sensations of soaring over water, and a telltale "warm touch" in the air. Sour could not detect any allergies, infections, or insect bites.

Barrie, one of the campers, had the sense at last to consider what had changed in their lives that might have caused such ecstasies. She described, with unintended irony, their habits and activities over the past few days, and then she revealed the secret, the scouts had not been the same since they discovered a statue buried on the other side of the lake.

Later, when the campers gathered to clean and examine the figure, their secret treasure, some of the girls swooned and fainted right at the table. The emotions were so contagious that the campers buried the statue and worried that they were being punished by some demon of the tribal land. "Some demon who hated outsiders from the cities." Clearly, these were signs of posttraumatic ecstasies.

Barrie, who was a senior scout, drew a very detailed map of the secret burial site. She blushed as she marked the trail to the mound near a cedar tree. Then she fanned her cheeks with the map. The mere thought of the trickster statue caused her breath to shorten.

Cozie located the crystal trickster in a shallow grave. She bound the statue in a beach towel, and we returned to the hospital. She was ecstatic on the backroads, certain that the treasure was the very crystal trickster that had once transformed the mundane in so many native stories.

She locked the trickster in a laboratory and reported to the director that there were no diseases to treat at the camp, nothing but blushes, short breath, and mild posttraumatic histaminic ecstasies. Later, the camp leaders reported that the girls were much better and that a cook-out was being prepared as a distraction. The scouts swore that they would never reveal to anyone the stories of the crystal trickster.

Almost was right, the heat was a crystal trickster.

Burn unbound the trickster when she finished her rounds in the hospital. She told me to observe in silence the entire event that night. The room was dark with one examination light over the statue. She soaked the trickster in warm water and as the mire washed away the pure crystal seemed to brighten the laboratory.

The crystal trickster was named *oshkiwiinag* in the stories we heard on the islands and on the barony. The ancient statue warmed her hands and face. She was bright with the light of the crystal healer. The trickster was smoother than anything she had ever touched. Smoother than a river stone, otter hair, even smoother than ice cream.

The *oshkiwiinag* was about seventeen inches high and each part of the crystal anatomy was polished with incredible precision. The arms, legs, head, torso, and penis were perfect interlocking parts. For instance, the bright head could not be removed unless both arms were raised, and the arms could not be removed with the head attached. The pure crystal penis was the most precise and intricate part of the trickster. She could not determine that night how to remove the penis from the body of the crystal trickster.

Burn polished each part with such pleasure that she lost her sense of time and place. She carried the shrouded trickster between her legs as she drove home, and then placed the statue in a locked closet. She asked me to consider the best way to present the crystal trickster to her great uncle at Wanaki Island.

Cozie and the thirteen camp scouts who had touched the *oshkiwiinag* were pregnant, and nine months later their trickster babies were born at almost the same hour. The coincidence became a scandal in the media, and hundreds of reporters roamed the reservation in search of wicked tricksters. The native government was cursed with nonfeasance, and the hospital was sued for malpractice by several mothers of the trickster babies. Cozie was portrayed as a native witch on several radio and television shows, a nurse who hated the light and caused those innocent scouts to become pregnant. One television host asked my cousin, "Are you an Indian vampire?" She was worried at the time, but we coached her to say, "Yes, your worst nightmare, a native princess as vampire."

Cozie was forced to leave the only job she ever loved at night. At the same time she had a clever daughter and an incredible trickster who could conceive a child with a crystal touch. She trusted that *oshkiwiinag* was the real father of her child, because she had not been with a man for three years, two months, and nineteen days. Her memories were precise.

Several months later the state medical examiners concluded in their report that the conceptions were curious cases of parthenogenesis. There is medical evidence that ecstasies and even terror have caused innocent conceptions. Such trickster stories have been heard in native communities centuries before the coincidence of parthenogenesis.

The Naanabozho Express was at the station near the hospital for a few hours that night. Gesture invited her to dinner in the parlor car. Cozie told him about *oshkiwiinag*, and the medical investigations on the reservation. He insisted that she establish her own clinic on the train and present trickster conceptions to women who would rather not bear the sensations and tortures of sexual intercourse. She moved to the train that very night and painted two signs on the side of the parlor car. The signs read, "Parthenogenesis on the Crystal Express," and, "Conceptions in Motion with No Fears or Tears."

The Naanabozho Express circled the reservation for several more months, and in that time thousands of natives had their terminal teeth repaired free by the one and only acudenturist in motion, and many women boarded the train to touch the crystal *oshkiwiinag* and conceive a child without sex. Some women had their teeth renewed and touched the trickster at the same time, ecstasies on one end and a better smile on the other.

Then, as you know, the luxurious seven coach train lurched out of the lonesome Ozaawaa Casino Station once more on the last wild run from the White Earth Reservation to the White House in Washington.

11

Headwaters Curiosa

 Almost told me that the Holy Rule of Saint Benedict was announced by veracious monks in the fifteenth century at the headwaters of the *gichiziibi*, the "great river" in the language of the *anishinaabe*, near the barony. Later, in colonial histories, the source was named the Mississippi River.

My cousin was almost convinced that our ancestors were touched by those monks, as most of our stories about the *debwe* have been traced to a monastic manuscript created at the headwaters. "That might be the reason, but not the cause, that my mother was a nun and your father was a priest, and the reason we are in the blank book business." The stories of the monks made more sense than conversions at the Stations of the Cross.

The monks had encountered by chance of their vision and the ironies of their devotion the mighty shamans of the *anishinaabe*. Many generations of tricky stories were inspired by this uncommon union, and the once pious monks wrote about their erotic connection with animals at the headwaters. The natives and the monks at the *gichiziibi* created new stories and a manuscript of authentic curiosa histories of this continent.

The *Manabosho Curiosa*, the monastic manuscript of their sensual pleasures with animals, was discovered by the antiquarian book collector Pellegrine Treves at an auction in London. Many historians considered the manuscript to be blasphemous, and others were more cautious, to say the least, because there was no evidence that monks were ever at the headwaters. Indeed, to surmise the very notion of an erotic conversion with animals was heretical at any time.

Manabosho is an earlier variation of *naanabozho*, the name of the protean trickster in the oral stories of the *anishinaabe*. As the name of the trickster was *heard*, the sounds, intonation, and articulation were uncertain representations in translations and written language. Curiosa, of course, is derived from Latin. The word, in the sense of this incomparable manuscript, means unwonted erotic trickster stories.

Treves, an honorable man who was much admired by other rare book collectors, was convinced that the manuscript was authentic, although he would not take a position on sex with animals. Scientific and historical studies of the parchment and the descriptive stylistics and patterns of the calligraphy revealed that the manuscript could have been created in the fifteenth century. The parchment was made with the skins of animals common to the headwaters. The animals represented the erotic union, the conversion, and the very manuscript of the stories. Eroticism has never come closer to the presence of visual memories in a monastic manuscript.

Moreover, the chemical composition of the paint that illustrated the manuscript, and the *anishinaabe* trickster stories that were recorded by missionaries and ethnologists much later, contributed to the evidence that the curiosa was authentic.

Hagal Williamson, a conservative scholar who underestimated tribal populations and once scorned oral histories, turned to trickster stories and the curiosa late in his career as a professor of colonial histories. He studied the original manuscript and ruled that the erotic stories were "transitional testimonies of uncertain circumstances" that could, in the absence of other monastic documents, "inspire a landscape of simulated evidence at the headwaters of the Mississippi River." He reasoned that the "ecstatic manner of the stories was not inconsistent with the inspirational flourish of certain monastic manuscripts."

Hesitation, in this instance, became a virtue, as he announced several years later, and much to the surprise of his colleagues, that an archaeological report on a recent excavation revealed evidence of monastic remains at *maazhi mashkiki*, or Bad Medicine Lake, on what is now the White Earth Reservation in Minnesota.

The Black Death and the tyrannies of government had driven the monks to sea with their venerable manuscripts and a sublime vision of silence at the common source of their own presence. The monks sailed west on the obvious course of the sun, over the ocean to the woodland lakes, and landed at the headwaters late in the summer two decades before the navigational adventures of Christopher Columbus.

The monks heard the warm rush of creation over the smooth stones in the river, a natural communion that heartened them to declare their monastic rule at the headwaters. The first monastic library was established there in the autumn. These were the first ascetic monks on the continent, and their contradictions of survivance were a source of humor in tricky native stories, the wild interior penance of their uncommon conversion.

Monasteries are reputable in histories because of the extremes of devotion, and because of old women. The men of unnatural silence are avoidable without the presence of old women, their memories of mortal creation and the ruins of erotic aversion. These circumstances were even more crucial at the headwaters. There, as natural as the stones, an old *anishinaabe* woman raised the river mire with her beaver stick and taunted the crows. She created the *debwe* or heart dance to mock the pious services of the monks, and then she seduced them with erotic animal stories.

The wind was tender in the birch when the monks landed at the headwaters. The bright leaves turned, the lonesome comedies of late summer, and shimmered in the clear water over the river stones. The crows bounced on the shore, more secure in their presence at the rush of the seasons than were the monks in their silence. Over night the snow touched the shadows of the great glacial boulders, and the river was hushed at the shoreline.

"The winters are never so wicked as men," the monks recorded in their manuscripts. "His mighty creations are heard in the silence of our seasons. His hand is our touch in the resurrection of the leaves and seasons. Spring is our benediction with the crows, the winds of our natural salvation, and the mercies of our sacred words melt at the source and run with the great river out to the sea."

The Holy Rule of Saint Benedict at the headwaters of the *gichiziibi* was parsed in tricky stories, an erotic humor that crossed the abstinence of the monks, and then, in the course of natural reason and mild seasons, the silence of the monastery was converted in the third winter by the rules of the *anishinaabe* trickster.

Naanabozho is the trickster of creation, the natural traces of men, women, bear, and birch, a wild tease heard on the wind and in the tricky stories of the seasons. Tricksters are stories, the chase of chance and visions, the traces and hum of the seasons, and the cover of winter. Tricksters are the chancy ruins of silence. The crows and animals are the trick-sters of human pleasure. The monks touched the animals with stones and teased the seasons.

Trickster stories are survivance, not salvation, pleasure not absti-nence, imagination not devotion, humor not termination. The trickster is on the rise, not the end of stories. Trickster is the wind, not the other, not mortal, not immortal, the natural tease of the obvious. Trickster is an erotic trace with no presence or salvation. Naanabozho is our carnal creation in tricky stories that never end in silence.

Saint Benedict of Nursia founded monasticism in the sixth century and was once misperceived as a wild animal in the extremes of his sepa-ration and devotion. Nine centuries later the stories of that obscure pose in a cave would become an erotic observance in the monastery at the headwaters.

Saint Benedict, at age fourteen, denied his presence and became a notable hermit in monastic hagiarchies. He withdrew from the com-mon world to avoid the evil of his time, abandoned his studies, turned to the solitude of a cave, and dressed in coarse hides, an unnatural rever-sion to the beast at the time. This pious and austere man, who mounted briars to distract his mere memories of a woman, was named the abbot of the monastery at Vicovaro in Italy.

The *Regula Monachorum*, his rules of monotheistic devotion, was composed for the monasteries. These same rules, a celebration of sanc-timonious manners, unnatural silence, obedience, fear, and humor en-cumbered with severe pieties, were overturned in tricky stories at the monastery near the *gichiziibi* headwaters. A century later the rules were converted to chance, and the praise of animals, natural comedies, thun-derstorms, and carnal pleasures in tricky erotic stories. The monks learned to shout at the seasons, lust at night in the river water, tease ani-mals with stones, and the erotic, once constrained in silence, became a virtue of meditation in the curiosa stories.

Fleury, the first monastery, was a *wiigiwaam*, an arched structure built by an *anishinaabe* woman who lived alone near the headwaters. The monks were amused by the old woman who carried a beaver stick. She was forever in the company of birds and animals. Not domestic creatures, but curious beaver, otter, wolves, bears, and nosy birds at their escape distances in the trees. She mocked the aversions of animals and monks in a heart dance. She laughed most of the time, and at every-thing, the mortal silence of the monks and the hides that covered their monastery.

The monks read their manuscripts several hours a day in the summer, the old monastic rules were carried to the headwaters. They intoned their words, and the old woman laughed at these men who read out loud their manuscripts, lived in silence, and were scared of sex and animals. The heart dance mocked the psalmodies and sounds of their sacred manuscripts. She danced their hearts back, a nude and erotic dance that mimicked the sexual movements of animals.

The monks lived in other structures that were connected in a circle to the monastic library in the main *wiigiwaam*. There, late in the third winter of the old rules of silence and obedience, several monks were tormented by the erotic pleasures with animals in their dreams. The monks intoned the rules, over and over, but even the parchment of their manuscripts was a sensual presence. The abbot reasoned that dreams were the metes and measures of devotion, and the eternal fear of starvation in the wilderness. His monastic silence was the assurance of salvation.

"The sacrifice of an animal is lust and sustenance without consecration," the monks wrote in their manuscripts. "His greater sacrifices are our eternal memories at night, and at first light, our silence and devotion is our everlasting nourishment."

The monks would never sacrifice animals or birds. "His mighty creations are not here to entertain our hunger," the monks wrote with a flourish on parchment made of animal skins. These severe rules and words of devotion might have been the end of the monastery at the headwaters. The monks, who considered the animals in their dreams a penance, prayed in silence for their deliverance from starvation.

The first two winters were mild, as sure a tease of the seasons as the humor of the old woman at the headwaters. The third winter was incessant, the snow crusted in wicked contours, and the wind was so cold that their best survivance stories would bear no shadows or humor. Roused from their extreme devotion that winter, the weakened monks heard the sound of laughter one night, then the slow beat of a hand drum, and a native rattle, in the monastic library. The laughter seemed to come from inside the manuscripts, and the sound of the drum surrounded the monks. The abbot turned his head from side to side to locate the source of the sounds. The overtones worried the abbot, his neck muscles shivered, but otherwise he was unmoved. He ruled that the obscure echoes were signs of their contrition.

Almost hears the same laughter at the headwaters. We have been there in the winter, at the actual site of the monastic library. My cousin sounded his rattle, and we heard the laughter of the monks buried in the snow.

Outside the *wiigiwaam*, on the other side of the headwaters, the monks saw the old woman at the treeline with the animals. Later, they found *baatewiiyaas*, dried meat, and *manoomin*, wild rice, in a birch bark bundle. The monks endured the winter in the murmur of their manuscripts.

Saint Benedict, the monks reasoned, had done the same in his cave. He might have starved without the service of others, and he never would have written his *Regula Monachorum*. A faithful monk from a nearby monastery brought bread to the young hermit. The abbot at the headwaters was not so hospitable that he would compare a pagan woman with the gestures of a pious monk. Nonetheless, this man of renunciation ate the meat that winter. Benedict, a thousand years earlier, ate bread, otherwise starvation would have been the termination of his monastic devotion. Likewise, the old woman had to save the monks that winter at the headwaters, otherwise there would be no manuscript of tricky curiosa stories.

"Benedict made his home in a narrow cave and for three years remained concealed there unknown to anyone except the monk Romanus, who lived in a monastery close by under the rule of Abbot Deodatus," wrote Saint Gregory the Great in the *Life and Miracles of Saint Benedict*. His dialogues on the lives of the saints were written in the sixth century. "With fatherly concern this monk regularly set aside as much bread as he could from his own portion; then from time to time, unnoticed by his abbot, he left the monastery long enough to take the bread to Benedict. There was no path leading from the monastery down to his cave on account of a cliff that rose directly over it. To reach him Romanus had to tie the bread to the end of a long rope and lower it over the cliff. A little bell attached to the rope let Benedict know when the bread was there, and he would come out to get it."

Fleury at the headwaters was a precise renunciation of native survivance. The abbot and the old *anishinaabe* woman were never named in the curiosa stories, but their presence at the heart dance late in the third winter was mentioned by the monks in the old manuscripts. The erotic dance caused an absolute schism in the monastery.

Two monasteries were established as a result of the separation over the monastic rules. The common practices of devotion and celebrations of silence, obedience, and monotheism, were overturned by chance, eroticism, and animism. Fleury, the first monastery, continued under the direction of the abbot at the headwaters, and the second monastery of the heart dance was built that spring on the eastern shore of Bad Medicine Lake.

The abbot endured the heart dance and the curse of eroticism that winter, as the monks scurried naked in the snow and then masturbated more than once in a circle around the old woman at the headwaters. "She mocked our debaucheries with a carved wooden penis," the monks wrote in the manuscripts. "The snow was warmed and crusted by the first monastic semen cast on this erotic continent."

The monks were brushed with an errant trickster heat, and the curious animals, aroused by the scent and sounds of the orgiastic monks, moved closer to the old woman in the circle. Several monks touched the back of a beaver, and caressed the ears of a snowshoe hare, but no one reached out to the black bear at the treeline.

The monks crossed over the monastic course at the headwaters, in hand, heart, and erotic conversion, and could never return to the silence, obedience, and severe pieties of the abbot and the monastery at the headwaters. The braces of monotheism were overset in erotic trickster stories.

Monte Cassino, the celebrated sixth century monastery established by Saint Benedict in Italy, became the name of the fifteenth century schismatic monastery at nearby Bad Medicine Lake.

"Jesus Christ and the creatures of his creation never heard of the monks who would restrain their tongue in his name," the monks wrote in the curiosa manuscripts. "His creations are the sacraments of animism, and our eternal cause is to consecrate the beaver, the bear, and other creatures."

Monte Cassino, the *bagwaj*, which means "in the wild," the name of the new monastery in *anishinaabe*, was the center of seven creature stations in the woods, and more as the monks learned to touch and trust the humor and erotic pleasures of animals.

The monks built a new monastic library and another *wiigiwaam* on the eastern shore of the lake, and named the old *anishinaabe* woman their abbot, a natural choice of an ecstatic healer who could hear the stories of the animals and birds. The monks were convinced that no monastery could survive without an old woman of the seasons.

"Call me Jutta," said Gaaskanazo, the old woman. These were the very first words she spoke that summer at the monastery. The monks were nourished once more in the wild course of their conversion. At first the monks could not believe that the old woman caused them to remember the stories of their own austere past. She was the divine abbot of their wonted memories, even as she mocked their asceticism. The monks were in awe to hear a revenant name from their monastic histories.

Jutta was a twelfth century hermit, an old woman, who adopted and educated the Benedictine mystic Hildegard. Later, the mystic became the abbess at Rupertsberg. "The *Scivias* contains the ecstatic visions and stories of Saint Hildegard," the monks wrote in their manuscripts. "The *Manabosho Curiosa* embodies the erotic visions of Jutta, our *anishinaabe* mystic, and the abbot of Monte Cassino at Bad Medicine Lake." The curiosa manuscripts are the histories of an erotic conversion to the tricky stories of chance.

Monte Cassino soon became the native center of the autumn heart dance. Several hundred dancers, many from distant tribes, and thousands of animals came together at the monastery to mimic each other, to masturbate with stones at the creature stations, carouse in the water, embrace erotic stories, and to consummate their creation.

Fleury, the monastery at the headwaters, survived the winter and sustained the pious mission of the abbot and three of the seventeen monks. One of the three senior monks could not hear. His voice was so loud as he read the manuscripts that he could be heard at a great distance. The abbot was responsible for the original monastic library, but the old stories never reached the erotic revelries of the tricky curiosa in the new manuscripts. The three monks, in their turn, were converted by the heart dance and never returned to the headwaters. The abbot, who had never revealed his name, was alone, in his own silence, and that winter he was found dead in the river. The monks brushed the ice clear of snow and there, at the source of the *gichiziibi*, the abbot was consecrated in blue ice. He was nude, frozen solid with a wide smile, and the monks discovered for the first time that the abbot was a woman.

The monks were astounded at the consecration, that the abbot with no name was a woman at death, and her frozen smile was the ironic salvation of a monastic trickster. The monks circled the ice woman at the headwaters, their last turns in silence, a winter crown to the curiosa stories. They removed their cassocks and leathers and masturbated on the ice over the abbot. Their semen steamed and stained the ice over her face. At last, the monks shouted and danced at the headwaters. The ice cracked and wheezed, and the beaver hurried to the shore.

"Saint Hilaria lived as a man, a double hermit with seventeen monks, and he was buried as a woman," the monks noted in their new manuscripts. "The abbot earned this name at his death, an obscure name from the earliest records of the monasteries." The abbot was buried with her new name in the monastic library at the headwaters. The old manuscripts were moved from the *wiigiwaam* to Monte Cassino at Bad Medicine Lake. Fleury was burned that autumn, the end of monastic silence.

Jutta mocked the death of the abbot and the obscure excuses of her name at the heart dance. The monks were overheated by the dance, the chance of their conversion, and at the same time careworn by centuries of unnatural silence. The old *anishinaabe* woman undressed and stretched out nude, in the same position as the abbot, on her back in the shallows of the headwaters.

"Saint Hilaria smiled at his death, and so she mocked that smile. She wore an enormous wooden penis," the monks wrote in the curiosa manuscripts. The penis or *niinag* stood erect in the headwaters. The monks laughed, the animals bounced in the water, and the wooden *niinag* was spirited away by a beaver.

Jutta told the monks to search in the headwaters for a smooth erotic stone, an ancient stone *niinag* smaller than their own penis. That night, at the heart dance, she examined their stones, warmed and moistened them in her mouth. She laid the *niinag* stones in a circle near the fire and later, as the snowshoe hare shivered at the hands of the old woman, the monks masturbated on their stones.

The *Manabosho Curiosa* contains the actual stories of the sexual conversion of the monks with the animals at the heart dances. The entries in the manuscript were written by several monks at the monastic masturbatory. The calligraphic styles and signatures indicated that the curiosa stories were written over several generations, as one style would end, another style of calligraphy would appear in the manuscripts.

The language of the monastic calligraphers is one of the remarkable features of the manuscripts. The heart dance and trickster stories in the headwaters manuscripts were written in Latin. The actual curiosa in the new manuscripts was said to be a translation of a phonetic transcription of *anishinaabe* oral stories. Near the end of the curiosa manuscripts several stories are written in Spanish, French and English. The second generation of monks, the continental native crossblood monks, made use of *anishinaabe* words in the manuscripts. Italian was the original language of the monks. The other languages of the manuscripts reveal a colonial presence at the headwaters.

Pellegrine Treves, the antiquarian book collector, circulated one copy of the translated manuscript to selected authors and scholars. His conditions were explicit, that the manuscript was not to be published, but he allowed fair and reasonable use of editorial selections from the curiosa manuscript. He seemed to be more concerned with manners and taste than with the commercial protection of the curiosa.

The *Manabozho Curiosa* reveals that there were several manuscripts completed at the headwaters and the monastery at Monte Cassino. The curiosa parchment, however, is the only extant manuscript. The monks are never named, and the mammals at the heart dance were never given domestic names in the curiosa. The monks held to their reduced vows of celibacy, no sexual intercourse with women, but near the end of the manuscript there are insinuations and elusive hints in the turn of pronouns that the monks had sex with other monks, native women, and mammals at the heart dances.

Almost has heard many native stories about the wild monks, and the priests at the mission have told some of the same stories, but my cousin and other tricky storiers at the barony told that the erotic communion of the monks and animals were more than mere traces and translations of the original curiosa manuscripts. My cousin created in his stories a seductive sense of presence.

The rare opossum, the least sociable of the arboreal marsupials, was one of the most erotic mammals at the monastery. The opossum were the first mammals "traded for spotted fawns and other sensual creatures at the autumn heart dances." The elusive opossum turns to the side and "raises the whiskers on her narrow snout at the touch of excitement." Several monks were aroused by the slow manner of these stout mammals with short legs, clawless big toes, and "the most erotic naked prehensile tails." The opossum have no hair on their ears either, a feature the monks raved about in their carnal trades at the heart dance.

When the monks heated their stones and touched an opossum she reached out with her tail and hung onto an erect penis. The manuscript names two opossum trained to grasp a wooden *niinag* with their prehensile tails.

"That morning on the third day of the heart dance, two monks were seated on the shore. They were naked with their feet pressed one to the other. Inside their withered white legs, the monks inserted their stones into the sexual organs of two opossum. The mammals shivered, moved to the erotic touch, and then their tails searched for a *niinag* to hold. One tail held the penis of the older monk, and when the opossum waggled and tightened her tail, the monk ejaculated on her back. The other monk was so excited by the scene that his orgasm was premature and the second opossum reached for his penis too late."

The elder monk who could not hear pursued the "obscure sensual pleasures of the stout porcupine. Earlier, he had teased a masked water shrew for a time, and then he was very much excited by the starnosed mole." Once he brushed his crotch with moist earth and "the mole searched his entire penis and testicles with her wet nasal saucer and fleshy pink papillae."

The monk prepared a portable white pine tree decorated with water lilies for the porcupine to climb during the heart dance. The porcupine, a nocturnal creature, eats the inner bark of white pine and, as a delicacy in the summer, water lily pads. This solitary mammal was seduced by the loud voice of the old monk. When he read the manuscripts out loud the porcupine heard him at a great distance. She recognized the sound of his voice and the acrid odor of his wrinkled body.

The monk would sleep with that small white pine tree between his legs for several nights before the heart dance. Then "he would read and the porcupine, who craved salt, would waddle to the circle of the heart dance and lick his erotic sweat from the white pine." The monk touched her genitals with his stone, "a delicate reach under the barbed spines, as she licked the sweat, hugged the tree, and urinated on his hand and stone." Later, he masturbated with the scent of the porcupine on his stone.

Several monks were aroused by the snowshoe hare and masturbated on her soft coat. The autumn hairs were silken and white, a natural for the eroticism of the heart dance. Everything about the snowshoe was erotic. The monks told stories about her large soft feet, and the warm underside as the hare reached to browse on bark. "The reach of the hare was considered to be the most sensual pose at the heart dance."

The reach of the snowshoe, poised on her long rear legs, was so erotic that some monks would masturbate at the scene, even at a distance with other mammals at hand. The one monk who dared to tease a black bear with his stone wrote that "my hesitation with the bear over me, and the erotic moves of the snowshoe hare at the heart dance, raised the wild pleasures of my orgasm."

The monks and the bears were natural masturbators. The shamans said the bear taught man how to masturbate when the two spoke the same language. The smaller mammals at the heart dance bounced, shivered, and wriggled with sensual excitement, but the bear roared and pounded the earth with his huge paws. "One monk turned from an older voracious wolverine, an uncommon union, to the bear, but no one else had the carnal hardihood to arouse a massive creature with a mere smooth river stone." The monk once teased the bear too much at the heart dance. Later, he was beaten at the treeline, and the bear held him down in a sexual embrace for most of the night. Since then the monk shouts and then shows his penis to the bear.

The same monk masturbates with the bear over him at the treeline. "This portentous position is the way bears once mated with humans in the trickster creation stories. The bears were human then, the primordial scent of a natural union." The bear was over the monk, nose to nose, and the monk tasted acorns and berries on his breath. The monk masturbated with one hand, and with the other touched the overheated sexual organs of the bear. The bear stone was wet and warm. The monk shouted and the bear roared at the heart dance. The abbot mocked the shouts of the monk under the bear, and the other monks joined in the chorus. "Twice, in the stories of the monastery, enormous male bears heard the shouts and masturbated with the monks at the heart dance."

Most of the monks, and even those who are not aroused by the river otter, would take part in the water games. The monks and the otter slide down the river bank into the water. The otter are sensitive and loyal to one monk, but there have been instances of communal sexual encounters with more than one monk at the heart dances.

"The most erotic features of the river otter are their webbed toes, and the sensual way they lope to the heart dance." One of the stout monks, the only one at the monastery with a tattoo, could not contain his lust and jealousy. He masturbated at least once, sometimes twice a day, and he was bothered that the other monks, or even other otter, had "unclean thoughts of pleasure with his favorite river otter." The monk carried his erotic stone in a leather pouch close to his penis. The stone was used to arouse him as much as the otter.

The abbot mocked his extremes at the heart dance. The other monks loped like otter around the fire, and several monks wore simulated webbed toes. Others pretended to be aroused by his stone pouch and teased him, "what do you have, a bigger penis in that pouch?" The monk with the tattoo was overtaken with erotic extremes. "He lost his humor and heard no other creation but a river otter."

The next summer the monk lived in the river and slept under a tree trunk. He ate fish and salamanders and strained to swim with the lithe movements of an otter. No other monk at the monastery came closer to a reversion to the other creation. Over the years the extreme course of his imagination in the river changed his body. The monks celebrated his creature conversion only months before his death. He was named a saint, the first at the monastery, because his toes were webbed, his nose was broad, he was lighter on the underside, playful on the river bank, and he had grown a thick tail covered with brown fur. Saint Lusus, the curious saint of the erotic river otter, was his name in the curiosa manuscript.

The lynx waited at the treeline and never came into the erotic rush of the heart dance. The monks who were aroused by the lynx were solitary masturbators, elusive hunters, but they were much more erotic and treacherous than a wild cat. One of the younger monks at the monastery "tracked the lynx for months because he was aroused by her huge paws, short tail, and tufted ears. He became the very stealth of the lynx as an act of extreme eroticism." He pretended to be a lynx and hunted the snowshoe hare. The monk sucked on his cat stone, ambushed a snowshoe at the heart dance, and masturbated on her huge ears. Some of the other monks were so excited by his rush as a lynx from the tree- line, that they waited to masturbate with him, the predatory lynx over the monastic hare.

One monk possessed a white tailed deer and her fawn at the heart dance. The other monks were enticed by the mature nature of the deer, and many watched with great excitement as "the monk raised the thick white underside of her tail and inserted his smooth red river stone," mounted her from behind, and "cried out a sudden orgasm."

The white tailed monk never masturbated with the other monks, not since his pleasure with the deer. He cared for his deer and her fawn, an eccentric reversion to a feudal family. The other monks teased him over his orgasmic cries, and the abbot mocked his moves under the white tail. Soon the monk pranced as the deer on horny toes.

"The deer and fawn lived with the monk as a family at the monastery. He would hunt by day for white cedar browse, and at night read to the deer from the manuscripts. He was the only father the fawn had ever known." The other monks were touched by his extreme sense of rumi- nant paternity.

Almost told stories about a new and unusual turn in the erotic histo- ries of the monastery. The white tailed deer delivered a fawn with the ears and penis of the monk. That autumn at the heart dance the monks were "dressed as white tailed deer, mounted each other, and cried out faux orgasms." The deer monk was so pleased with the humor that he presented his first born fawn to the abbot and created a new passion play.

The Monte Cassino Passion was enacted by a melodist at the head- waters of the *gichiziibi*, the great river. The first passion play, as you know, was based on the original medieval liturgical drama, a histrionic and "mimetic crucifixion," composed by an anonymous playwright in the twelfth century at the Benedictine Abbey.

"The audience is already initiated into the mysteries that the play seeks to dramatize, and it is aware of such elements as plot and character," wrote Robert Edwards in *The Montecassino Passion*. "Rather than create scenes and characters solely within the play, the dramatist allows his audience to identify them from its own experience." The native *debwe* passion converted the play into an erotic initiation of monks and animals.

"The element of music is the bridge between the discrete actions of the episodes," wrote Edwards. "It establishes a continuity against which the fragmented, iconic action can be placed and acts as an interlude between scenes. It can even accelerate or retard action as needed. In addition, music adds another dimension to the flow of narrative and dramatic action. As a mirror of universal order, it connects the play's spectacle and visual qualities to literal, moral, and anagogic truth."

Lumina Romanos, the native melodist, chanted the erotic themes and stories of the passion that autumn. The monks who had turned to animals were honored, a natural glory, and the waves of countenance were marvelous at the pleasurable play of ruminant paternity.

UNIVERSITY PRESS OF NEW ENGLAND

publishes books under its own imprint and is the publisher for Brandeis University Press, Dartmouth College, Middlebury College Press, University of New Hampshire, Tufts University, Wesleyan University Press, and Salzburg Seminar.

ABOUT THE AUTHOR

Gerald Vizenor teaches Native American literature at the University of California, Berkeley. His novel *The Heirs of Columbus* (1991), collection of stories, *Landfill Meditation* (1991), collection of essays, *Manifest Manners: Postindian Warriors of Survivance* (1993), and *Shadow Distance: A Gerald Vizenor Reader* (1994) are also published by Wesleyan. *Griever: An American Monkey King in China,* his second novel, won the Fiction Collective Prize and the American Book Award.

ABOUT THE ILLUSTRATIONS

The title page illustration is a reproduction of an *anishinaabe* pictomyth first published in *Chippewa Music* by Frances Densmore, Bureau of American Ethnology, 1910. The wavy lines from the mouth of the mythic figure show the sound of a song, the spiritual power of the voice.

The chapter illustration is a reproduction of an *anishinaabe* pictomyth first published in *Chippewa Music* by Frances Densmore, Bureau of American Ethnology, 1910. The pictomyth shows the *manidoo,* the spirit in *anishinaabe* songs and stories. The horizontal figure is *waaban manidoo,* the east or dawn spirit. The vertical figure is *zhaawans manidoo,* or the south spirit.

LIBRARY OF CONGRESS CATALOGING-IN-PUBLICATION DATA

Vizenor, Gerald Robert, 1934–

Hotline healers : an Almost Browne novel / Gerald Vizenor.

   p.   cm.

ISBN 0–8195–5304–2

I. Title.

PS3572.I9H6   1997

813'.54—dc20   96–43955